THE STORRINGTON PAPERS

Sarah found herself looking into a face like
a Japanese netsuke, ivory-coloured and carved
into innumerable wrinkles, blurred eyes sunken
in hollows. The wary, suspicious and perplexed
eyes of a very old woman.

'Who was the dreadful Miss Knox, and what
did she do?'

The dim eyes looked up out of their deep pits.
'Oh dear, oh me. Oh dear, oh me. You must be
careful of Master Dolly. He may be in danger.
Oh dear, where does it all end?'

Fascinating, fascinating. The woman old
nanny referred to, and who seemed to hold
deep alarms for her, must be the new governess
Cissie had written about, Miss Knox who was
small and neat and quick, like a brown bird.
That didn't sound the description of someone
who was potentially dangerous.
But 'her eyes are big and notice everything'
Cissie had written . . .

**Also by the same author,
and available in Coronet Books:**

The Storrington Papers

Dorothy Eden

CORONET BOOKS
Hodder and Stoughton

Copyright 1979 by Dorothy Eden

First published in Great Britain
1979 by Hodder and Stoughton Limited

Coronet edition 1980

Printed and bound in Great Britain for
Hodder and Stoughton Paperbacks, a
division of Hodder and Stoughton Ltd.,
Mill Road, Dunton Green, Sevenoaks,
Kent (Editorial Office: 47 Bedford
Square, London, WC1 3DP) by
Richard Clay (The Chaucer Press), Ltd.,
Bungay, Suffolk

ISBN 0 340 25014 3

For AMANDA

who is to be a writer one day

I

Sarah

THE OTHER DAY a friend asked Sarah to witness his will. She had to put her name, address and occupation. Sarah Goodwill, Pemberton Mansions, S.W.3. Housewife.

She thoroughly disliked the name Goodwill (Simon's name) now that it had proved so false. Lately there hadn't been much goodwill in their marriage. Even more she objected to her occupation "housewife". It sounded as if she were married to a house, and that she was not. She was an indifferent cook, a worse bedmaker, and if Simon were to be believed, a thoroughly bad bed partner. Though he had only made that accusation over the last unhappy year when what the judge had called an irretrievable breakdown in their relations had occurred.

It was true that she was bored with housekeeping, and wanted to go back to her old job of journalist and writer. She had a strong creative urge which needed satisfying, and Simon would never believe that she couldn't write in that gloomy flat which had always oppressed her, even when she had been a relatively happy wife and mother. Simon was not a mover. The flat had belonged to his parents, he himself had lived there since he was a child. It was spacious and comfortable and most women, living on the draughty first or second floor, or in the basement, of converted houses, would have envied her.

Perhaps. She didn't envy herself. Although the flat was only a symptom, not the cause, of her discontent. And the fact that Simon didn't want to, indeed couldn't face moving, suggested disturbing limitations in his character.

Not that Sarah regarded herself as perfect or always right. But she had grown increasingly appalled at the thought of them spending a possible fifty further years in each other's company. They had made a mistake. Okay, they were young enough and honest enough to admit it, and hopefully make a fresh start. Simon's first infidelity hadn't been too shattering because he had confessed to it, and wept in Sarah's arms. The next had been less forgivable. And the next. From feeling humiliated, Sarah became angry, then disgusted. She had discovered that Simon got rather a kick out of relating his misdemeanours.

That was when she knew for certain that the world outside Pemberton Mansions could be nothing but full of opportunity. This explained why she was in Brook Street that morning, approaching Claridge's Hotel and the interview with Major Charles Storrington who had advertised in *The Times*. "Wanted, experienced writer or journalist to assist in preparing family history, also for secretarial and other duties. Must be willing to live in."

She had wondered what the other duties might be. The intriguing address was Maidenshall, near Maidenhead, Berks. She imagined a mock-Tudor house, swimming pool, stables, the river running past the bottom of the garden.

Although family history could also suggest a ruined manor house, ghosts and all. She would prefer that. The trouble with her, Simon had said, was that she was a suppressed romantic. He made it sound like being an alcoholic or a drug addict.

A week after answering the advertisement she had a reply, a handwritten letter, the writing disappointingly uneven, suggesting an elderly or even aged scribe. Well, of course. Family history. What would you expect? The playboy heir?

Dear Mrs Goodwill,

If you are still interested in the work I have in mind, would you be able to meet me at Claridge's Hotel on Tuesday, the 14th, at 11 a.m. Ask at the desk and someone will direct you to my suite.

Yours sincerely,

Charles Storrington.

So there she was, on that sunny May morning, dressed in what she thought might be suitable ghost-writing attire, a dark blue polyester suit with a bright scarf, her last pair of Gucci shoes (no more of those now that she had to live on alimony) and a patent leather shoulder bag. Her outfit for visiting Jane at her boarding school. And that was another reason why she needed to work. The school was expensive, and Simon as a company manager had already indicated that he couldn't pay all those fees and her exorbitant (his word) alimony, too. But Jane was happy at her school. She had green playing fields and trees, masses of space, and the Sussex downs just beyond the walls. She had had to escape from the gloomy flat. That was the principal reason Sarah had chosen that school, and that was where she intended her nine-year-old daughter to stay.

The man behind the desk at Claridge's said that Major Storrington was expecting her. He was in suite number six on the third floor.

"Knock loudly," he said, and Sarah's heart sank. That, coupled with the feeble handwriting, suggested that the Major was deaf. She wasn't very good with deaf people.

However, when she knocked loudly, a very vigorous voice called, "Half a minute. Coming," and presently the door opened. In the small hallway sat a man in a wheelchair. The wheelchair didn't entirely surprise her, for the man at the desk had prepared her for some disability, deafness, blindness, an arthritic hip, or even this apparent paralysis.

What did surprise her and give her a sharp feeling of pity was that this man was relatively young.

"Mrs Goodwill?" he said. "Come in. I don't suppose you expected a cripple."

It didn't take much intuition to be aware of the taut anger beneath his routine politeness. Sarah imagined it was kindled afresh every time he had to explain his condition to a stranger.

"Permanently?" She tried to make her voice matter-of-fact, as if it were no great thing to be crippled at the age of – say thirty-five, thirty-six.

"Very permanently." The wheelchair moved fast, without

9

sound on the carpet. They went into a sitting room which was pleasant though anonymous. "They're very good to me here. Always give me the same rooms so that I know my way about. With the bathroom fittings etcetera, which are a major hazard in the life of the disabled." He was staring at Sarah with very brilliant dark eyes, daring her to show too much morbid interest in his condition. His face was extremely thin, as if he didn't, or perhaps couldn't eat enough. Or was in pain.

She said, "I imagine that must be so about bathrooms," and sat down where he could see her clearly. She would have preferred to see him clearly, too, but they couldn't both face the window.

"I'll ring for some coffee. Now tell me about yourself. Not your qualifications. You told me those in your letter. They seemed fine except that you don't seem to have had much practical experience. Some articles in magazines, and the Sunday papers. A job for six months on the *Observer*. What made you give that up?"

"I got married."

"And did that dry up your creative flow? Your husband objected to a working wife?"

"I had a baby."

"Oh. How old is it now?"

"She. She's nine and at boarding school."

"Does she like it?" he asked rather unexpectedly.

"She loves it."

"Splendid." He had springing dark hair that matched his eyes. He looked as if he might have been a politician, one of the whizz kid kind, if it weren't for the wheelchair. "I have a son of the same age. I want him sent to school but my wife doesn't care for the idea. Says he's too sensitive. Sensitive! He's just spoiled, I'm afraid. I can't make anything of him. Although perhaps his behaviour isn't so surprising when he sees his father like this."

"How did it happen?" Sarah hadn't meant to ask too soon, but here she was doing so.

"A tank fell on me. In Germany. A slight variation of the car accident, much more spectacular actually, but the result is the same. Anyway, I would have got out of the army before long. I wasn't a dedicated soldier. What caused your own particular crash?"

"My crash?"

"You said in your letter that you were in the process of getting a divorce. I appreciated your honesty. That's what made me decide to see you first."

Did he regard her as a fellow sufferer? Why not?

"Oh, that's just the usual thing. Married too young. We didn't know each other properly."

"How do you know each other until you marry?" He said this with some feeling, striking his hands together. "Who could have guessed how either my wife or I would react to a situation like this? Fortunately I haven't lost the use of my arms, which I am constantly reminded is a blessing. I remain a reasonably functioning human being. Or so the doctors say. Well, I don't have to be fed – heaven forbid – and I can, as they say, enjoy a drink."

Sarah heard a tap at the door.

"That must be the coffee. I'll go."

But the waiter, evidently familiar with the occupier of this suite, was already half way in. He set down his tray, handed a chit to the Major to sign, said "Thank you, sir," and withdrew.

"Albert," said the Major. "He's always on this floor. He knows me. Will you dispense? And then you might tell me more about yourself. When is your divorce coming through?"

"It has. It will be final in three months."

"You look upset. Does it still hurt?"

"It hurts to be a failure."

"Could you have sorted it out?"

"No!" she said vehemently.

"Then it seems to me it must be your husband – your ex, I should say – who's the failure. The guilty party."

"I suppose so. We were in no trouble for co-respondents. But basically that must have been my fault." Sarah thought of the first two years of their marriage which she had believed to be happy. At least she had been happy with her beloved baby daughter. Simon, she realised, had been jealous of Jane.

A not unnatural state with husbands, people told her. But it had seemed to her so petty and so cruel to be jealous of a pearly-fleshed morsel so full of innocent friendliness towards him. He was extremely and permanently possessive, she had discovered. He was so immature or insecure that he must be the only one in his wife's world. When he was no longer that he taunted her with failed devotion. Yes, the Major was right, one had to marry to find the kinks, the shadows beneath the attractive exterior.

"There are always faults on both sides," she said.

"So that's why you call yourself a failure?"

"Both of us must be, mustn't we?" She frowned, then said lightly "What is this, a visit to my psychiatrist? I thought I was here to discuss my merits as a writer."

"It's all part of it, isn't it? If you can't analyse yourself you can't be expected to analyse other people. I have an Edwardian grandfather who requires a bit of sorting out."

The coffee was good. And Sarah was extremely glad that she didn't have to hold his cup for him. That would have destroyed the superiority he required over her, as a prospective employer. She found she was enjoying this interview in a wry kind of way. She hadn't discussed Simon like this, even with her solicitor. And he needed discussing, airing, shaking briskly, and then filing away. Permanently.

What was Maidenshall like? she wondered. She realised she wanted this job very much.

"Tell me about your grandfather."

His eyebrows were expressive, nicely-curved black ones that wrote persuasiveness or impatience or a little gentle teasing across his forehead. Sarah suspected they could also display a sharp anger. Even apart from his grave disability, she guessed that he would not be an easy man. She began to wonder about his wife.

"My grandfather? I can guess what you're thinking. Mention the word Edwardian and everyone immediately sees the Prince of Wales. Grandfather was certainly a playboy, but he was also a hard-working industrialist. He had a violent temper and I should think he terrified the whole house on occasions. I know my father had good reason to be nervous of him. I never knew my father. He died soon after I was born. He hadn't married until he was forty and then he had the bad luck to be killed in the first year of Hitler's war. He was a war correspondent for *The Times*. So my mother was left with a six-month-old baby. She arranged for me to stay at Maidenshall with a nurse and a skeleton staff, and went off to join the W.A.A.F.'s, and got killed in an air raid. So I was brought up entirely by servants, and a guardian I didn't often see. Then I went to school, of course."

A lonely child, Sarah was thinking. "Tell me more about your family."

"Well, there was a Victorian ancestor who established the Storrington Munitions Company and made his pile supplying arms in the Crimean War. He longed to be rewarded with a knighthood, but since this didn't happen he consoled himself by building a Victorian Gothic pile on the site of a medieval nunnery, and impudently calling it Maidenshall. It's quite near the town of Maidenhead. He filled the house with expensive and rather nasty treasures, so that now it's an example of Victorian tastelessness and smells of money. All the same, I care about it. My family always has done. The Victorians were great property worshippers, and we all inherited the trait, especially grandfather Charlie."

"Grandfather Charlie?"

"The Edwardian chap. He went on adding to the family fortunes, so even in these rotten days of high taxation I suppose we live in some luxury. Grandfather was indirectly responsible for my career in the army because without his money I'd have had to do something more profitable, like being a stockbroker. You could infer, therefore, that he is responsible for this damned conveyance I'm forever doomed to sit in." His thin hands pressed on the arms of the chair. The laconic voice shook with suppressed vehemence. "It would be in keeping with some of the melodrama that went on in his lifetime."

"He sounds quite a person," Sarah said.

The Major gave her a probing look. "You're not nervous, Mrs Goodwill?"

"Of your grandfather?"

"No, of me. A lot of people are, nowadays." For the first time he allowed the pain to show in his eyes. "My temper's pretty vile."

"Fair enough, under the circumstances. No, I certainly wouldn't be nervous of you, Major Storrington."

"Well, that'll be a relief. I don't like cowed people. You'll understand that I can't decide on you immediately. I have two other applicants to see. But I'll write to you in a day or two. If you come I would suggest a three months' trial. Would that be sufficient to decide whether we have a book?"

"It should be. It will certainly decide whether you like my style. Or I yours," she added.

He seemed to find that thought interesting. Then he reverted to being an army officer, his voice brisk and impersonal.

"You would live at Maidenshall, of course. I might occasionally want to work late at nights or at weekends. Would that be acceptable to you?"

"Perfectly. Except for school holidays."

"Oh, your girl? Well, don't worry about that. She can come to Maidenshall. Plenty of room. She'll make a companion for Dolly."

"Dolly?"

"Adolphus. A family name. All the male heirs were either Charles Adolphus or Adolphus Charles. Dolly is a lonely difficult little devil. Needs straightening out."

"And that's to be Jane's job?"

"Jane will be a bonus. My wife has suggested that part of this job should be to keep an eye on Dolly. Will you take that on?"

"But of course. I'd enjoy it."

"Splendid. Then I'll let you know."

He did, and promptly. One had known he would not be an indecisive man. He wrote,

Dear Mrs Goodwill,

      The other two applicants were out of the question. One was stupid, and the other offended my eye. Could you come in two weeks' time, on the seventeenth? Catch the ten

forty-five from Waterloo. My chauffeur will meet you. We didn't discuss salary but we can come to an amicable arrangement.

Yours sincerely,
Charles Storrington

P.S. No need for a lot of gear. We don't entertain much. My wish. My wife does what she likes in London.

"I am to look after a *boy*!" came Jane's incredulous voice on the telephone. "Honestly, Mummy, have you lost your marbles?"

"Is that the kind of expression they teach you at St. Anne's?"

"Penny says it. And Barbara. But truly, Mummy, who is this boy?"

"His name's Dolly."

"Dolly!" Jane was now giggling uncontrollably.

"Don't do that, darling. His name's Adolphus, it's a family name, and it isn't funny. And he isn't funny, either, because his father's a cripple. So be a love and say you'll be nice to him. We'll be living in a very grand house. You'll enjoy that. You can boast about it to Penny and Barbara who might then try to speak the Queen's English."

"Ghosts?" said Jane, and Sarah knew she was being won over.

"I expect so. Of some sort or other."

"Daddy won't be coming?"

"Darling, you understand that you only see Daddy for a weekend now and then. And only if you want to."

"I don't want to," said Jane flatly. "He's always been beastly to me."

If shutting her out, ignoring her, or being sarcastic at her expense deserved the word beastly, then Jane was right. Sarah shivered, remembering Simon's small intentional cruelties. But how would Major Charles Storrington, reluctant invalid, behave towards Jane? Or, indeed, towards herself?

"Darling, give this a trial for me. If you hate it I promise not to make you stay. We'll both leave. But right now we need the money and this seems an interesting way of earning it."

"All right, Mummy, I'll try not to push awful Dolly down the stairs. When do I have to come?"

"I'm going next week. You'll come on your first long weekend."

2

MRS STORRINGTON RECEIVED Sarah in the drawing room. She sat at a circular rosewood table, dispensing coffee with deliberate formality.

She was a tall very slender woman, in her early thirties Sarah guessed. Her face was long and narrow, made interesting by a high forehead, smoky blue eyes, and raven hair puffed out over her ears, and drawn into a French knot at the back. Her hands on the coffee pot were narrow, too, as were her immensely fine ankles. She had a great deal of style and one couldn't see her adapting her life very happily to an invalid husband. She looked entirely the jet set type, more at home in luxury hotels than this Gothic mansion.

Yet she showed frank interest in her husband's new secretary, staring at Sarah without apology. Finally she gave a small nod and said she was glad of her husband's project, it would keep him occupied, temporarily at least.

"I don't know too much about his ancestors. He's never talked about them until lately, when he's begun reading old letters and balance sheets, and so on. His ancestors were very successful business men, and now that Charles can't do active things I am cherishing the hope that he might have inherited their skill. He might invest in some business. It would be a hobby at least. But not only business took place in this house. I believe it was one of the fashionable haunts of the Edwardian smart set – naughty weekends and all that. Don't you think it is hideous, a sort of miniature Mentmore?"

Sarah murmured that Victorian Gothic was not quite her thing, not adding that she had been sadly disappointed when Major Storrington's chauffeur had driven up to the front door of the sprawling over-ornamented pile. She had been hoping for something warm and mellowed and ivy-covered,

but realised she should have known better. In the mid-nineteenth century rich men had enjoyed building these showy places. Yet this room, with its long windows looking over a terrace and formal gardens, was rather lovely. Or could be, if several heavy pieces of furniture and some large opulent paintings that looked like Rubens were exchanged for Queen Anne walnut and Sheraton mahogany, and perhaps a Constable or a Reynolds. The faded Aubusson carpet was beautiful, and the marble fireplace with a wide mantelpiece was embellished by some nice pieces of Meissen and Sèvres porcelain.

Sarah hoped that her bedroom would not be too vast and too filled with heavy dark furniture. And Jane was going to hate it unless there was a cosy nursery wing.

"Charles, of course, will never move," Mrs Storrington was saying. "He has this family thing. Anyway, who would buy a place this size except an oil Sheik? They seem to be the new aristocracy nowadays. So I wear myself out keeping things going here and dash up to London four days a week. I do a job on a fashion magazine. I have to go to Paris, Rome, Florence. It's all exhausting, but fun, after those dreary years of being an army wife abroad. Cyprus was appalling. That was where Dolly was born prematurely. I was supposed to have flown home, but I didn't make it. So I gave birth in a temperature of a hundred degrees, and nearly died. I believe poor Dolly was born with permanent sunstroke, or something, and that's at the bottom of his troubles."

"Troubles?"

"He's so difficult. Didn't Charles tell you? He can hardly read and he's eight years old."

"Doesn't he go to school?"

"Impossible. We tried him at a day school in Maidenhead, but it was a disaster. They asked us to take him away. So now he has a private tutor who costs the earth. I believe you have a daughter the same age."

"Yes. Major Storrington kindly said she could come here for her holidays."

"Good. That might be just what Dolly needs to make him work. He surely won't enjoy a girl being superior to him."

This brisk cool mother, Sarah thought, would intimidate a nervous child. And he had the added problem of his father in a wheelchair, poor little beast.

"Major Storrington didn't tell me how long ago he had his accident."

"Eighteen months. But that isn't the reason for Dolly's behaviour. He was odd before that. It's something in his genes, I suspect. Charles's, not mine. My own family is boringly normal. Perhaps you and Charles will dig out what it is. Or it might be something in this house. I've always maintained it's spooky."

She was sharp and cynical. Sarah thought she might have been wrong in suspecting that she was happy enough with her busy life. She was the sort of woman who would keep up whatever she thought were the appropriate appearances.

"Charles says you're divorced," she was going on.

"In the process of. I'm waiting for the decree absolute. That somehow sounds like a benediction, doesn't it?"

"But it isn't? It's painful?"

Sarah shrugged. She could keep up appearances too. "It's a good deal a matter of wounded pride. A failed marriage. Not something one boasts about. The loss of love," she added thoughtfully. But had true love ever existed between herself and Simon?

"You'll find someone else."

"I've no intention of doing that for a long time. Jane and I will get along very well."

Mrs Storrington seemed amused.

"I'm beginning to see why Charles chose you. You're dis-enchanted with the male sex, and he . . ." She pressed her lips together. She wasn't amused, after all. She was a more complex person than one would have suspected.

"I should warn you that my husband has foul moods. Not surprisingly. He used to be impossible to keep up with, lived twenty-three hours a day. They thought the world of him in the army. Then the gods struck, the thunderbolt fell."

"It's often people like that who have these things happen to them," Sarah said ineffectually.

"My God, that's not much help, is it? To him, to me, to

Dolly who'd rather run a mile than meet his father in that damned chair."

And you? Sarah wanted to ask. Do you want to run a mile? If so, your husband, poor devil, will know. But then he, too, might want to make himself invisible to a beautiful wife.

Mrs Storrington was giving Sarah a sharp look. "Now, Mrs Goodwill, you look as if you want to run away, too. I only wanted to warn you about Charles's moods. They don't last long. He's terribly stoical, really. What's your first name?"

"Sarah."

"I'm Cressida. Since we're going to be living in the same house, let's act like friends."

Act? Was there some reason they couldn't genuinely be friends?

"You know, at night when I can't sleep, I imagine all the things that have gone on in this house for the last hundred years. I expect there have been tragedies as bad as Charles's. But there must have been a lot of fun, too. I wish I were one of those gay Edwardians with their nocturnal prowling. It would be better than listening to Charles in his wheelchair, or Dolly screaming in a nightmare."

Sarah was slightly startled. She could see this smart, sophisticated woman with her throw-away manner in army barracks on the Rhine, or pregnant and complaining in Cyprus, but not as a sensitive over-imaginative wife haunted by ghosts in an old house. Besides, Charles's chair didn't make any sound on carpets.

"I love parties. We never have any now."

She was dwelling on another grievance.

"Why not?"

"Because Charles objects. Anyway there hasn't been much chance. He's been in and out of hospitals until recently."

"Perhaps seeing his old friends would be good for him. If they're close friends –"

"Who wouldn't mind talking to the poor old boy in a wheelchair?"

Sarah stiffened. "People do talk to paraplegics and enjoy

it, especially one as mentally alive as your husband is."

"I can see he impressed you," Cressida said, lifting an eyebrow. "Actually I think it might have been kinder if he had been left a bit of a vegetable, then he wouldn't feel things so keenly. And I am not being a monster, Sarah. I'm just realistic. After all, my life has also crashed. So if I'm a bitch now and then don't blame me. I'm floundering as much as Charles. But you may be right about a party. Do you like parties?"

Sarah shrugged. "The last one I gave was a disaster. My husband, my ex-husband, was in a mood – and it pervaded."

"I'm afraid Charles will do that, too. If he deigns to appear at all."

"The circumstances were different, Mrs . . . Cressida. Simon was moving on to pastures new and couldn't have cared less about my friends. But your husband has to be rehabilitated. Isn't that the dreary word hospitals use? And it's summer, and that's a lovely terrace. I could help. That's if you'd like me to."

Cressida was looking at Sarah thoughtfully. "You'll risk the displeasure of your employer? You might find yourself out on your ear."

"I hate people being hurt, suffering more than they need to."

"Oh, my! You're not too intense, are you? If you didn't have that rather nice dimple in your left cheek I'd think you were."

"I am," Sarah admitted. "Over some things, some people. I'm sorry." She wondered who was getting the best of this conversation. "I don't even know if I can do this job properly, without presuming to organise Major Storrington's social life."

"Let me tell you something. You won't do it properly if you get too intense over Charles. He'll loathe that, and you'll both get fraught. You have to be like doctors and nurses, remain uninvolved. Encourage him to develop another kind of life. At least that's what they told me. So you're here for that purpose, and I don't intend to interfere. I'll keep out of the way as much as possible." Cressida sprang up. "Now I must fly. I'm due in London for an appointment at two-thirty. Charles is expecting you down for lunch at one. Dolly will be there, too, and Jeremy."

"Jeremy?"

"Charles's valet, nurse, male companion, you name it, he's it. He's a nice fellow. Kind. Kinder than me because he truly isn't involved. I expect your bags have been sent up. Come and I'll show you your room. We've put you in the nursery wing because that will be more convenient when your daughter comes. She'll be next door. The old nursery isn't used now. Dolly found it too lonely. He uses the study on the ground floor. But your room," Cressida was leading the way up the main staircase, her slim body moving beautifully inside her silk dress, "was always given to the resident governess. We've had it done over, of course. It makes a very good guest room since it's away down the passage from our suite, and the other bedrooms. Guests who like quiet prefer it. I thought you might like to work in it, rather than share the library all day with Charles. You may irritate each other. I warn you he can't bear the slightest noise when he's working."

Cressida seemed to be something of a compulsive talker, no doubt because she could no longer communicate easily with her husband. But this house, the wide stairway, and the long carpeted corridor which turned into what seemed to be another wing of the house, needed voices prattling, as the silence would be overpowering.

Cressida opened a door and Sarah followed her into a large room, its windows looking over a tennis court and a croquet lawn. It was pleasantly furnished with chintz-covered chairs, a desk, a well-polished dressing table and stool, and a comfortable-looking bed. The walls were painted apple green.

"How nice," Sarah said appreciatively.

"Yes. It used to be ghastly, all dingy chocolate brown. We even had that enormous wardrobe painted to match the walls. It used to overpower the room. As if any governess had enough clothes to fill it."

She opened the door and Sarah had a quick strange

22

impression of some limp sober-coloured dresses and shawls hanging there. Rows of buttoned boots on the floor and drab bonnets on the pegs. She took a deep breath of private relief when Cressida, as if she had sensed Sarah's thoughts, said "I don't think the ghosts of any Victorian governesses will worry you if they see this." She opened the door of a modern bathroom with primrose-coloured fittings. "No mahogany throne, you see."

"En suite," Sarah said approvingly.

"Shared with the room next door, which will be – what's your daughter's name?"

"Jane."

"Then it will be yours and Jane's. Dolly sleeps near us. I have to listen for him. Nanny's too old."

"Nanny?"

"Old Miss Galloway. She lives on the next floor. Just above your head. She's ancient now. I'm sure she remembers the Crimean War. But you know what families like this are about old retainers. She was Charles's nanny. Still, it's rather admirable, isn't it, not sending her off to one of those ghastly twilight homes. I'm sure you will approve of that."

A little sarcasm? But Cressida's eyes were friendly.

"If she doesn't fall out of bed in the night just over my head," Sarah murmured.

Cressida laughed. "She isn't a secret tippler, thank goodness. But I will tell you one thing, if we give a party Charles will insist that she be there. She was at our wedding in the clothes she probably wore for the occasion of Queen Victoria's funeral."

"You don't mean it! She isn't immortal, is she?"

"That's a secret fear I have. No, I'm joking. She's a good old thing when she isn't being weird. She still knows what's going on most of the time, and she's more active physically than poor Charles is now. Okay then Sarah, I'll leave you to unpack. Sorry I can't offer you the commodity that used to be taken for granted in this house, a lady's maid. But I believe it's going to be nice having you here. You'll brighten us up. Now I've really got to fly."

There was only time to wash in the pretty bathroom, and

23

tidy her hair and touch up her lipstick before going down to lunch. Sarah didn't want to be late. She had a feeling that Charles (now she was privately calling him Charles) would have a thing about punctuality. She must make a good impression on her first day, a cream silk shirt and beige skirt, a smooth hair-do. But there was the child, too. She didn't want to look governessy. Boys, even little boys, liked a touch of femininity. Some gold chains, a string of pearls?

Sarah rejected both, knowing she would have been ornamenting herself for Major Storrington, not a retarded small boy. That wouldn't be the most sensible thing to do, and why should she want to do it for a maladjusted paraplegic? Before she had answered that question in her mind she heard a window pushed up over her head. That must be Nanny. Briefly she imagined the old face, ravaged like the crumbling gargoyles under the eaves, peering out at the sunny landscape. She must meet this old lady for if she had been here so long she would be a source of information about the family. Why, for instance, hadn't Charles Adolphus Storrington who had served his country so well in industry been ennobled? Would he have been the type to refuse such an honour? It hardly seemed likely since his style of living had obviously been luxurious, not to say ostentatious. Perhaps there had been some scandal as there had been about several men linked with the court of that royal roué, Edward the Seventh. Would his grandson know, or was that something for them both to discover? Or to conceal? How was old Nanny's memory? Good, one hoped, for servants knew things that even wives did not.

Warming to her work, Sarah felt more alive than she had done during any of the grey weeks since leaving Simon. Then she had thought her spirit was failing her. Now she felt alert and optimistic as she ran down the stairs, afraid she would be late after all, and not knowing where the dining room was.

Instinct, and the sound of voices, took her past the drawing room door, across the hall with its black and white tiled floor and massive fireplace, and through a half open door into another panelled room, gloomy and far too large for cosiness.

It needed at least twenty people around the long oak table to make it seem comfortably populated. Instead there were three, four now she had arrived.

Major Storrington sat in his wheelchair at the head of the table. On his right sat a little boy with tousled black curls, wearing a distinctly grubby sweater and jeans, on his left a very blond young man with a charming smile (he was watching Sarah's entrance), and curious wintry eyes. He looked very athletic and rather calculating. Or was that an instant and inaccurate impression?

Charles waved Sarah to the place laid beside the young man. There was another place laid beside the little boy, she noticed.

"I'm glad you could make it, Mrs Goodwill." The Major's voice was polite and perfectly pleasant. "We thought you must have missed your train. This is Jeremy Lundren, my nurse." He raised his hand good-humouredly as the young man made to protest. "True, Jeremy. Let's face reality. That's what the doctors said I had to do. One must learn to accept unalterable facts. Oh, and this," he laid his hands on the small boy's tousled head, "is Adolphus Charles, the youngest Storrington at present extant."

Oh, Major! Sarah protested silently. Don't emphasise to that troubled little face that he must grow up and procreate. Shades of Grandfather Charlie. But no – she had anticipated wrongly, for he added with almost a touch of tenderness, "Dolly to us," and the child gave a lop-sided grin, not looking at Sarah. He seemed a rather nice little boy, grubby and bashful, not at all the problem his mother had suggested. All the same, if he couldn't read . . .

"I'm sorry I'm late. Your wife was talking to me and showing me my room."

"You've just about made it. I'm a bit neurotic about punctuality. I know that doesn't make much sense since I've the whole day and nothing to do in it. Jeremy, ring the bell and pour Mrs Goodwill some wine. Which do you prefer, Mrs Goodwill, red or white? Or both? The Chablis is pleasant. Are we having a meat course, Jeremy?"

"I think not, sir. Mrs Storrington is rather firm about that.

25

Just soup and fish and cheese, or you'll have a weight problem. I have to agree professionally."

"So the rest of you must suffer with me. How's that, Dolly? No meat for a growing boy."

"He'll have his lamb cutlets for supper, sir."

"And so will we, I expect. If my wife wants to run a hospital she might at least be here to supervise."

Sarah felt her confidence ebbing. She had forgotten how angry Major Storrington's eyes could be. If this went on at every meal when his wife was absent it wasn't going to be much fun. For she suspected his anger was because of Cressida's absence. Fortunately a maid had answered the bell. Or was it the cook? She was a buxom fortyish woman wearing a white apron over a print dress. She was smiling and saying familiarly,

"Cold consommé today, since the weather's so warm. But I've a nice Dover sole to follow. Shall I take it off the bone for Master Dolly?"

"Certainly, Agnes. This is Mrs Goodwill, Agnes. Our cook-housekeeper, general factotum, Mrs Goodwill. You look surprised. But Maidenshall doesn't have an army of servants any more. We make do with Agnes and some ugly old crones known as cleaning ladies from the village. And Jeremy, of course, who does a little gardening and grows some rather nice roses in his spare time. And now you. And old Nanny upstairs. She comes down to the kitchen for her crust. Doesn't she, Agnes?"

"Yes, she does, sir. When she deigns to. I take a tray up as often as not. The stairs are getting a bit much for her. She's ninety-one, after all. Or so she says."

"I'd be the last to dispute that," Major Storrington said. "She seemed pretty ancient even when I was a child, and that's more than thirty years ago. I ran rings around her. Just the way Dolly tries to do with his tutor, poor old Crankshaw. Has he been, by the way? Have you had your lessons this morning?"

"Yes, father." The little boy's voice was subdued, but polite. "He's just gone. Didn't you see him on his bicycle? He wouldn't give Joseph a ride."

"Is that so?" Major Storrington's voice had an edge. Dolly hung his head over his soup plate and began eating his soup noisily. A pity that tutor doesn't teach him table manners, Sarah thought, and asked pleasantly, "Is Dolly expecting a friend? There's a place laid beside him."

There was even a bowl of soup placed on the linen table mat. Sarah, mystified, had watched Agnes putting it there. Was there to be a sole taken off the bone too?

"He's here," said Dolly loudly. His eyes, amazingly blue and beautiful burned upwards. "Aren't you, Joseph? Speak up, boy."

"Okay, old chap," Jeremy said in an oddly placating voice. "Let Joseph enjoy his soup."

Major Storrington was frowning, his face sharply thin and vulnerable.

"We're going down to the river this afternoon," Dolly went on. "May we, Father?"

"You announce your intentions and then ask permission. Get your facts in order. You must ask Jeremy if he has time to keep an eye on you."

"If you don't need me, sir," Jeremy answered.

"I don't need you. Mrs Goodwill and I will be working in the library. If you have no objection to beginning at once, Mrs Goodwill?"

"But of course. That's what I'm here for."

Sarah watched Agnes scoop up the empty soup plates. The untouched one next to Dolly was left until last. When she reached it she said in a perfectly sober voice, "Doesn't your little friend feel hungry today, Master Dolly?"

"He doesn't care for chicken soup. He doesn't care for fish either. He'll just have ice cream."

"He'll be lucky to get it, since he doesn't speak up for himself."

Dolly began to giggle, turning his face to the empty chair beside him and conversing in a whisper.

His father gave a resigned shrug.

"Well, the rest of us do care for fish, Agnes. Mrs Goodwill, as you may have guessed, my son has a faithful shadow called Joseph. They are inseparable. How long it will last . . ."

Since Dolly seemed to be so absorbed in his giggling whispering that one almost saw the imaginary child beside him, Major Storrington went on in a lower voice, "I believe this sort of thing isn't uncommon with an only and lonely child. At least that's what the last doctor told us. That psychiatrist Cressida had down, Jeremy."

"I remember, sir. He seemed to be a good man."

"Yes, well it's a bit weird, but we have to live through it. They suggest my accident may have had something to do with it. Highly disturbing for the child, since he was accustomed to seeing me pretty active, and now I never get out of this damn chair. So he has compensated by inventing Joseph. He's never even met anyone called Joseph, as far as we know."

"He must have heard the name, sir," said Jeremy. He spoke in polite slightly subservient tones. Perhaps that was the best way to deal with an invalid of uncertain temper.

Sarah was wondering what Jane would make of all this. Perhaps, indeed, that was why she was so welcome here. If no one else could, she might be able to dismiss the invisible Joseph. She was a very healthy extrovert little girl.

But it was strange how uncanny it was, at mid-day, in this formal setting, hearing the excited childish gabbling at the empty chair. If one weren't careful one could easily believe that there were, in truth, two little boys at the table.

3

Immediately after lunch Charles asked Sarah to come to
the library. The room faced west, the afternoon sun gleaming
on the faded leather of the hundreds of books lining the walls.
They may have been bought for appearance rather than
erudition, but they must represent a century or more of literature. Sarah longed to browse. She hoped that Charles enjoyed
this inheritance. It seemed made to order for a sedentary man.

As well as books there was a small arsenal, models of field
guns of the type used in nineteenth-century wars and of more
recent types of gun, beautiful little bronze toys that reminded
Sarah of paintings she had seen of horses straining down
muddy roads as they dragged these deadly long-snouted guns
behind them. There was also an open case of faded tooled
leather containing a pair of duelling pistols chased in
damascene and mother-of-pearl, and obviously heirlooms.

Above the mantelpiece hung an oil-painting of a man in
middle age. He looked over plump and pampered, as if he
were nourished on the best food and wine – no cold soup and
fish only for him at luncheon. His eyes were brilliant and
mesmeric but the full lips were pouting, sensuous and had a
hint of cruelty. A heavy gold watch, the symbol of affluence,
hung across his stomach. He was undoubtedly Grandfather
Charlie.

Charles, watching Sarah, confirmed this. "What they
called a fine figure of a man," he said. "And these were his
toys." He picked up a model of one of the tanks used in
France during the First World War. "Grandfather lived for
his weapons and liked to think he was a British Krupp. He
certainly did nicely in terms of success. And without too
much respect for other people's feelings. My father, when he
was a small boy, was partially deafened by a gun going off.
He never regained his full hearing and couldn't be passed as
fit for the army."

"Ironic justice?"

"Oh, certainly. Actually, Grandfather's last field gun made in too much of a hurry because the Great War was raging, had a tendency to blow up and kill more of our chaps than the enemy. It's suspected that that's how Grandfather died. He got into the army, became a temporary colonel and was killed on the Somme."

Charles took a book from his desk. "I'd like you to read this, since you ought to learn about weapons. It's an account of the Storrington works before they were merged with a bigger concern after the Great War."

"Weapons of death," Sarah murmured.

"Artistic creations, Grandfather would have insisted. Don't be squeamish. I'm going to call you Sarah, if you don't object."

"Please do."

"And I'm Charles. No formalities. We're going to be collaborators."

He was nice, like this, interested in his project, his face keen and alive.

"I may expect a lot of you. I'd like you to get some ideas on the personal side of this book while I concentrate on the hardware. I'm not much good on people. Women have more curiosity."

"But I don't know anything about your family."

"So you do research. Family documents, church records, old letters. I have some written by my Aunt Cissie and my father when they were taken to St. Petersburg as children. It was before the assassination of the Czar and his family. But there must be other caches of letters and diaries to be discovered."

"In the traditional attics?" Sarah said, excitement stirring.

"That's mostly where the old stuff is dumped. There may be locked drawers, too. I don't think there's ever been a thorough cleaning out in this house since it was built. As we've shrunk in numbers, surplus things have been pushed into empty rooms. Cressida hasn't any interest in dusty old papers, as she calls them."

"Muniments," Sarah murmured.

"Exactly. I really want this record for Dolly, and whoever comes after him. I'd never have thought I was that sort of chap, family proud. But it's easier right now to concentrate on the past and the future, than on the rather unacceptable present."

"I've never had the luck to live in a house like this," Sarah said.

"Luck? Is that what you call it?"

"It has such a lovely name, Maidenshall. That comes from the nunnery, I suppose?"

"Naturally. I don't think anyone has seen any coiffed ghosts, but there'll certainly have been young and old maidens living in this house, as well as in the nunnery in earlier times. Governesses, elderly servants, nannies. They were always spinsters. Even my Aunt Cissie was one, because she died in the influenza epidemic after the war, before she had time to be married."

"I have my own traumas, but being a spinster isn't one of them," Sarah said.

"Where did you live as a child?"

"In the Cotswolds near Cirencester. My father was a country doctor. We lived in an old rectory, six bedrooms. My brother and I thought it enormous. But you could almost put it in the hall and the big drawing room here."

"No family —"

"Skeletons? Was that what you were going to say?"

"No, I was going to say family trusts or obligations. Duty to history, or whatever you call it. I suppose skeletons, too."

The sound of Dolly shouting in the garden was closer. He seemed to be arguing with someone. "No! I told you, no! I don't want to do that. You're being very bossy today, Joseph."

"Come along now, old chap," came Jeremy's mild voice. "If you'll rake up these clippings I might take you out in the boat."

"That is kind of you, Jeremy. We'll like that." Dolly had an old-fashioned politeness, almost as if he had been born in another century. It must be the result of always being in the company of adults.

"Perhaps you could leave Joseph behind today," Jeremy suggested.

"No! No, no, no! He'd be angry."

Sarah saw Charles's gesture of irritation. "Open the window and tell Dolly to play farther away. Noisy little brat. Never has a thought for anyone else. As for the famous Joseph – they seem to fight as much as they love one another. Typical small boys, I suppose. If Joseph is a small boy," he added, "I sometimes think he's a monster."

Apart from that interruption, the afternoon passed quietly. Sarah had the distinct feeling that Charles found peace in this room, even being able to temporarily forget his tragedy. He had seemed to enjoy talking about his family, as if having an audience stimulated him.

He had dictated some letters to her, made notes, talked about possible chapter headings, then had pushed his pad away, abruptly tired. At the same time they could hear Agnes calling Dolly in for his supper. It was six o'clock, the sun was slanting across the green lawns and Sarah could believe Charles's weariness, for she was stiff and tired herself. It had been a demanding day.

"We dine at eight, Sarah. Drinks at seven-thirty. Why don't you go out and get some fresh air?"

"Wouldn't you like some too? I could push you –" she saw the lift of his chin "– or call Jeremy."

"No, thank you. I'm perfectly able to take an airing on the terrace unaided. There's a ramp especially arranged by my thoughtful wife. And I'm past the age for being taken down to the river to feed the ducks."

Sarah ignored that rather poor joke and asked if the river were a tributary of the Thames.

"Yes, it flows into some water meadows half a mile away. A place called The Marsh. It's a pleasant spot in the summer but damned cold and miserable and misty in winter. It's a strict rule that Dolly – and your girl, when she comes – must never go there alone in the winter or after heavy rain. The weeds are deceptive. They look like grass, but they cover very wet bog. It's now become out of bounds for me as well, which is a bore. I enjoyed an early morning shoot. Wild

32

duck for dinner. Now that isn't self pity, it's a statement of fact."

"You're entitled to some self pity," Sarah exclaimed. "Good God."

"*Good* God? Sarah, you're looking angry. Is that on my behalf? That's decent of you. Well, off you go, but mind the marsh."

As she went out through the garden door she looked back and saw him wheeling his chair to the window. From there he could get a view of the long drive that led to the ornate entrance gates and the London road. She knew he was watching for his wife's return.

The sadness that had touched her in the library refused to be shaken off. It was a beautiful evening, the roses glowing in the golden light and filling the air with their scent. In the distance, at the bottom of the sloping lawn, water gleamed. The river, neat and tamed here, was spanned by a charming humped bridge. Only clumps of marsh marigold and reeds bordered it, but a pathway beneath the willows and elders led to a narrower weed-infested stream that wound, shining darkly, into the distance.

Although curious to explore, Sarah's melancholy mood deterred her. Tomorrow, she thought, she would find the kitchen and make tea and carry a tray into the library. That was what was wrong with both her and the man sitting in the window practising his difficult discipline. They had needed refreshment. Thoughtless of her. She should have looked after him better.

She turned back and went into the house by the front door, and upstairs. She would finish unpacking, bath and change. Did they dress for dinner? Not too elaborately, she hoped. She hadn't had much occasion to wear evening clothes over the past year.

That poor devil sitting alone in the library. When did Cressida get home?

It wasn't the sound of a car in the driveway that aroused Sarah, having a brief rest after her bath. It was someone screaming. Surely it could be no one but Dolly. The sound came from the other side of the house, probably from the

33

little boy's bedroom. The long corridor was empty. No one was hurrying to his aid.

Sarah passed several closed doors. The walls were hung with a great many water colours, large and small. She would study them another time. The door from which the distressed sounds were coming was at the far end of the corridor. Now they had clarified into words.

"Let me out! Let me *out!*" Dolly was imploring in a frantic voice.

Sarah opened the door and rushed into the room. The little boy was flinging himself about, the bed in a state of disarray. His eyes were wide open but he was not immediately aware of Sarah. She had to sit beside him and try to wake him gently from his nightmare.

"Dolly! It's all right." She held his hand. "You're safe in your own bed. See! Wake up!"

Slowly the look of blind panic left his eyes. They focused on Sarah and became puzzled.

"Who are you?"

"I'm Mrs Goodwill. Don't you remember me at lunch?"

"Oh yes. Jane's mother."

"That's right. You've been having a nightmare. You were screaming."

The briefest flicker of fear crossed his face, a memory of darkness.

"I thought I was locked in."

"Where?"

"In a room."

"A room you know?"

"Sort of. I'm not sure. But someone locked the door, and I banged my hands on it and shouted."

He was rubbing his hands as if they hurt him. But he was calmer. An odd look of maturity had come into his eyes, an old weary look, uncannily like the one his father had worn in the library an hour ago.

"I'm better now, thank you, Mrs Goodwill. Is Mother home?"

"I don't think so. She'd have come to you, wouldn't she?"

"I don't know. Sometimes Nanny does. She's old. Joseph doesn't care for her very much."

"Joseph?" Sarah paused a moment. "Does Joseph have nightmares too?"

"Oh, yes. He screams. Didn't you hear him? He wakes me up."

A queer thought came to Sarah. Hadn't Dolly known it was he himself who had been screaming?

"Well – I suppose I did."

"Mrs Goodwill –" He was wide awake now, and obviously about to use some ploy to keep her. At least that was healthily normal. "Will I like Jane?"

"I hope so."

"I'm afraid Joseph won't."

"Goodness me, you can't run your life to suit Joseph."

Dolly's face, flushed and tense, seemed deeply perplexed. As if he were carrying a burden far too complex for his tender years.

"I really think I'm happier with just Joseph. Could you tell Jane – politely?"

"No, I couldn't. I want her here. She's my daughter. So if Joseph doesn't like her, he will just have to lump it." Was it too soon to adopt such a firm attitude? But, really, this obsessive nonsense about an imaginary playmate and not a particularly nice one, had to be moderated.

"You will like Jane," she said gently. "But of course she'll have to like you, too. Do you think you can make her?"

But suddenly the child was falling asleep, his face soft, his long black lashes touching his cheeks. He was a cupid with black curls – a slightly wicked cupid. There was something about him, even in this quiescent state. What was it? Surely not what she sensed, a deep and disturbing lack of innocence.

The moon was up and flooding the garden with white light. It was warm enough to sit on the terrace. Sarah, in the light voile dress she had worn to dinner, sat a little apart from Charles and Cressida. Jeremy was busy with the coffee tray. It seemed to be his task to take the dishes out and bring in the coffee. Agnes, after what must have been a twelve hour day, had apparently taken herself off to her room and her television set. Vague sounds of actressy voices and synthetic laughter came from an open window in the distance.

"Agnes is addicted to the most boringly awful TV comedies," Cressida said.

She sat on a low chair close to Charles. His hand occasionally strayed to her hair. She jerked her head once, as if she didn't like her hair, obviously fresh from a London hairdresser, being disarrayed. She had been so late home she had apologised for not changing for dinner, although her silk dress, cleverly suggesting the curves of her body, would have taken her anywhere.

"It was ghastly in town," she said. "Hot and airless. Charles, you're wearing your velvet jacket. Is that for Sarah?"

"Of course."

"Well, it's nice, even if it isn't for me. Poor love, I know what an exercise it is for you to change."

"Not an exercise at all."

"No, he didn't even need help this evening, Mrs Storrington," came Jeremy's voice, the male nurse trained to be soothing. "Shows how he's getting on."

"Getting on is hardly what I would call it." Charles's voice was tight. "However, since you seem determined to talk to me as if I'm an infant learning to walk, I'll eventually prove I can, and Jeremy might find himself out of a job. How about that?"

They laughed dutifully, Cressida and Jeremy. Cressida, standing behind her husband, looked towards Sarah with eloquently raised eyebrows.

Later she came over to Sarah and said in a low voice, "He seems in one of his moods. Has he behaved himself this afternoon?"

"Yes, indeed. He seemed to enjoy working. Planning how to shape his book, and so on."

"I expect he will behave himself with you. He does, with people he isn't involved with. They all think him wonderful."

"If he can't cry on his wife's shoulder –" Sarah began.

Cressida looked annoyed. "That isn't crying. That's just

36

bloody-mindedness. But poor love," she added, dutifully it seemed.

Naturally, he'll be bloody-minded if there are too many poor loves being tossed about, Sarah thought. Really, Cressida, you're too intelligent for that. Or don't you care? Any longer?

However, on the terrace in the dim scented night light, the conversation faltered and died out. The coffee cups chinked, the owls called from the willow trees at the river's edge.

"Brandy, sir?" asked Jeremy.

"Yes, a large one. Cress?"

"Yes, please."

"And one for Sarah."

"Oh, it's Sarah now, is it," said Cressida good-humouredly "So you two are getting on."

"She may not be so happy when she sees what I want her to read this evening, or before breakfast."

"What's that?" Sarah asked with interest.

"Some diaries. They are voluble and endless. I've had them locked in my desk for years. Never got round to deciphering them. The writing is rather childish and almost illegible. They belonged to my Aunt Cissie. There are no dates, but she seems to have been born with a pen in her hand and everything is recounted. She had absolutely no gift for selection. They finish while she still had a governess. I suppose girls always did in those days."

"Yes, they did. Now they wear chastity belts – hopefully." That was Cressida's ironic drawl. "Lucky we didn't have a daughter, darling."

Sarah noticed the past tense. Cressida was still young enough to bear a child.

"Will you begin reading them, Sarah?"

Sarah sprang up to take the shabby books from Charles.

"I'd love to. I'd like to begin at once. Would you excuse me if I went upstairs now?"

"Why not?" That was Cressida again. "There's nothing to do down here, unless you like listening to owls."

Sarah could hear the owls through her bedroom window, too. But she was not aware of them for long. Propped up in bed in the tastefully refurbished governesses' room, she strained her eyes over the faded childish writing, gradually becoming immersed in the other world that was springing up around her.

"Today Miss Knox arrived. On my asking, she told me that her first name is Hannah. And she said that she would call me Cissie instead of my real name Celia, because everyone else did. She is small and neat and quick, rather like a brown bird. But her eyes are big and notice everything. I saw the way she looked round her room and didn't seem to care for it. I suppose I shouldn't have followed her in, uninvited. She told me to go away, but I decided I still rather liked her."

I believe, she thought, tingling a little as she lay in the old-fashioned bed, with its polished brass knobs at head and foot, that this must be the actual bed in which the governess with the big eyes had slept. She had a good old-fashioned plain name. Hannah Knox . . .

4

Hannah

HANNAH'S BOX HAD been carried upstairs while she was in the morning room being given instructions by her new mistress. Now she was shown to her room by an elderly servant whose name was Barker.

She stared at Hannah a good deal. Her face was narrow and humourless. She had a knot of grey hair wound tightly on the top of her head and she wore an unadorned dark grey dress. Her only sign of liveliness came from her black eyes, which were keenly observant. She had thought Miss Knox would be older, she said.

"I'm twenty-five," Hannah said. Surely that was old enough for anybody. "This is my third position." Because the woman was obviously waiting for this information to be enlarged upon, she added, "I was with a family in Leicester, the Drews, for three years, and then with the Woodcocks in London for two and a half years."

"And before that?" Barker asked.

These were questions her employer should ask, and indeed had done so. They were really no business of Barker's, but there was something about her that made not answering unthinkable and rude.

"I had a good schooling. Then my father unfortunately lost most of his money in a business deal. I had not married, so –" She flung out small child-like hands, her prettiest and most disarming feature, "– with no fortune and few looks" (and no special gift for attracting masculine attention, she thought privately), "this is the kind of life I chose."

"You like living in good houses" Barker observed shrewdly.

"Why do you say that?"

"Because otherwise wouldn't you have gone into business? Been a dressmaker or a typewriter, or even a hospital nurse?"

"I sew very badly, I can't typewrite and I don't care for illness. Besides, with those kind of positions one has to pay for one's own board and lodgings, which leaves one with little enough to live on and nothing at all for luxuries. Yes, I do like good houses. And I am a good teacher. I'm quite content with this way of life. Why are you looking at me as if you're sorry for me?"

"It's not you, it's your kind. You come to grief. Get envious, get ambitious, want what you can't have. Because you're all the same, aren't you, neither fish, flesh nor fowl. You've never been taught your place. If you ask me, it's better to start out as a plain servant and know which is your side of the fence."

"I am a mature woman with a superior education," said Hannah crisply. "I think I know how to behave in any situation. And I'm not sure that your many years of service here give you the right to speak to me like that."

"I've seen them come and go," Barker observed. "And you're just a little sparrow of a thing, aren't you, in spite of your grand education. Well, maybe that's for the best."

She didn't add in what way it was for the best. However, Hannah, rather bitterly, could guess. As it happened, she had never been put to the task of repelling advances from straying husbands or amorous guests. Of course, her two previous households had been strait-laced and frankly dull. She was fairly certain that this one would be neither of those things. She had only to look at Mrs Storrington, with her air of distraction and dishevellment, her reddish hair tumbling over a very white forehead, her sea-green gaze scarcely resting on Hannah as she seemed to seek beyond her for some more amusing and desirable form. A self-absorbed woman who had little serious concern for her children's education, Hannah had decided. Although when she had mentioned the youngest one, Boy, she had frowned in a preoccupied way.

"Celia, we call her Cissie, is my eldest," she had told Hannah. "She is thirteen. Adolphus is eleven and Boy is not quite ten. Adolphus will go to Eton next year. He goes to a tutor in Maidenhead, but with your really excellent references, Miss Knox, I am sure you will be able to help him a great deal. My husband says that his Latin is deplorable. I'm not in a position to judge that." She shrugged charmingly. "I'm quite uneducated. My mother thought that all that was required of a girl was to shine in society. Will you remember when you speak to Adolphus that he is a little deaf? My daughter Cissie has no particular talent. She's quite average, but she's going to be reasonably presentable and there I agree with my mother – it's the most important thing for a girl. What do you think?"

She didn't expect an answer. Her lazy eyes (slightly malicious, or was it amusement that flickered in them?) took in Hannah's neat and modest appearance. "But we can't all be wild beauties, can we? I do congratulate you on your scholarship, Miss Knox. Cheltenham Ladies College, I believe. And you excelled in music and the classics?"

"Yes, madam."

"Did you enjoy learning? And call me Mrs Storrington."

"Yes, Mrs Storrington, I did."

"Then you'll enjoy teaching. My husband agreed that you were quite the best of the applicants. Your predecessor was splendid at tennis and cycling, and dancing, too, but she was quite hopeless in the classroom. We want discipline and hard work, Miss Knox, especially for Adolphus who would be at a preparatory school except for his deafness."

"Of course, Mrs Storrington."

So she had been chosen not so much for her scholarship as for her inconspicuous looks. She was not to waste her time playing tennis or dancing all night.

"We spend the summer here and part of the winter abroad. But we will see how you get on this summer before we talk of future commitments. You won't find it too dull here. We have house guests most weekends. I'm afraid I'm a great butterfly. And this hideous house is only possible to live in when it's full of pretty people. The Victorians had absolutely no taste and Charlie's great-grandfather who built this house had even less than most. All vulgar ostentation.

But I flatter myself I have made it liveable. Now I'll ring for Barker to show you your room and the schoolroom. Don't let her bully you. She was nursemaid to my husband when he was a child, and then to my children, so she's inclined to give orders, even to me. Well," the beautiful eyes surveyed Hannah again, with that touch of patronising pity, "do you think you can manage?"

"I will have to wait and see, Mrs Storrington."

Manage? When had she ever failed to?

But suddenly she wished deeply that she had some more attractive clothes. She had had an amber silk once, in which she had looked well. But such a dress would be superfluous here. Mrs Storrington had hinted pretty plainly that she was not meant to have any part in the gayer life of the household.

It wasn't until she had followed the uncompromising Barker upstairs that she realised Mrs Storrington had not given her any specific instructions about her youngest son, Boy. She had mentioned neither his mental ability nor her plans for his future. But then he was only nine years old, and the baby of the family. Probably shockingly spoiled.

Hannah hung her clothes in the cavernous wardrobe. They scarcely filled a quarter of the space. Her bottle green coat and skirt and matching straw hat, her blue crepe dinner dress with its modest neckline, her blouses and skirts for the schoolroom, her well-polished buttoned boots. Not an evening bag, not a fan, not a fluttering feather stole.

"Oh," came a voice behind her. "I had hoped you would have had prettier things."

Hannah turned sharply to face the girl who stood behind her watching her inquisitively.

"Who are you?" she asked coldly.

"I'm Cissie. Didn't you know?"

"How should I, since we haven't been introduced. And do you usually burst into other people's rooms without knocking?"

"I didn't mean to – I didn't think. Miss Shepherd didn't used to mind. Are you angry?"

"No," said Hannah, "But you've reminded me to put manners on the agenda."

The child – she was really only a child, with pigtails, freckles, and the lingering awkward angularity of childhood – looked abashed. She was very unsure of herself, which was not surprising with a mother like that tempestuous beauty downstairs. What was the father like? She wondered for the first time.

"So you're Celia," she said.

"Yes, but everyone calls me Cissie. And Adolphus sometimes gets called Dolly, which he hates. Boy, of course –"

"Yes?"

"He's just Boy. He's rather spoilt, did Mamma tell you?"

"No, she didn't."

"I suppose she wouldn't since he's her pet. He has the most awful manners."

"Then we must not only put manners on the agenda, but at the top."

As Cissie fell into a little explosion of giggles, her face became lively and attractively dimpled. Her mother had said she might be quite presentable. Well, Mamma might be startled and perhaps not too pleased by what her angular young daughter eventually became. For there could be an arresting personality here. Hannah was feeling an impulse to bring it out prematurely. To set the cat among the pigeons. That was one of the irresistible games that governesses, ignored and seemingly invisible persons themselves, could play, given the right material. And if they had sufficient grievances, which was unfortunately often the case.

Hannah had realised this when she chose her career. But her last two households had been tepid and unprovoking. Now, a precious six years had gone by virtually wasted, and she was rapidly heading for permanent spinsterhood. She really must find some amusement on the way, if only by administering some uncomfortable pricks to that supremely confident, vain and insensitive woman downstairs, who, unfairly, had everything. And what quiet sport, she found herself wondering, might the master provide?

Hannah was a little shocked at her thoughts. She had never been contented, but neither had she been deeply

43

discontented. She had taken comfort from her good intellect, her pleasure in books and music, her feeling of mental superiority over pupils and parents.

But from the moment of entering this house, restless, curiously excited feelings had stirred in her. In contrast to its ugly heavy exterior, the interior of the house had been so surprising with its luxurious overflowing contents, rugs, flowers, ornaments, pictures, cushions in exotic colours, that one had known the glorious woman sitting in the midst of all that profusion had created the warmth around her. Someone like herself would be as invisible in that setting as a chrysalis on the bark of a tree. The idea of her making any impact on this household was so improbable that suddenly she was determined to do so. She would burst out of her chrysalis and show her true self, subtly coloured, brilliant, desirable.

The fanciful thoughts were like a spell. She hadn't the faintest idea why she had this feeling of challenge and madness, unless it were that she had had her twenty-fifth birthday a week ago, and Daisy, her younger sister (who had married a solicitor's clerk and sensibly settled for security rather than romance) had observed that even a cab driver or a gardener would be better than no husband at all, although she shouldn't plan to set her cap at the butler in the big house, because they usually got at the port.

"Try and bring out your looks, Hannie. You scare men off with your brains."

Looks. Yes. As she talked carefully and earnestly to the dazzling Mrs Storrington at that first interview, taking Daisy's advice was exactly what she intended to do.

When she heard two weeks later that she had been successful in her application, that foolish excitement had vanished and commonsense had taken its place. She would go to her new position in her usual way, neatly and inconspicuously dressed. Her blue crepe would last another season. She had four white immaculately starched and ironed shirt waists, and two good skirts, one tweed for outdoors, one merino wool in a serviceable dark grey for the schoolroom. She would seldom, she supposed, be eating with the family, but when she did she could dress up in her crepe or her worn

44

brown velvet, with a shawl and her one piece of jewellery, her garnet necklace.

However, guessing that Cissie's estimation of her wardrobe was more sympathetic than contemptuous, she knew she had made a mistake. She should have invested some of her precious savings in a couple of new dresses and possibly a new hat. Caution should have been forgotten. Here, if ever, was a house in which to preen for those gay weekends and parties of which Mrs Storrington had talked.

The game's afoot, she murmured under her breath, and like a blaze of sunshine the quite unjustified excitement seized her again.

"Miss Knox, you aren't angry, are you? Your eyes look so bright."

"Yes, I am angry. But only with myself for not having the pretty clothes you wanted to see. I shall get some at the first opportunity."

"Oh, Miss Knox, may I come with you? I know a lovely shop in Maidenhead where Mamma goes when she wants something in a hurry, and hasn't time to go to London."

"One thing I will not have time for is to go to London."

Cissie giggled again. "You looked so funny when you said that. Your eyes twinkled. I believe I shall like you."

"I hope so."

"Then Adolphus will, too. He always likes people I like."

"And Boy?"

"Oh, he never likes anyone. Except Mamma, of course."

The last items in Hannah's box were her books and photographs. Cissie, who was too inquisitive, had been sent off at this stage of the unpacking. The books were far too advanced to interest her (the Oxford Book of Verse, Middlemarch, all of Jane Austen, Hazlitt's essays, the diaries of Samuel Pepys, Shakespeare, of course and Keats and Tennyson). The photographs of her mother and father, herself and Daisy as two loving sisters, arms wrapped about one another, and a faded one of their brother who had died at the age of six years after short distressing illness which had shocked her beyond words because, when everyone knew that little children gladly went to Jesus, his dying should not have been so

45

full of pain and fear, were put on show because they gave her a sense of identity. They also proved that she had had a loving family, even if Daisy, intolerably smug about her pedantic husband, was the only other survivor. Daisy, one knew, found Hannah nothing but an irritating appendage while she remained a spinster. So the feeling of identity was not particularly satisfying or strong. But it was there.

It was late afternoon now, and the sun had moved round to this wing of the house. The sound of voices took Hannah to the window. She saw that Mrs Storrington had guests to tea. A table was laid under a freshly-leaved chestnut where dappled sunlight could fall across the snowy cloth. Two maids, cap ribbons flying, were carrying laden trays, the contents of which they proceeded to set out on the table. The chink of porcelain sounded distinctly, sharp facets of light struck from the silver tea service, a large fruit cake was placed in the centre of the table.

Presently Hannah heard Mrs Storrington's warm rippling voice.

"If we don't spend too long over tea we may have time for a game of croquet. Reggie, will you partner me?"

"Certainly, dear lady. I'd rather have you as my partner than my opponent. Violet's lethal at this game, I'd have you know."

Mrs Storrington, accompanied by a tall blond man, obviously Reggie, came into view. She was wearing a broad-brimmed flower-decked hat, and a trailing gown. Ridiculous for croquet, Hannah thought. The other woman, in pale green, was far more suitably dressed, indeed almost as modestly as Hannah herself. She was not saying anything to her partner who surely was not Mr Storrington. Mrs Storrington would never have married that slight and insignificant figure. Unless she had done so for this rich house and plenty of money, an act of which Hannah was sure she was capable.

Reggie, with whom she was now flirting, was a much more likely sort of man for her to have married.

Too interested in a scene that should not concern her, Hannah nevertheless kept being drawn to the window to watch until tea was finished and the four adjourned to the croquet lawn which was partially out of sight. Then only an occasional flicker of a gown, the ringing crack of mallet on ball, and various shrieks of indignation or dismay, told her that the game was in progress.

"Reggie! Reggie! Reggie!" Mrs Storrington cried once, on a note of pure triumph.

An intuitive and startling thought came to Hannah. That was the kind of cry which could come from a wife and husband at their most private moment.

She had no idea why she should think that. Her cheeks had become burning hot. She felt she had been eavesdropping unforgivably. And Reggie's response to Mrs Storrington's cry hardly bore out her fancy.

"Well done, Vi, old girl. I told you she was madly dangerous, didn't I? Do you two want to give up before you're slaughtered?"

There were indistinct murmurs of assent.

"Anyway," came Mrs Storrington's voice, "we must go in. Charlie will be home soon. He has to meet the new governess. She arrived this afternoon."

"Promising?" asked Reggie.

"Yes, promising for the children."

"No more tennis-playing amazons, eh?"

There was a ripple of laughter, knowing, slightly sniggering. The heat rose to Hannah's cheeks again.

Someone knocked at her door. A maid stood there.

"The mistress said you was to dine with the family tonight, miss. Will you be down at seven o'clock?"

"Very well."

Very well, indeed. Now was she to enhance her blue stocking appearance by wearing the blue crepe dress, or begin defying it by wearing the more dressy brown velvet, though that was shabby enough.

Before she could decide a rifle shot sharply and shockingly broke the evening peace. A colony of rooks flung themselves into the air, cawing discordantly. Hannah's hand had flown to her mouth. She could scarcely speak.

"Whatever was that?"

The maid, quite a young girl with pink cheeks, was giggling irrepressibly.

"If you could see your face, miss. I was the same when I first came here. It's only the master home. He fires a gun to warn everyone, although he only does it when he is in a good humour, so he lets you know about that, too. It's his kind of joke, really."

"Really," Hannah echoed.

"He makes guns, didn't you know? Mad on them, too. Can't talk of much else. That's why Master Adolphus is deaf. His father fired off a gun too close to the little chap's head once. Cracked his ear drum. It's a downright shame."

Hannah wanted to know more.

"What's your name?"

"Elsie. I'm the first floor maid."

"What's Mr – the master like?"

"Well, he can be ever so nice. Or not. You need to mind his temper."

"Oh! Will I –"

"Don't suppose you'll ever get in his way, miss," Elsie said kindly. "He doesn't take much interest in the schoolroom. If you ask me, Master Boy's the one you'll have to mind."

5

WHEN HANNAH PRESENTED herself punctually in the drawing room there was only the master there. Mr Charles Storrington. He could be no one else. The ugly dark face fitted exactly the kind of man who would fire a gun into the air as a warning that he was home. Rugged, keen-eyed, heavily built, this man would always announce his presence, although even without announcing it in some flamboyant or eccentric fashion, he would not be overlooked.

Hannah felt her heart jump beneath the modest bosom of her blue crepe. She knew she looked timid and tongue-tied. She wished that she could have let this man, who was staring at her with unconcealed disappointment, be aware that there was more to her than appeared on the surface. But would her suppressed qualities of wit and mental agility appeal to him? Of course not. She recognised his type at once, extrovert, uninhibited, physical. Overpoweringly physical. It was a type she thoroughly disliked. Yet she stood there like a voiceless schoolgirl, wishing she could have maintained his interest for at least a few minutes while they were alone.

"Good evening. You must be the new governess. Did my wife tell me your name?"

He didn't care whether he should have remembered it or not. He only needed to know it for convenience. And already she knew that his disappointment was giving way to an expansive relief. She would present no problems. (What, she wondered, had the tennis-playing Miss Shepherd been to him?)

"I am Miss Knox, sir."

"Ah! Not a descendant of the preacher, I hope."

"No, sir." Her lashes lay demurely on her cheeks. "Would you be afraid I would try to convert you?"

He suddenly gave a roar of laughter, almost as noisy and

explosive as his gunshots. "Small chance you'd have." But he didn't look at her again. He was at the sideboard where an array of decanters and glasses stood. "Can I pour you a sherry? Everyone seems to be late tonight. I can't stand unpunctuality."

She took the glass of sherry with a murmur of thanks. When she lifted her eyes she saw that he was giving her a quick second look. His eyes were a very dark brown, almost black. He had stopped laughing. Indeed, his interest had faded and he was clearly relieved when Mrs Storrington, followed by her three children, came into the room.

The glorious hair was tumbling already, Mrs Storrington's face was distracted.

"Charlie, I'm sorry we're late. Reggie and Blanche brought a rather dim house guest, Edward Flint, and we stayed too long on the croquet lawn. I see you have made Miss Knox's acquaintance. Cissie tells me she's introduced herself, so you have only to meet my two sons, Miss Knox. Adolphus and Boy."

Adolphus was tall, thrusting already into the thin vulnerable height of adolescence. He was dark-haired and dark-eyed like his father. His sulky mouth expressed his scorn at being forced to endure another governess. That was a healthy attitude which Hannah appreciated. What she didn't care for was the anxious listening look of the hard of hearing. He was too young for such an expression. And that unthinking brute, his father, was responsible. Rather than make amends for his guilt one was pretty sure that all he did was to shout at the boy to pay attention and not to daydream.

However, in spite of his disability, Adolphus did have the manners to shake hands and mutter some sort of welcome. The younger boy was another character altogether. He clung to his mother's hand and seemed unduly shy for his age. At first he refused to look at Hannah at all, then suddenly he lifted an exquisite pink and white face, like a girl's, and gave her a long stare. He was utterly beautiful. His tousled red-gold curls were his mother's. His eyes were a lighter blue than hers, but even more brilliant, like a summer sky. He made no attempt to come forward or to speak to Hannah, but his tongue flicked in and out between his lips, like a lizard's about to catch an insect. The grotesque comparison didn't seem wrong to Hannah. Boy was difficult, Cissie had said. And spoiled rotten by an anxious adoring mother, Hannah was now able to add privately to herself.

Though why did his mother show such anxiety, frowning and smiling at the same time. Was this over-dressed little boy (he wore a frilled shirt under a velvet jacket) going to ruin his beauty by staging a tantrum?

But no. His mother relaxed visibly when he put his hand out in a curiously puppet-like way.

"I am pleased to meet you, Miss Knox," he said in an impeccable voice, and for a moment it seemed, absurdly, as if everyone were going to applaud with relief.

Did he seldom show good manners? Hannah knew that if she were to be a success in this position she must begin by weaning Boy from his mother's influence. Boy! The very name proved that he was still regarded as a pet, something between a perennial infant and a lapdog.

Tomorrow she would assess his real capabilities. Tonight was obviously intended to be an exercise in friendship.

"If he misbehaves at table —" she heard Mr Storrington saying in a low voice to his wife as they went in to dinner.

"S-ssh! He's being angelic."

"But she'll have to know —"

"No, Charlie, not now." Mrs Storrington raised her voice. "Miss Knox, will you sit between Adolphus and Boy."

"— sooner or later," Mr Storrington finished stubbornly.

"And Cissie, you can face Miss Knox. I can see you're unable to keep your eyes off her."

Did she use this artificial raised voice because she thought everyone was a little deaf, like Adolphus? And that no one would hear the low private exchanges between herself and her husband?

Boy ate his food untidily and noisily, but otherwise behaved well enough at table. Although he now totally ignored Hannah when she spoke to him, and significantly was not reprimanded by his mother, almost as if she did not dare to do so. Conversation was not easy, for the

51

better-mannered Adolphus failed to hear Hannah's remarks to him, and rather than ask her to repeat them he flushed with painful embarrassment.

"He didn't hear you, Miss Knox," Cissie said mildly, and Hannah had a sharp feeling of pity for the silent boy.

"I have a rather soft voice," she said apologetically. "People often fail to hear me."

Then Mr Storrington surprised her by giving her a warm and intimate smile.

"Don't get a shrill voice. Can't bear that in a woman."

"*Fee, fi, fo, fum,*" said Boy unexpectedly. "*I smell the blood of an English mum*! That's you, Miss Knox." He went into peals of laughter which seemed to Hannah to border on hysteria. Then, with a bewildering change of mood, he said to Hannah, graciously, "I grew out of fairy stories when I was five years old. I hope you will have something more grown-up for me to read."

"Boy!" Cissie was shocked. "You're telling fibs. Don't believe him, Miss Knox, he can hardly read or write. He just remembers what's read to him."

"Cissie!" Mrs Storrington was angry. She was not going to have her favourite criticised.

But her father came quickly to Cissie's defence, his voice changing as bewilderingly as Boy's had done. It was deep and full of love, caressing, almost sexual. Hannah defined this last quality although she had never had a man speak sexually to her.

However, it was plain to see what was happening in this household. The father adored his daughter, the mother her exquisite younger son. Poor marred Adolphus was in the middle. His confidence must be built up. It might take a long time. But she was going to be here for a long time. Already she was finding this unusual household fascinating. She had broken out of the grey area of her life even if she were still to live vicariously.

But why not live in reality? It seemed that if ever she were to have the opportunity, it might be in this house.

Although she was still being treated as if she were as deaf as Adolphus, for, after dinner, while Cissie stumblingly and too ambitiously played a Chopin ballade, Mr and Mrs Storrington's voices were perfectly audible.

"Well, what do you think, Charlie?"

"She's a bit mousey, isn't she? Can she control the boys? Adolphus can't hear her, Boy can hear but won't listen. And she's only really visible in a strong light."

He gave a low rumble of laughter. Mrs Storrington said acidly, "Cissie likes her. That should please you."

Again his voice went deep and soft.

"It does. Well, I suppose Adolphus has his tutor, and Boy is your responsibility. You've always said so." His voice rose, suddenly, "My God, that child is playing badly. Miss Knox, are you a good pianist?"

"Only moderate." Hannah hesitated. "Shall I show Cissie what she's doing wrong?"

"I wish you would. Cissie, my dearest, come and sit on my lap and listen."

Hannah seated herself at the piano and let the quiet notes ripple beneath her fingers. What heaven to be playing again, to allow the confused day to come to an end with the calm lovely music entering her soul. The colourful crowded room, so full of strange and disturbing undercurrents, melted into the prisms of a rainbow, there was beauty, serenity, a faint melancholy, love . . .

The composition came to an end. There was a short silence. Then, "That child is too big to be sitting on your lap," said Mrs Storrington irritably. "Cissie, get off, you're showing your legs. Anyway, it's bedtime. Yes, Boy, I promised you a sugared plum for being good and you shall have it. Come along, all of you."

With goodnights, and a loving "Goodnight Papa, *darling*," from Cissie the children and their mother departed. Hannah stood up uncertainly.

"I enjoy the piano when it's well played," Mr Storrington said from the depths of his chair, "It has a soothing effect on jangled nerves. Do you find that, Miss Knox?"

"I am a great admirer of Chopin," Hannah said primly.

The dark eyes in the ugly creased face regarded her.

"You're a young lady of surprises, aren't you?"

"Am I?"

Again, his momentary interest in her had gone.

"Yes, well, I expect my wife will get up a concert one night."

And I certainly won't be asked to play, Hannah thought, her own elated mood fading. Mrs Storrington, she guessed, hadn't expected so much musical talent from a mere governess, and it would not be encouraged. So after all she was there to live vicariously, even when playing that beautiful Steinway Grand.

"Goodnight, Miss Knox," said Mr Storrington. Unexpectedly he added, "Don't let that little devil Boy get the better of you. He has to be locked up sometimes, you know. Just tell Max. He looks after Boy. He knows what to do. Don't send for his mother. That's the worst thing."

By candlelight, in her room, Hannah resorted to what she considered her worst vice. Setting down her thoughts in her diary. After all, what other outlet had she? No friends, no one in whom to confide. Her diary had to be her comfort, virtually her confessional.

"This room," she wrote, "although quite large has none of the sumptuousness that I have seen in the rest of the house. The walls are a sober brown, the furniture austere, a brass bedstead with a white bobbled cotton quilt, a washstand, a small writing desk with an upright chair, on which I am now sitting, a lamp with a pink globe at the bedside, and these two pewter candlesticks whose candles I have lighted, preferring their gentle softness to the harsh electric light. There is also a rocking chair by the window, and a bookshelf for my books. I daresay it is all good enough for a governess. I shall be perfectly comfortable, and shall not indulge in melancholy thoughts about how many previous young women have shed lonely tears within these four walls. For my uncomfortable second senses are working again and I imagine a strong aura of past unhappiness – or is it yet to come?"

"Not to me, please God!" Hannah wrote vigorously, her pen stabbing the paper and making an untidy blot. "I am determined to be happy here. I may be mousey, as Mr

Storrington unkindly said, and nothing much to look at, but he, all of them, will discover that I have an extremely strong will, and intend, no matter what the odds, to be happy. I feel it is my last chance." She paused, sighed, then took up her pen to add, "I wonder why Mr Storrington said that sometimes Boy had to be locked up . . ."

6

AT BREAKFAST, WHICH she took downstairs with the children, Hannah indicated that she wished them to begin work that morning.

Cissie was eager to have any kind of occupation. She found Saturdays dull and Sundays worse.

"But I meant to play cricket," Adolphus objected.

"You may, after luncheon. I merely want to establish your proficiency so that I can arrange a programme for you."

Boy was eating his breakfast with single-minded concentration, porridge followed by scrambled eggs, to which he had helped himself from the sideboard. When he had finished he looked at Hannah impatiently.

"When do we begin?"

Hannah was anxious not to dampen this apparent willingness. If she had had opposition from anyone, she had expected it would come from Boy.

"At once. Cissie, I'm sure you have eaten enough, if you want an eighteen-inch waist when you're a young lady."

"Is that what yours is, Miss Knox?"

"Well – a trifle more. I'm beginning to be middle-aged, after all."

"Miss Shepherd was much more, she was like a feather bolster, Papa said." Boy was grinning cheekily.

"Shut up," Adolphus muttered in embarrassment.

"You're a terrible liar, Boy," Cissie scolded. "Really he is, Miss Knox. He makes up terrible stories. I'm sure Papa never said anything of the kind."

"Miss Shepherd was middle-aged, too," said Boy. "Hurry up, Miss Knox, you said you were coming. After I've done some reading and writing you can leave me alone. I have many things I want to do today."

"Such as?" Hannah asked pleasantly.

"Many things." He was half way upstairs already, his thin body as quick as a weasel. Weasel? Why did that rather nasty little animal immediately spring to mind?

By setting a series of small tests, Hannah made her discoveries fairly quickly. Adolphus was a good average at mathematics, and better than average at languages and the classics. His tutor in Maidenhead must be efficient. Unfortunately he would always be at a disadvantage in a class room because of his defective hearing.

Cissie was rather less than average, probably because she had been indifferently taught for most of her life. Also she was very female, caring more about getting ink on her fingers or creases in her dress, than about learning French, music or literature. But she was amiable and obedient and had a good measure of charm, which Hannah knew was all her parents desired for her.

Boy was a mystery. It was true that his writing, spelling and reading were that of a six year old, or less. Yet he could make sudden sophisticated remarks as if he were deliberately hiding his abilities. He appeared to delight in flustering people. He was also excessively restless, darting from one activity to another. Finally, with obvious intention, he upset his inkwell, and after transforming the blots on his exercise book into surprisingly clever and imaginative little drawings he suddenly announced that he was bored and would like to leave the room.

"When I give you permission," said Hannah. "First I would like a rag to mop up this ink."

But Boy had turned on his heel and disappeared. Imagining he had gone to the water closet, Hannah let him be for a few minutes. She would finish the morning session with a short lecture on obedience, and then allow them all to go. It was a beautiful day, and to tell the truth she would like to be outdoors herself, exploring the garden, the croquet lawn, the tennis courts, the river walk.

Boy did not return.

Arrogant little beast, she thought. Adolphus was despatched to investigate the water closet. He came back, saying that Boy was not there.

"He'll be away outdoors, Miss Knox."

"Does he often do that in the middle of lessons?"

"Quite often," said Cissie. "No one can keep him if he wants to leave. It isn't your fault, Miss Knox."

"Then he will have to learn to obey, won't he?"

"Mamma says he doesn't have to," said Adolphus, who was proving to be a quiet, serious boy. "It isn't fair, actually."

"It's better than his scenes," said Cissie under her breath.

The door opened and Barker stood there.

"If you're looking for the boy, he's gone."

"But I won't have it, Barker, he must ask permission."

"Wasting your words, miss. You could as easily stop a bird flying free. So long as he's happy."

"Happiness is hardly the point."

"You'll come to think so, miss." Barker's cynical eyes went from Cissie's neatly pinafored figure to Adolphus, resentful but obedient. "Can't you let Master Adolphus and Miss Cissie out, too, miss? Keeping them caged up on a sunny day."

One would think they were all wild birds, Hannah thought irritably. And why hadn't Barker called Boy Master Boy? She had simply said 'the boy' as if he were a stranger in the family. A temporary visitor.

She began closing her books with sharp, snapping sounds.

"Very well, if my authority is going to be undermined in this way, you may as well all go. But I intend to speak to your mother about rules and regulations."

Mrs Storrington was not available until an hour before luncheon, which seemed to be her time for coming downstairs. Then she agreed to see Hannah in the morning room.

"I warn you I can't have you running to me all the time with schoolroom problems, Miss Knox."

She looked luscious, like a sun-flushed peach, in a ruffled pink blouse and beige skirt. She would change again for tea, and once more for dinner. It made a busy day. No doubt complaints from any department of the household were given minimum time.

"But I find I'm not in charge, Mrs Storrington. Boy pays

no attention when he's there and leaves when he pleases. I'm sure my predecessors must have mentioned this."

"Never mind your predecessors. They were a hopeless lot, anyway. I thought you looked as if you had more intelligence."

I have plenty of intelligence, Hannah thought silently, but am I going to be allowed to use it?

"Then I may punish Boy as I think fit?"

To her astonishment Hannah saw the lovely face break up in grief and bewilderment. Mrs Storrington put her head in her hands, and for a moment appeared to be weeping.

Then she raised a flushed face and said passionately, "No, you may not, Miss Knox. You may not. Boy must never be punished. He has the most acutely sensitive nature. A harsh word, any opposition, and we have the most dreadful tantrums." She raised wet eyes. "You may think this is just a fond mother speaking. It is not. It is on doctor's orders that my son must be treated with the utmost gentleness and understanding. You may think him semi-illiterate, but this is simply because he isn't interested in books and words. If he is interested in a particular subject, then believe me, Miss Knox, he can be a genius."

Hannah felt dazed. "In what things is he interested?"

"I can't entirely explain. No one can. He knows some things as if he's known them always. He occasionally has an ancient look that frightens me. Anything mechanical he can master in minutes. I gave him a camera for Christmas and he can operate it as well as any trained photographer. He has his own dark room and develops his own plates. It has proved an absorbing hobby, thank goodness. He gets tired of most things so quickly. Then he says he sees and hears things that no one else does." Again Mrs Storrington pressed her face in her hands. "He has nightmares that terrify him, and he screams. He is so beautiful," she said in a muffled voice.

After a moment Hannah said, "Mrs Storrington, why didn't you tell me this at the beginning?"

"Isn't this the beginning?"

"Yes, I suppose it is."

"Well, now I have told you. And I hardly know why you

are complaining since Boy didn't make a scene this morning."

"How do you know?"

"I would have heard him," she replied simply.

"Well, if knocking over an inkwell can be called a scene –"

"Certainly it can't. Let him be, Miss Knox. He's probably down at the marsh."

"Where's that?"

"Where the river flows out. It's a piece of swampy ground, water meadows actually, and it's very peaceful in the spring and summer. Boy loves it. He catches butterflies and dragonflies."

"Is it safe?"

"Perfectly, for anyone who knows it as well as Boy. It is dangerous in mid-winter, or after floods, but he doesn't go down there then. He only likes the sun. I used to worry but now I don't. We've learned that it's best not to stop Boy doing anything that makes him happy. You'll understand as time goes by. If you stay with us."

Boy screams, he has nightmares, he has violent rages, sometimes he has to be locked up . . . He was the kind of pupil about whom nervous governesses themselves had nightmares.

Hannah took a deep breath. "Oh, I intend to stay."

There was just time before lunch to explore. Hannah had a great desire to see for herself the marsh, after which the house was obviously named. She preferred the description, water meadows. A marsh suggested something more sinister, treacherous hidden pools, or sucking mud beneath innocent green weeds.

She took her parasol, and wandered down the sloping lawn to the river's edge. Although it was less a river than stream, amber and damp-smelling, with a humped bridge in the Chinese manner flung across to a small island. As a delightful surprise, a gay little red pagoda emerged from the greenery.

This was the most charming discovery Hannah had made. It showed a far more graceful imagination than the heavy sprawl of the house. It had surely been the idea of a

Storrington wife, for the man who had built Maidenshall had been concerned only in showing the world how successful he was. He had been an arms merchant at that. Not the kind who built follies.

But one could easily imagine it to be the whim of an earlier Violet Storrington, a romantic soul who was probably bored with her stolid Victorian husband.

Hannah crossed the bridge and went up a winding path through rhododendrons to the little pagoda. It was open to the four winds, its stone floor sprinkled with catkins and faded blossoms. It didn't seem as if anyone came there. It was merely a decoration in a wild garden. Although there was a heavy wooden chest in the centre of the floor. Hannah tried the lid, found it unlocked, and lifted it to disclose a stuffed medley of furry rugs and gay cushions.

So on summer afternoons there must be picnics here. Or was this a quiet refuge on warm evenings for guests seeking solitude? There were no doors to be locked, which gave the little edifice an air of complete innocence. The amours of guests, or erring husbands, who came down here, must of necessity be decorous. The love pavilion, if it was intended as such, was a charming sham. Yet it was pleasing, and Hannah, who had had her share of lonely prowling in other people's houses, on the edge of other people's lives, had perhaps developed a too emotionally charged imagination. She could imagine Violet Storrington, in her camellia pink blouse, flickering in the greenery here. Not alone, of course.

The path along the edge of the river was more predictable, rush-edged, willow-hung, bird-haunted. It took ten minutes to emerge into the sunshine and the expanse of the marsh, where the little stream spread untidily through green meadows.

She immediately understood its fascination for the small boy who was perched on a grassy hummock staring intently into a pool. There were larks and lapwings, small water-fowl wading on weed-thin legs, a pair of mallard ducks making peaceful observations to one another. Butterflies and cabbage moths were like blown leaves. A frog was croaking in deep-throated pomposity. The wiry marsh grass and rushes were brilliantly green, the sky reflected in the still pools. There were buttercups and marsh marigolds. The heat of the early summer brought out a not unpleasant odour of stagnant water. In the distance, rotund shapes in a pastoral setting, cattle grazed.

"Hi!" Hannah called in a friendly manner. "Boy!"

The small form on the hummock tensed, then flung round. Even from a distance of twenty yards Hannah could see the child's angry face and sense his fury.

Oh, goodness, what have I done? Provoked his terrifying rage? She scarcely had time to wonder before he came hurtling towards her screaming, "You spoiled it! You spoiled it!"

"Spoiled what?"

"I was just about to catch a frog. He was spotted. I haven't *got* a spotted frog." He paused, his face so scarlet and contorted that Hannah feared he was holding his breath, and would explode. But he was merely gathering strength to express what was an almost maniacal anger.

"You're not allowed here. It's my place. I shall tell my mother and she will lock you up. Serve you right, you're ugly and I hate you. Go away, go away, go *away*!"

However, without waiting for her to retreat, he decided to leave himself, and was gone leaping over hummocks and pools, as graceful as a young deer, but surely there had never been a deer so angry.

Half amused, though distinctly shaken, Hannah watched the flying form. Of course he was angry that she had disturbed his frog. But that display had not expressed just the disappointment of a spoiled little boy. It had been so violent that it had seemed sinister. She believed he would genuinely have liked the blaze of his eyes to burn her to ashes. He was too small, as yet, to be dangerous, but one day . . .

The mild sunny noon had turned to disaster. Chastened and not a little apprehensive, Hannah retraced her steps. Did she, in future, have to ask Master Boy's permission to come to the marsh, his marsh? Was there going to be an almighty row at luncheon, with Mrs Storrington consoling her tear-stained dishevelled evil child?

Evil. That word came spontaneously to Hannah and would not be eradicated.

Yet, bewilderingly, at the luncheon table where there was only Mrs Storrington and the children and herself, Boy was quiet and well-behaved. Someone had washed his face and brushed his golden curls, and exchanged his mud-stained apparel for a clean white jersey and knickerbockers. Now and again he fondled his mother's hand with a touching tenderness. Only once did he look fully at Hannah and then it was with an innocent blue gaze that held no shadow of enmity.

Beneath that innocence there must be a cunning mind, plotting future enormities. There had to be, after that scene such a short time ago. She was not going to be taken in by his display of angelic goodness.

The thought came to her that he was like the marsh, sunny and benign on a fine day, dark, lowering and dangerous in a storm. A disturbing child, indeed. Was she going to hate him as, for that frenzied few moments, he had her? Or was she going to attempt patience and understanding? Only time would tell.

But she said now, "I upset Boy a little while ago by disturbing his frog. He badly wanted to catch it."

"A jolly good thing," said Cissie. "He's horrible to things he catches."

"He's a boy," said Mrs Storrington fondly.

"I'm a boy and I never wanted to poke out a frog's eyes," Adolphus said.

"He'll grow out of that sort of thing. Won't you, dearest?" Boy lifted his bland blue gaze.

"If it would please you, Mamma. May I have another plum?"

When he was allowed to take one of the red-flushed hothouse nectarines from the dish, he didn't eat it but held it in the palm of his hand, gazing at its glossy surface, and then rubbing it caressingly against his cheek. He apparently had an extreme tactile appreciation of soft and glowing surfaces. Yet he could torture small animals . . .

Mr Storrington had not come to luncheon.

"My husband works all the time," Mrs Storrington said.

She gave a slight shrug. "Therefore I am forced to find ways to amuse myself. Next weekend we're having a house party. We dance in the evenings, or play cards. Do you play bezique, Miss Knox?"

"Yes, I do."

"Splendid. You may be useful." Boy had just left the room. Mrs Storrington took the opportunity to speak more frankly. "Certainly I'll want you to keep a constant eye on Boy. I won't have time, and he can be a little jealous of me devoting myself to other people."

"He doesn't care for me much," Hannah said, still shaken by that scene on the marsh.

"He takes violent likes and dislikes." Mrs Storrington sighed. "Give him time. He hasn't got to know you yet. But we don't want any scenes in the drawing room, do you understand?"

Hannah nodded. She and the children were to be relegated to the nursery for meals during this glamorous weekend. She would catch only tantalising glimpses of the guests. Unless, of course, as a last resource, she was drawn unwillingly into a game of cards.

She wondered how Mr Storrington, who was so obsessed with business and making money, behaved as host to a houseful of smart guests. She imagined him being alternatively jovial and impatient. One would have thought that he could not help being besotted by his lovely wife, but he was not. She had been an observer of people's emotions and behaviour for too long to be mistaken. But she was also enough of a cynic to know that this couple didn't need her pity. Both had enough vitality and sophistication to make the best of an unfortunate situation. Married bliss, after all, was a very rare condition.

Everyone, even Mrs Storrington, was at breakfast on Monday morning, although Mr Storrington did not linger long. After swallowing a cup of coffee and eating only one boiled egg he jumped up and kissed his wife, then Cissie (more lovingly), and announced that he would be spending the next two nights at his club in Pall Mall.

"Some foreign buyers," he said, adding for the benefit of

the children, "Russians, all the way from St. Petersburg."

"You are clever to speak their language, Papa," Cissie said adoringly.

"I don't, moppet. I have a chap from the Embassy to interpret."

"Where are the Russians fighting a war, Papa?" Adolphus asked.

"They have just finished one against Japan. They lost it, so they need more guns. Perhaps they mean to fight Germany one day. The Czar is foolish enough. He's a weak man, and therefore dangerous. But then he has a petticoat kingdom."

"You mean he *wears* petticoats?" Cissie giggled.

"He has a wife and four daughters. How does the poor man get a word in edgeways?"

Mr Storrington had an attractive teasing grin, Hannah noticed. But his and his wife's sense of humour were not compatible, for Mrs Storrington merely looked bored.

"And supposing the Russians turn your guns on us, Charlie?" she asked indifferently.

"Not while Czar Nicholas is on the throne. After all he is our King's nephew. That would be worse than incest."

"What is incest, Papa?" Cissie asked.

"Never mind. Well, I've given you your history lesson for today. I am doing Miss Knox's work for her."

"Could I speak to you, Mrs Storrington?" Hannah asked, when Mr Storrington had gone.

"If you make it brief. I have a conference with cook. I don't suppose you have any idea, Miss Knox, how much food is needed for a houseful of guests."

"No, I haven't. But what I wanted to say is that the schoolroom is very badly equipped. There are almost no suitable books for children of Adolphus's and Cissie's ages. We need pencils, too, and exercise books, and a box of paints and drawing pins. Could I go to Maidenhead this morning and make some purchases?"

"Story books, Miss Knox?"

"Novels by Charles Dickens and Robert Louis Stevenson. Lamb's Tales from Shakespeare. They're very much part of a child's education."

"They weren't in my day. I was told books made a child too dreamy, too wrapped up in fantasy."

"I think they may be particularly good for Boy, Mrs Storrington. I believe he would enjoy poetry. He would find it soothing."

The bored green eyes softened.

"If that is your opinion, Miss Knox. Very well. Go to Bates and charge your purchases to me. Using your discretion, of course."

"Naturally, Mrs Storrington. Thank you."

"Mamma! Mamma!" Cissie cried, "May I go with Miss Knox? Miss Knox, will you take me?"

"Do as you please," said her mother, her interest vanishing. "You may as well go in the dogcart with Adolphus when he goes to his tutor. But be sure to tell Barker that Boy will be home alone."

Boy slid off his chair.

"I shall spend the morning with you, dearest Mamma. I shall help you to order the food. Stuffed plovers' eggs and caviare, and the best Scotch salmon, and jugged hare and chicken in aspic, and gigot of lamb, and Aberdeen Angus roast beef, and peaches and strawberries and lemon sorbet and two dozen pineapples and plenty of sherry trifle."

Mrs Storrington gave Hannah a proud but bewildered look. She was laughing helplessly.

"Do I need a chef?"

Cissie tucked her hand in Hannah's.

"I'm so glad to be coming with you, Miss Knox."

"Does Boy really know so much about food, or is he being a parrot and reciting menus he has heard?"

"Yes, he really does. He's terribly greedy. He's like an elderly gourmand, Papa says. What does that mean?"

"Someone who enjoys food rather immoderately."

"That's Boy. He's going to be a very fat old man. Are we only to buy school things, Miss Knox? Can we stop and have hot chocolate at Mrs Munn's?"

"Certainly. And I'll tell you a secret. I want to buy a dress for this weekend. Since you thought my wardrobe so inferior, and since I may have to come downstairs."

Cissie nodded with pleasure. "How jolly! I'll take you to Miss Featherstone's. She sells hats too. I think you might be awfully nice to look at in pretty clothes. Not like a governess at all."

"I think that's a little too much to be hoped for," Hannah said drily. "What's wrong with being a governess, anyway?"

"I expect if the Russians buy Papa's guns," Adolphus said, as they jogged down the green country lanes in the dogcart, "they'll all go deaf, too."

"Poor Dolly," said Cissie, as she walked beside Hannah down the High Street. "He does so hate being deaf. He thinks Papa should have at least given up firing his gun when he comes home. But Papa doesn't mean harm, he's just high-spirited and does things impulsively. He says Dolly must have weak ears since no one else has gone deaf. And he makes it up by being kind to Dolly. He doesn't get angry with him the way he does with Boy. But Boy would try the patience of a saint. I hope he doesn't manage to drive you away, Miss Knox."

"Could he?" Hannah asked, not entirely in amusement, remembering the morning on the marsh.

"He might if he set his mind to it. He's a very strange boy. An enigma, Mamma says. I don't know what that means. But she does make him her pet. So I adore Papa. Even when he is in a rage."

"Lucky Papa, to have a daughter like you."

"I'm just telling you the truth, Miss Knox. Look, this is Miss Featherstone's shop. Let's go in now, before we buy the boring old school things. Oh, look, Miss Knox, look! Here's Papa."

Mr Storrington, very tall in the small low-ceilinged shop, showed one moment of startled guilt.

Then he smiled with apparently unconstrained delight, and exclaimed "Cissie! Miss Knox, what are you doing here with my daughter?"

Cissie had, as usual, flung herself into his arms. "We're here shopping. Are you shopping, Papa?"

He could hardly deny it since a middle-aged woman in black, obviously the proprietress of the shop, was in the act of showing him a hat, a delectable affair of wheat-coloured straw trimmed with an amber silk rose and amber velvet ribbons. But he adroitly avoided the question by asking the saleswoman to try the hat on Hannah.

"Model it for me, Miss Knox. What does a mere man know about hats?"

Before Hannah could protest – aghast at the thought of her small pale face diminished by this elegant creation – Miss Featherstone had whipped off her modest sailor and arranged the light-as-air concoction on her head.

She caught sight of herself in the mirror, aware of her dazzled eyes, the exact shade of the ribbons. She had become an instant lady.

Mr Storrington was watching with amused interest.

"You have remarkable eyes, Miss Knox. Like rich brown sherry of the very best vintage. You must keep the hat."

Hannah pulled it off in a fluster.

"How ridiculous! I couldn't possibly."

"Oh, do, Miss Knox," Cissie begged. "It looks so wonderful. Doesn't it, Papa?"

"Cissie, don't be so foolish," Hannah exclaimed. "Apart from it not being at all the thing, where would I wear it?"

Mr Storrington's voice was deep with the quality that Hannah had already identified as unmistakably sexual.

"Isn't it rather amusing to do something that isn't the thing? And don't women find that, having something ravishing to wear, they will find the occasion to wear it? Miss Featherstone, this young lady is my daughter's – what – chargé d'affaires? Will you put the hat in a box. Did you two come in the dogcart? Then Cissie won't mind being your delivery lad."

"You would like to see something else, Mr Storrington?" Miss Featherstone was asking. Hannah realised she was almost as fussed as Hannah was, though for a different reason. She must have known that the hat had been intended for another lady altogether.

"Not this morning. I couldn't have enjoyed myself more.

Besides," he added smoothly, "my wife has an infinite supply of headgear. Now," he consulted his watch, "I have ten minutes to catch my train. Be good, my children."

My children! With such a twinkle in his eyes he could be forgiven even that familiarity. It took five minutes for the flush to leave Hannah's cheeks and for her to regain her customary commonsense.

"I can't accept this, of course."

Miss Featherstone, carefully arranging the circle of straw in a nest of tissue paper in a hat box, tut-tutted.

"If I were you," she said drily, "I would enjoy my good fortune. Mr Storrington is a very generous man. His eccentricity is quite attractive, to my way of thinking. And his judgment is always correct. You did look very well in this creation. One of my most successful, I think. You could wear it to Ascot – no, I see. But to a garden party, surely." Her narrow eyes, suddenly shrewd and sharp, sent an unmistakable message, allying herself with Hannah. "Outdress your mistress for once," she seemed to be saying.

"Now, what else can I do for you?" she asked.

Cissie was having a marvellous time. Fortunately she was totally unaware of undercurrents.

"Miss Knox wants an evening gown, Miss Featherstone. Something the same colour as the ribbons on the hat, don't you think? Since Papa thought it was right."

"This young lady is nearly old enough for an evening gown herself," Miss Featherstone commented. "But certainly. A dinner gown, or a ball gown? You are perhaps travelling abroad with your employers?"

"No, I am not travelling abroad, and something quite modest and suitable for my position."

"I understand. All the same," Miss Featherstone was drawing back curtains and rummaging among a display of gowns, "you do seem to be fortunate in your employment."

Hannah, who had neglected her diary for a couple of days, wrote in it:

"Last night I dreamed about Mr Storrington. Charles. Charlie. I was wearing the new hat and a trailing gown, and holding his arm as we walked down the street of some foreign city. There was a river running on one side, and elegant classical buildings on the other. It was not a city I had ever seen. I have never been abroad in my life. The dream seemed like a strange prescience, but surely it could be attributed to the small river running by the Chinese pagoda, and to Miss Featherstone's slightly impertinent remarks. Although the dream was brief, I woke feeling hot and restless and extremely disturbed. That wretched hat is a most unwelcome possession. I have hidden it, wrapped in its tissue paper, at the very back of the top shelf of the wardrobe. I have put my own modest sailor, and my velvet toque (intended for church) in the box, pretending that that makes it respectable. Anyway, it would be difficult to get rid of that receptacle since it has bright pink stripes. Barker or Elsie would see it. But is Mr Storrington going to expect me to wear that very expensive creation, or will he forget he gave it to me in that moment of embarrassment which he was so clever at concealing? I am sure he will forget it because his mind will command him to do so . . ."

7

WHAT HAD HANNAH expected, a group of gay friendly people who begged her to join them at tea in the garden, where blossom fell and was crushed in the grass, and wasps made the ladies scream, or after dinner in the drawing room where she might have been able to display her facility for witty conversation?

Cissie had assured her that she looked charming in the new coffee-coloured lace with which she could wear her garnets. But as yet she had had no opportunity to wear either the dress or the garnets. She had merely been required to make a brief appearance with her pupils in the drawing room after tea, and before the company disappeared to dress for dinner.

Adolphus and Cissie had been bored, Boy, red-cheeked and looking alarmingly on the edge of a tantrum. She had wished herself anywhere but answering the polite indifferent questions of ladies in long ruched and ruffled teagowns and gentlemen who looked over her head. Her answers were drowned, anyway, by the hubbub. There was a great deal of merry badinage going on.

Hannah had recognised the two people who had played croquet the other day, Reggie and Blanche Mainwaring, Reggie blond and handsome in flannels, Blanche thin-lipped, with a sharp nervous look. The rest of the guests were strangers. There were some good-looking women, but none who could outshine Mrs Storrington. Mr Storrington was not there.

For the rest of the evening, from her lonely window, Hannah saw the flicker of pale dresses in the garden, and heard snatches of music and laughter. After midnight, when she still lay awake, her room too near the guest wing, there were whispers and giggles in the passages. A door opened, someone exclaimed in an agitated voice, "Don't! Don't you dare." The door shut softly.

No one came down until mid-morning. Breakfast could not be cleared away until midday, and then the maids muttered audibly that it was time to lay the table for luncheon. For this meal the children went downstairs, Adolphus reluctantly because with all the noise he couldn't hear what was said to him, Cissie dimpling and confident in the party frock that she *knew* Papa would expect her to wear, Boy in a sailor suit that was slightly muddied. He, too, was muttering under his breath. He had been down at the marsh out of everyone's stupid way. But this afternoon he intended to take his camera out. There was a sudden sly look in his beautiful eyes. People were awfully funny playing croquet. Someone always lost his temper and looked angry, and that made a jolly good picture.

It proved interesting to observe Boy's tactics. He carried the camera on a tripod to a fairly obscure position beside a rhododendron, the sun in the right direction, then disappeared beneath the black velvet cloth like a small magician. The click of the shutter went unnoticed, the players unaware that they were trapped on film. Boy, for all his tender years, had something of the voyeur about him.

"Oh, I've dozens of pictures of all sorts of things," he told Hannah.

"What sort of things?"

"Things people don't know they're doing. It's much more fun that way."

"May I see them some time?" Hannah asked. She had been very wary with Boy since the episode on the marsh.

"Perhaps. If I can trust you not to tell."

"To tell what?"

"The things grown-ups do, of course. Don't you understand?"

He looked as innocent as the ten-year-old child he was. But there were times when Boy was infinitely older than ten years.

The extreme tedium, after the usual charade of presenting the children in the drawing room for their hour of polite conversation, and of eating supper in the nursery to the accompaniment of bursts of laughter from the terrace, was relieved that evening when Elsie came up with the message that Miss Knox was wanted downstairs.

What for? To play the piano, Elsie thought. It was the master who had made the request.

What should she do? Go down as she was in her afternoon blouse and skirt? Change?

Cissie answered her problem.

"You must put on your new dress, Miss Knox. Papa will expect it."

"Papa doesn't know about it."

"Then surprise him, dear Miss Knox." Cissie could be as persuasive as her father.

"You are lucky to be joining in the fun. When I am fifteen Mamma has said I can always eat with company. But that's two years away."

"Be thankful," said Hannah, pulling open the door of the wardrobe and taking out the new dress, "I have ten minutes."

She hesitated at the drawing room door, then lifted her head and walked in boldly. Why not? She could hold her own with these women, most of whom made nothing but trivial conversation, and all of whom looked a little overblown. She was at least ten years younger than them, she was certain, and her waist three, four or five inches smaller. Her hair style was less elaborate, her dress much simpler, her garnets humble compared to the flashing diamonds and aquamarines. And she had no husband at her side. But she had confidence in her taste and her superior intelligence, and, given the opportunity, could coquette with her eyes as well as any of them.

Mrs Storrington was sitting on a couch with a man on either side of her, the handsome Reggie Mainwaring, and another, less good-looking, but just as assiduously attentive.

At first glance, Mr Storrington did not appear to be in the room. Yet it was at his request that she had come down.

Suddenly she wondered if the lady who had been the intended recipient of that hat were here, and a warm embarrassed flush coloured her cheeks, as if she had caught the unknown lady and Mr Storrington flirting on the terrace.

73

Mrs Storrington had seen her.

"Miss Knox! Is anything wrong?" There was a pause as she frowningly took in Hannah's party attire. "Are the children – is Boy all right?"

"Perfectly, Mrs Storrington. I had a message from Mr Storrington that I was to play the piano."

"Oh! Oh, did you?"

"Not Chopin. What about some Strauss waltzes?" came the deep, now familiar voice behind her. "Miss Knox plays as proficiently as I shoot," Mr Storrington told the assembled company. "And that is the highest compliment I can pay her."

"Charlie!" Mrs Storrington was not trying to conceal her irritation, "I was just about to ask Eddie to give us the latest George Robey songs."

"Delighted," Mr Storrington said affably, "but later. Now let's dance. Where's Perkins? Why doesn't the lazy devil open some more champagne?"

He was a little drunk, Hannah realised. And more than a little bored. The special lady was not here after all. How could she be, since she was probably an actress or even a secretary?

But presently, as she played, he tried to enliven the party by swinging one after another of the ladies, even the wan Blanche Mainwaring, into a waltz.

"A glass of champagne, Miss Knox? You look hot."

"Oh! No thank you." Hannah pushed back a damp tendril of hair. The night was warm and she had played vigorously for half an hour. "I haven't a spare hand."

"Then have a rest. You've done splendidly." The pushed back furniture and the tumbled rugs were evidence. "Perkins! Where is Perkins? Every time I want him he has disappeared."

Hannah realised that most of the guests had disappeared, too. After she had stopped playing they had strolled out on to the terrace, no doubt to cool themselves after the exertion of dancing.

"And how do you like Maidenshall?" asked Blanche Mainwaring, approaching Hannah. She was wearing a light-coloured dress, and looked thin and tapering like a white candle. Unlit.

"Very much, madam."

"And the children?"

"They're very agreeable. And bright."

"The little one. Boy? Is he bright?"

"Very, madam." (And I will never admit anything else to you because you have a secretive jealous look in your eyes.)

"Then you're lucky, if you haven't seen him in one of his attacks. Poor Violet. She calls them tantrums, but Reggie and I both know . . ."

"Your champagne, Miss Knox," said Mr Storrington. "I have brought it myself. And well earned, too. I'm going to deprive you of Miss Knox, Blanche. I have something to show her."

"Is one of the children —" she began.

"You're not their nursemaid. Come this way."

He made her precede him into the hall and through a door at the end. She was aware of thousands of books from floor to ceiling.

"I wanted to rescue you from that acidulated old maid."

"But she —"

"—has the money. Mrs Reginald Mainwaring." He was laughing softly. He was drunker than she had thought.

Quickly she swallowed the glass of champagne she had carried from the drawing room. Her head buzzed.

"How fortunate for her," she murmured.

"Meaning?"

"That she has the money. I am only one half of your description. An old maid without the fortune."

His restless intoxicated eyes had stilled.

"But witty instead. Well, well. Have you found an occasion to wear the hat?"

"Where would I have done so?"

"No. I see. A pity. We must contrive something."

We? Hannah's hand had given a sudden nervous jump, almost spilling the last drops of the champagne.

"Drink it," he said, amused. "I'll get you a refill. Or would you prefer brandy? That's what I'm drinking in here.

Courvoisier 1881. I refuse to waste it on those ignorant louts."

His wife's friends? Certainly she had guessed that they were not his. He would rather be at his club in London – or in some cosy pied-à-terre. She knew that, too.

"No, not brandy, thank you."

"Scared, Miss Knox? It would make those magnificent eyes of yours shine."

"I really ought to go upstairs, Mr Storrington."

"No, no, I want to show you something."

He opened a drawer and took out a long box. Inside, in the faded crimson velvet bedding, was a pair of duelling pistols.

"My great-grandfather made these. Aren't they a beautiful piece of work? The finest ever made in England, that's certain. The Germans and the Spanish were best at this sort of art."

"Art?"

"What else? Look at that gold damascening and mother-of-pearl on the stock. If you study the lock you will see an engraving of St. George and the Dragon. You're not going to faint at the sight of a gun, are you?"

"Certainly not." She took one of the pistols in her hand, smoothing her fingers over the elaborate workmanship. "Have these ever been used?"

"I don't know of any specific occasion. Duelling was outlawed in England when these were made. Grandfather kept them as a showpiece. Not that I wouldn't have liked to use them myself, now and then."

His face brooded. He was no longer joking. He would be capable of using the deadly toys. Hannah was half repelled, half elated.

"Why are you smiling, Miss Knox?"

"Was I? I believe I was thinking of my last employer. He had a hobby, too. It was painting and cataloguing wild flowers. With their correct Latin names of course."

The blurred brown eyes (no, black, in this light, or in this state of intoxication) stared at her. Then the uproarious laugh that no longer irritated but instead had become strangely infectious broke out.

"Well, now you have an employer who plays with guns. A

bit different from *Heleborus viridi*, eh? But it was a damn shame about Dolly's ear. The boy must have had a weakness. Violet didn't need to be so unforgiving. Well, come along, Miss Knox. Better get back to the party."

"If you will excuse me. I really must go upstairs."

"If you wish. But I wasn't going to –" His eyes glinted as he changed the word she had half-expected to hear – "deafen you, Miss Knox."

She could hear him laughing still as she reached the top of the stairs.

Half an hour later reality – or a different kind of fantasy – struck her. Boy was screaming.

In spite of all those half-spoken warnings about Boy, Mrs Storrington's, Cissie's, Blanche Mainwaring's, Barker's, and in spite of what she herself had experienced down at the marsh, no one had really explained to Hannah what Boy's attacks were.

His room was at the far end of the nursery wing, as far as possible from the guest wing and from his parents. She hadn't known who occupied the room next door. Tonight she discovered not only why a small boy was given such an isolated room, but also who slept within earshot. Not Barker, but a heavy-set young man whom she had previously seen wearing a baize apron and polishing floors or brushing the stair carpets. Just another servant, she had thought. But now, as she flew down the corridor in her hastily-donned dressing gown, she saw this young man, also wearing a dressing gown, emerge from his room and go into Boy's.

Immediately Boy's screams intensified. Hannah got there to find a scene of chaos, the bed clothing thrown on the floor, a table overturned, a multitude of toys flung about, and, most sinister of all, the curtains dragged back from barred windows. Barred!

Crouched at the top of his bed, and stark naked, was Boy. His fists were dug into his eyes, and he was shouting, "No, Max! No, Max! Don't lock me in! Please don't! Please don't, Max!"

The young man, his face expressionless, had picked up Boy's nightshirt and, most curiously, began tying it round the slight naked body. Like a bandage, like a winding sheet.

For a moment Hannah couldn't speak. Anyway, she would not have been heard above Boy's screams. Then she realised that if the child was demented, it was with fear, and she rushed to tug at Max's arms.

"Whatever are you doing, tying him up like that? Can't you see he's terrified?"

She got an impassive look from the stolid young man.

"It's for his own good, miss. Otherwise he'll hurt himself. Cut his hands on things. It's not me he's terrified of, miss."

"Then what?" Hannah gasped.

"Things he sees. Or thinks he sees." Boy was silent, momentarily, regarding them both with wild eyes. But not seeing them, Hannah was sure.

"It's always stones, miss. And water. Stones tumbling down to crush him. Or rocks, perhaps. And the water underneath like glass."

In a corner of the room Hannah saw the tripod of Boy's precious camera, tipped over, and thought of his cleverness. Then she remembered vividly how he had screamed hate and defiance at her on the marsh. Was it her, or a toppling rock he was seeing?

"He's getting quieter now," Max said. "I'll get him some of his medicine if you'll hold him."

"H-hold him?"

"His arms are tied down." There was a hint of scorn in the young man's voice. This, shockingly, was not a servant but Boy's nurse, his keeper!

Nervously Hannah sat on the edge of the bed and took the slight and violently shivering body in her arms. The child was as cold as ice, and judging by the fixed look in his eye, still seeing some unfathomable terror.

Without knowing why she did so, she began half singing lines of poetry to him:

"When I behold upon the night's starred face
Huge cloudy symbols of a high romance
And think that I may never live to trace their shadows.
And when I feel, fair creature of an hour,
That I shall never look upon her more."

78

The shivering was growing less. Max had a spoon containing some thick dark liquid at his lips. He seemed astonished when Boy swallowed it.

"Well! Usually he fights like a spitting tiger cub."

"What is it?"

"Something the doctor prescribes. Just an opiate. He'll be asleep in a few minutes. You can lie him down, miss. What were you saying to him?"

"Just quoting some poetry. Keats. I find it soothing, too."

Hannah was covering the now limp child with blankets when she saw that Mrs Storrington was in the doorway. She had taken long enough to arrive, Hannah reflected.

But Mr Storrington was not with her. Perhaps he never came.

"You've got him quiet, Miss Knox?"

"He is now."

Mrs Storrington stood looking down at her son, his curls damp and shaggy like a bedraggled chrysanthemum, his face unnaturally flushed. His heavy eyelids were almost closed.

"Boy, darling. It's Mamma."

A spasm crossed the small face. Then he was asleep.

"How long this time, Max?" Mrs Storrington asked.

"Not long at all, ma'am. The young lady helped."

"How did you do that, Miss Knox?"

"I just recited some verses of poetry to him. It was purely instinctive, but they seemed to soothe him."

"That's interesting. You weren't frightened? The others always have been. Miss Shepherd screamed louder than Boy."

"I was startled," Hannah admitted. "Can't the doctors do anything for him?"

"Doctors! They just mutter about periodic derangements and give him sedatives. They never find the cause. I was a long time coming because I was down at the river."

(In the Chinese pagoda? The thought flashed through Hannah's head.)

"Go back to your room, Miss Knox. Max will clear up here. I think the door had better be locked, Max. Until midday, anyway."

"This seems to be a short attack, ma'am."

"We can't be sure. He'd better be kept out of the way until the guests have gone."

Mrs Storrington's plump hand lay heavily on Hannah's arm as she led her down the corridor.

"I'm afraid I may have to give up having weekend guests. Doctor Peters seems to think Boy's attacks could be provoked by jealousy. He's acutely jealous about anything concerning me."

"You said to keep him locked up until midday." Horror lingered in Hannah's voice.

"Just for his own safety. Sometimes the attacks last for days when he seems to be in a passion of terror. He breaks glass, and cuts his hands. He goes about carrying bits of broken glass." Mrs Storrington seemed about to weep, her lovely face crumpling. "But what am I to do if I have to bar the house to guests? I shall go mad with boredom." No, she wasn't weeping, she was petulant. Wasn't her child's sanity enough for her happiness?

"Perhaps you could go to London now and again with Mr Storrington?" Hannah suggested, without any intention of irony.

But there was irony enough in Mrs Storrington's lifted brows.

"Do you think so, Miss Knox?"

There was no sound from Boy's room all the next morning. He must have been sleeping off the drug Max had given him. Barker went about with a morbidly long face, and hushed the two elder children, although they, accustomed to this situation, were quiet enough. Indeed, they went off to church with the grown-ups, and after luncheon, which was a prolonged meal, the guests departed. There was a good deal of flurry in the courtyard, with luggage being carried down and carriages brought round. Most of the guests were taken to the railway station to catch trains to their various destinations. Reggie and Blanche Mainwaring drove across country to their estate, Steening, five miles away.

After they had all gone, and the house was quiet, Boy came

80

downstairs, dressed in a clean sailor suit, and looking pale, heavy-eyed and subdued.

"Has everyone gone?" he asked in surprise. "Oh, bother, I wanted to take some more photographs."

"Then you shouldn't have slept so late," said Cissie.

Mrs Storrington had her arms out. "Boy was tired. Weren't you, dearest? Come to Mamma."

Cissie said under her breath to Hannah, "And now he looks quite saintly. He always does after one of his attacks."

"I think he's acting most of the time," said Adolphus. "He only pretends he doesn't remember the scenes he makes."

But it was not pretence, Hannah was sure. She remembered too vividly that wild haunted face and the shaking body, naked and slippery with sweat. The sweat of pure terror. She was more than a little frightened herself. The child could become dangerous.

A week after Boy's illness (what else could it be called?), Mrs Storrington agreed to Hannah's request to visit her sister Daisy who had just suffered a premature confinement and lost her baby. Mrs Storrington had a generous nature and a kind concern for Daisy's health.

Daisy was interested in Mrs Storrington, too. Hannah readily answered her immediate eager questions because they took her sister out of her depressed state. Anyway, Mrs Storrington was an absorbing subject and Maidenshall's luxurious vastness contrasted acutely with this cramped uncomfortable house which seemed to overflow, although occupied by Daisy and her husband and two small children and an overworked maid of all work.

There would have been no room for the new baby. Perhaps it was just as well that it hadn't survived.

Hannah regretted, however, telling Daisy about Mr Storrington's habit of firing a revolver to announce his return home in the evenings, for Daisy was horrified. She thought he must be a great show-off always wanting to attract attention, and a bit brutal, too. She did not need to point out how different he was from her meek and quiet Albert, although she still looked a bit down in the mouth at the thought of the colourful life Hannah was leading.

It wasn't very colourful being a shadow in the background, as she was most of the time, but Hannah didn't remind Daisy of that. Neither did she tell her that the explosion of the gun, and the rooks clapping their wings and cawing, had begun to strike a shaft of pure excitement through her. On the nights Mr Storrington stayed in London the evening was dull and empty. And that lately she had begun to dream ambitiously, and to have far-fetched ideas.

Daisy knew all about her tendency to dream, and now said rather sourly, "You'll be twenty-six soon, Hannah."

"And I haven't got a husband. Is that what you're about to say?"

"Well, it seems a bit impractical to talk all the time of Mr Storrington. Don't you ever meet anyone suitable? What about Adolphus's tutor? Or Mr Storrington's valet? What's he like? Or isn't there an unmarried curate at the vicarage?"

Hannah pressed her hands together in suppressed anger. Daisy could talk in that patronising way when she was living in little better than squalor, with two whining ill-kept children at her skirts, a pailful of wet napkins in the kitchen, an inefficient maid who scarcely knew how to clean let alone cook, and a husband who would shortly, no doubt, sow the seed of another child.

Oh no, she would rather indulge in dreams. For instance the one that had been coming and going in her mind.

A few days before, in an expansive mood, Mr Storrington had talked of making a trip to St. Petersburg. It would be on business, naturally. He had a customer there, General Zoubetsky, who wanted to buy sporting guns and also discuss a new Storrington machine gun. Russia, after the disastrous Japanese war, was still depleted of arms. But there would be time for pleasure, too. Sleigh rides, the opera, the ballet, dinner parties in the grand homes of the aristocracy. Violet would enjoy it if she could be persuaded to accompany him.

Hannah had waited with some anxiety for Mrs Storrington's answer, thinking how dismal the house would be if they both went and she was left with the children.

But Mrs Storrington made an unhesitating refusal. St.

Petersburg would be so cold, the sea journey so stormy at this time of year, and besides the whole thing was quite out of the question because she couldn't leave Boy.

Mr Storrington had made it plain that he was disappointed, and impatient with her reasons which he regarded as trivial. If she couldn't leave that tiresome child now, was she contemplating being a prisoner here forever? Besides, he added, he didn't care for travelling alone.

His words made Hannah think what a waste it was that a fine-looking man should have no companion and that Mrs Storrington, supreme in her beauty, seemed to rather casually take him for granted. However, she had succeeded fairly well in putting the thought out of her mind until today in Daisy's house. Putting away the unneeded baby clothing and looking at Daisy's white face she had reflected on how dull and crushed life could be for some women.

A great desire seized her for adventure and excitement before she did as Daisy wished and got trapped with a husband she didn't love, a baby in her stomach, and endless dull household chores. If that was to happen to her, she was at least going to live first! By living she thought of words like glamour, brilliance, romance. And travel to foreign lands. If Mrs Storrington refused to go to St. Petersburg with her husband, she was thinking with flaring excitement, why shouldn't *she* go?

Daisy was staring at her and asking her whatever she was thinking of, she looked quite wicked.

"I believe that house is changing you, Hannah. You never used to look like that at your other positions."

"Perhaps it is," Hannah agreed. "Maidenshall is supposed to have been built on the site of a medieval nunnery."

"It doesn't sound the right name for it, the way you describe it."

"No, it isn't full of virgins," Hannah said flippantly. "And I certainly don't feel like a nun. Oh dear me, now you're looking shocked again. Shall we talk about the children instead?"

"Yes, do. What about Boy? Is he still being difficult?"

"Not since his last attack. He's really been quite saintly.

The doctors talk about dementia praecox. One day he's an angel, and the next a different person entirely, a little devil. We can never tell when these attacks are coming on, but Boy is the reason Mrs Storrington won't travel with her husband."

"Then she is a good mother."

"In her erratic way, I suppose she is. Although Cissie much prefers her father. She adores him, and he does her. Indeed," Hannah heard herself going on in a flash of inspiration, "I wouldn't be at all surprised if she persuaded Mr Storrington to take her to St. Petersburg instead of his wife. Cissie is old enough to benefit from foreign travel. So is Adolphus. It would be quite advantageous for him to have had a trip abroad before he begins his first term at Eton." Ideas were coming to her fast. "If this were to be arranged, I naturally would have to go also, to take care of the children."

When Daisy asked if she would care for that, Hannah said carefully that she would probably find it very strange and tiring. But Cissie's father never refused his dearly loved daughter anything, and if she set her mind on going, one supposed they would go.

"I would have to get a fur-lined cloak, but I have my savings. What are savings for but to meet emergencies?"

Looking at Daisy's face, open-mouthed with surprise, but not succeeding in concealing its envy, Hannah found herself just forbearing to relate the story of the hat . . .

8

Reggie Mainwaring was riding off on his horse when Hannah returned home, trudging the weary three miles from the station because no one had remembered to send the dogcart for her. He waved to her, without stopping. He was hatless and the wind caught his thick blond hair. He looked rather splendid. One wondered that his wife Blanche looked as pressed down by low spirits as Daisy did. Or did one wonder?

I'm getting worldly, Hannah thought, not without satisfaction. This surely would make her a more interesting person, a more interesting *companion*, she thought significantly.

For her idea, conceived at Daisy's, was growing more compelling the more tired she became and the more incensed by Mrs Storrington's forgetfulness. Violet (hush, are you calling her Violet now?), had been too occupied with Reggie Mainwaring's visit to think of a weary governess and a three-mile walk. She was not cruel, merely self-absorbed, with that slight distracted air of disorganisation and disarray which men seemed to find so attractive. What right had she, Hannah grumbled to herself, to be born within the charmed circle of beauty, wealth and lovers, while Hannah, with her excellent brain, and poor Daisy, a much more worthy female, were forever on the outside?

The blister on her right heel was stirring up a different discomfort in her mind. She had not allowed herself to examine these thoughts before. She had read romantic poems, and let their beauty mask her growing discontent, like certain drugs masking the symptoms of an illness.

Oh, bother you, Violet! she muttered angrily, as the pain burned in her foot and the blond dashing Reggie galloped out of sight.

They had been cuddling on the deep couch in the drawing room. Or on those rainbow-coloured cushions in the Chinese pavilion. This was another thing beautiful, idle women like Violet Storrington took as their right, lovers on summer afternoons. No such benefits for her, without home or husband, or for overburdened Daisy with her emptied and aching womb.

Why was I given an excellent scheming brain if not to use it? It may not bring me the life of Violet Storrington, but it could bring me – other things . . .

"Miss Knox, have you walked home? Wasn't the dogcart sent for you? Oh, Mamma, did you forget?"

Cissie's concern and indignation were balm. A genuinely nice child, Cissie, in spite of her father's spoiling. But Mrs Storrington (under the roof of Maidenshall she was quite naturally Mrs Storrington again to Hannah) moving languidly, and with a soft absent look in her eyes, said mildly, 'Oh, goodness me, I'm sorry, Miss Knox. Are you very tired? How was your sister?"

"Not in very good spirits, I'm afraid. I may have to –"

"Oh no, Miss Knox, you can't leave us!" Cissie cried. "You wouldn't, would you? Just as we are becoming devoted to you."

Hannah could not help a gratified smile.

"I wasn't saying anything about leaving. You do jump to conclusions. I was merely going to observe that I may have to make another visit to Daisy before long. If you will allow me to, Mrs Storrington."

"Of course."

"Thank you, Mrs Storrington. If you will excuse me I think I must go upstairs and bathe my heel. I foolishly wasn't wearing my walking shoes."

"Oh, poor Miss Knox!" That was Cissie, but Mrs Storrington said, "Now I can't stand sulks, Miss Knox."

Hannah opened her eyes wide. "But I am not sulking, Mrs Storrington."

"Or unspoken grievances, either. Oh dear, I am sorry, you poor creature." Mrs Storrington, if absent-minded and thoughtless, was always impulsively generous. "And I have had such a heavenly afternoon in the sun. It's been one of those golden autumn days. Cissie, I left my parasol down by the river. Be a good child – Oh, merciful heavens!"

The exclamation came the second after the familiar shot which cracked the stillness and sent the rooks complaining into the air. Mrs Storrington had her hands to her ears.

"Charlie is home. I never will get used to that barbaric custom of his."

"I can't get used to it either," Hannah murmured, her stomach knotted.

Mr Storrington would be home for dinner.

Cissie must be the one to sow the seed of her idea. But with the greatest subtlety. She must be carefully coached so that in the end it would seem entirely her idea. Patience was required, and this, in her excited mood, Hannah found difficult. On the evenings they were to dine downstairs, Cissie, when dressed herself, liked to be allowed in Hannah's room.

At first, her inquisitive lingering had annoyed Hannah. She liked privacy while she brushed her hair and dressed. She had realised that Cissie, who suffered from lack of suitable companions, was just at the age to form a crush on someone older than herself, as a prelude to first love, and that she was now fixing her affections on Hannah. For the desire to perform small services for her, doing up her back buttons, pinning her hair, tidying her dressing table, all expressed devotion. This could be a valuable weapon to be used in the future, though for what reason Hannah was not clear. She simply had a premonition that one day she would need someone passionately on her side in this house.

"Cissie," she said, as if the thought had just occurred to her, "Have you and Adolphus ever had a holiday abroad?"

"Once, a long time ago, we went to Brittany. But it wasn't a very happy time. We were all seasick on the Channel crossing, and then Boy behaved terribly. He was only little and the hotel frightened him, I think. Anyway, I heard Papa and Mamma quarrelling. Papa said he would never travel anywhere again with that howling maniac, and that Boy wasn't fit for civilised society. He said they could never risk a family holiday again, which is rather unfair to Adolphus and me. But it's the reason he wants only Mamma to go to St. Petersburg. I shall miss him dreadfully."

"Would you like to go to Russia?"

"Of course I would, Miss Knox. It would be the most exciting thing. I would go anywhere with Papa, even to the wastes of Siberia, or Mongolia."

"Dear me, you do know your geography. What about Adolphus?"

"He loves adventure. And he'd do anything to get away from Mr Beard for a while. He gives him so much homework. And then you make him read the classics, Miss Knox, but he doesn't mind that so much because you choose interesting books."

"A shipboard journey is the time to read books," Hannah said.

Cissie stared at her, wide-eyed.

"You mean we're going! With Papa!"

"No, nothing of the kind. I was only speaking at random. I expect the idea has never come into your Papa's head."

"Then couldn't we ask him, Miss Knox? Couldn't we?"

"I'm sure your mother would never agree to such a thing."

"But she wouldn't need to if Papa agreed. He doesn't listen to her opinions – well, almost never."

Was this really true? Had beautiful Violet no more authority in her own home than Daisy had in hers? But surely this must be their own fault, Daisy was too meek and Violet had an overbearing and strong-willed husband who wouldn't tolerate opposition. However, a clever woman . . .

Hannah dared not finish the thought. Because she wasn't that clever. Or not as clever as she would need to be. Although one never knew what one's powers were until one tried them. There had been times in her childhood when she would not be bidden. Nothing but death would have broken her will. Though that was only when she desired something with all her heart.

Such as a trip to a wonderful foreign city in the company of such a challenging personality as Mr Storrington. With his elder children too, of course. They didn't fit into the dream, but they represented the reality.

Yes, Cissie would have to be coached carefully. And the subject must not be broached tonight. There was a Cabinet Minister coming to dinner, Mrs Storrington had said. He was an old friend who liked to see the children. So they would all dine together and later the men would adjourn to the library to talk business. Something about Kaiser Wilhelm and his obsessive re-arming of Germany, she said indifferently.

With Charlie, business always came first. As it happened, immediately after dinner Mrs Storrington had to take Boy upstairs. He had been on the edge of a tantrum all evening, something had upset him. The rising wind, Hannah thought fancifully, because it did howl in a melancholy fashion around the big house. Leaves crackled like crumpled paper against the french windows of the drawing room, and branches of the larches were a moving frieze against the pale sky. It was an evening for fires and stories told sitting on the hearthrug.

But Boy had disturbed Hannah with that hint of held-back frenzy in his shining eyes. He had been clutching something in one of his hands and when Hannah had prised open his fingers she had found several pieces of broken glass and his palm was bleeding. She had feared an outburst as she had deprived him of his unnatural treasure and washed his hands, but he had remained silent.

After dinner he had gone quietly upstairs with his mother, and Mr Storrington and Mr Workman had gone to the library to have port and cigars.

Hannah thought of Mr Storrington showing Mr Workman his prized duelling pistols, and was startled at the desire she had to be with them. She wanted to listen avidly to what they were saying. She was not made to be satisfied forever with the conversation of children and adolescents. Perhaps that was doomed to be her fate, but who said one could not struggle against fate?

In the drawing room, however, she had to make do with her adolescents. She persuaded Cissie and Adolphus to amuse themselves with a game of dominoes, then went to the piano and began to play musingly, hoping to calm her restless mood. Deep in reverie she didn't hear the men come into the drawing room until a voice, not intended to reach her ears, murmured, "Charming creature. Where did you find her, Charlie?"

"Violet did that. At least she's an improvement on the last one. Meaning," Mr Storrington didn't realise what acute hearing Hannah had, "she pays attention to her work."

"Not much bosom. But a deuced graceful neck."

Hannah's fingers played more softly, her eyes half closed. She hoped she was giving the impression of being completely lost in the music.

Stupid creatures, men. Stupid. They thought she was deaf like Adolphus. Anyway, they both had had a little too much port, or brandy, over their discussions about guns.

"What do women like this do, Charlie? I mean – dried up forever, eh?"

"S-sh!" Hannah, her eyes on the keyboard, did not allow her playing to falter. Mr Storrington came across the room to stand over Cissie and Adolphus, and spoke loudly, "Well, you two, isn't it past your bedtime? Miss Knox, your musical expertise increases daily. Hasn't my wife come down again? She overprotects that boy," he said to his guest, the impatience he felt at any mention of Boy apparent in his slurred voice. "Will you allow me to say her farewells for her?"

"Certainly, my dear fellow. If I'm to catch the ten-thirty to London I must be off. It's been a good evening, Charlie. Try out my advice on the Russkies. But don't spend your entire time in St. Petersburg working, eh?"

There was a half wink, a waved farewell to Hannah and the children, footsteps down the hall, the front door opening and closing, then Mr Storrington was back in the room and saying in his expansive manner, "Well, then, what would you all say to a sea voyage?"

"*Papa!*" shrieked Cissie. "Not to St. Petersburg!"

Adolphus's head had come up warily. He never entirely trusted his father.

"What did you say, Papa?"

Hannah was keenly conscious that although Mr Storrington was answering Adolphus he was not looking at him. His bold bright eyes were on her, and the colour was flooding her cheeks. Rosy red, she must look. Like a schoolgirl.

"I was making the suggestion that you two should accompany your lonely Papa on an educational journey to the Kingdom of All the Russias. The thought has just come into my head. It's pure inspiration. Don't you think such a trip would do my children's education good, Miss Knox?"

"I haven't travelled abroad myself, Mr Storrington, but I have always imagined foreign travel would be beneficial." She flushed even more deeply beneath his satirical gaze. "Both for health and broadening the mind," she said.

"Perfectly splendid, Miss Knox. I'm glad you think that because you would have to accompany us. I have a lot of business to attend to and couldn't be with the children all the time. They would have to be amused. I imagine sleigh rides and going to the ballet and eating sticky cakes, and so on, would be enjoyable to them. Would you be capable of organising those activities, Miss Knox?"

"I – I imagine so, Mr Storrington."

He was staring at her flushed cheeks, and seemed on the verge of giving one of his uproarious laughs. Instead he said, "I'll have to put it to my wife, of course."

Cissie flung herself at him. "But, Papa, it's what *you* say, isn't it?"

"Minx. Well, sometimes."

"Would Mr Beard give me permission?" Adolphus asked uncertainly. He was not a boy with much confidence. Perhaps this proposed trip really would broaden his mind and give him some maturity. "He says I must work like a black until Christmas," he added.

"I'm sure he's right, my boy. But on this occasion you have my permission to tell Mr Beard that he is talking into his beard."

The atrocious pun made Cissie double up with laughter, and after a moment of astonishment at his father's levity, Adolphus joined in. Hannah felt no inclination to laugh at such schoolboy humour. But she was registering how attractive Mr Storrington was in this playful benign mood, a benevolent despot deciding to captivate his audience.

"Well, I must say you two make a more enthusiastic audience than Miss Knox does. I daresay she's full of fears of losing you over the rail of the ship, or in a Russian snowdrift. Come, Miss Knox, if I feel in the same mood in the morning will you still be so reluctant?"

Hannah took a deep breath. "I think it would be the most exciting thing I have ever done in my life."

What do women like this do? Dried up forever . . . The cruel words, like the sting of a wasp, echoed in her mind. She scarcely listened as Cissie, undressing in her bedroom, chattered compulsively.

"But, Miss Knox, after all I didn't have to persuade Papa into anything. He had the idea himself. It was just like fate."

The fate she thought she had to struggle against? It seemed to be on her side after all.

A sober thought, quickly suppressed, told her that it was later the struggle would begin. Just now she refused to spoil Cissie's pleasure by any qualms.

Anyway, it was possible Mrs Storrington would forbid the whole thing. Or decide to go herself, after all. Or that in the sober light of morning Mr Storrington would say it had all been fantasy. Neither of these things happened. When Mr Storrington told Mrs Storrington his plans at breakfast she exclaimed, "What an excellent idea, Charlie. Just the sort of enlarged horizon Adolphus needs. And Cissie will be safe with Miss Knox. You will promise to never let her out of your sight, Miss Knox? We must have a trip to London to buy fur hats and fur boots and gloves. We can't have you catching frostbite. No, I won't be too lonely, Cissie darling. Boy and I will think up some little treats to amuse ourselves. To tell the truth I'll be glad of a rest. It's been an exhausting summer . . ."

Making her frequent toilettes, playing croquet, holding her parasol up against the glare of the sun, welcoming and farewelling guests, planning the endless menus, dancing in the moonlight on the terrace, laughing and coquetting. Yes, it must have been quite an exhausting time. But Hannah didn't believe a word of it. For Mrs Storrington had the dreamy voluptuous look that she had worn on frequent occasions during the long warm summer. She was basking in some pleasant memory. Her reflective eyes suggested that she believed in fate, too.

But it would be too cold to spend evenings in the Chinese pavilion, Hannah was thinking.

Hannah's diary during those busy days was neglected. She only had time to scribble:

"I am so excited I can hardly write or think. This, I believe, is the high peak of my life.

"I am to get two trunks, one for myself and one for Cissie. Beale, Mr Storrington's valet, is to look after Adolphus. Today Mrs Storrington, Cissie and I went to London to shop, not only for warm outdoor clothing but for dresses suitable for the theatre. Mrs Storrington has generously insisted that my wardrobe be provided. Blue velvet was chosen for Cissie and dark grey taffeta for me. I would have preferred a gayer colour, but this is what Mrs Storrington decided was suitable. I thought it wise not to protest, otherwise she might suspect that I see myself, in St. Petersburg, as something more than a governess.

"I do not, of course. I am too practical for that. Yet I know that just as Adolphus is meant to widen his horizons, I intend to grow in worldliness. I haven't pursued that thought to any sort of conclusion. But it is a fact that I can brighten up the grey taffeta with my garnets.

"In any case it will be very obvious what I am, for I will always have Cissie with me, probably Adolphus, too.

"There is a crescent moon tonight. It is like a band of gold. I could pluck it out of the sky and wear it round my wrist. Or my finger . . ."

9

Sarah

IF SARAH HAD been expecting a breakfast in the tradition of houses like this, scrambled eggs, kippers, grilled kidneys and bacon, and kedgeree in silver dishes on the sideboard, she would have been disappointed. She found that Agnes gave Dolly porridge in the kitchen, and took trays of coffee and orange juice and toast upstairs to Cressida and Charles, who didn't come down until ten-thirty.

"There's plenty of coffee, dear," she said over her shoulder to Sarah, "but if you want a boiled egg you'll have to do it yourself."

"I'll have toast and marmalade, thanks, Agnes, and I'll get it. I don't know how you cope, single-handed."

"No more do I. And that lazy Jeremy don't help."

"Is he lazy?"

"Likes to sleep in. Goes to bed too late, if you ask me. And the poor Major waiting for some help. He's awake at dawn, that I do know."

Sarah tried to imagine the impotence of helplessly waiting for the morning, for footsteps, voices, signs that the night was over and one was not alone in the world.

"If Jeremy is lazy why does Major Storrington keep him?"

Agnes shrugged, her broad face cynical. "He's as good as they come nowadays. He's strong. He can lift the Major in and out of his bath and he does the garden, and he keeps an eye on Dolly. You can't have everything. He says he can't work more than twelve hours a day, and that's true enough. I have a fellow feeling."

"Perhaps I could take up the Major's breakfast in future," Sarah suggested. "Would that help?"

"You'll risk getting your head bitten off. He's in an evil mood until he's dressed and downstairs. A right evil mood, I can tell you. Seems to hit him most then, that he can't walk. Master Dolly, you finish up your porridge or I'll never give your little friend Joseph another bite."

"Oh, Agnes, you must, or he'll be in a mood," Dolly cried.

"What do you mean, in a mood? Haven't we enough with your father, and he has an excuse. But a healthy little boy — well, we must take that for granted, since we're not privileged to see him. Anyway, you've cleaned up your plate now, so you'd better get ready for Mr Crankshaw."

"Agnes, you are silly. It's Saturday. Mr Crankshaw isn't coming. Joseph and I are going to the marsh."

"The marsh?" said Sarah. "But I thought there was a rule you were not to go alone."

"I won't be alone, I'll have Joseph. Anyway, Father won't know. I never tell him when I go there."

"Then I'm coming with you just so that, for once, you obey rules."

Dolly quickly looked sideways and spoke to an empty chair. "Shall we let her come, Joseph? Shall you mind?" He waited a moment, appearing to be listening, and the uncanniness came over Sarah again. Then he looked up, saying brightly, "Joseph doesn't mind. But you'd better put on your wellingtons. It's a bit muddy in places. You can be sucked in the mud and never seen again."

"I'd call that exaggerating and I haven't got any wellingtons, but I'll put on my walking shoes. We'd better go now because I'll need to be back when your father comes downstairs."

Dolly slid off his chair and whooped like a perfectly ordinary small boy. In spite of the seemingly permanent company of the invisible Joseph, he was apparently pleased to have her come. She herself was becoming deeply intrigued by him. What, she wondered, did psychiatrists say about his condition? More practically, what would Jane say? If she laughed, as she was all too likely to do, would this volatile little boy forgive her?

It was a strange experience, that walk down the river path,

with Dolly running ahead and chattering to his unseen companion. Occasionally he looked back and hoped, politely, that they were not going too fast. Joseph, he said, loved the marsh and could never get there quickly enough.

Sarah could understand this when they came out of the dimness of the river path, for the enormous lift of blue sky over hummocks of emerald green grass, and the stretches of shining water edged with cowslips and marsh marigolds had a lonely compelling beauty. It was alive with the crying of seabirds, the cosy fussing of mallard and coots, and the occasional plop of a frog.

Dolly leaped lightly from hummock to hummock, pursuing dragonflies and early cabbage butterflies. He laughed excitedly, and kept up his restless conversation. "That isn't a tadpole, Joseph, that's a worm. Oh, look, did you see that frog on the dock leaf? Joseph, be careful or you'll fall in. You know what old Nanny said, that we'd better watch out or we'll both be drowned. Sarah!" He turned to look back, an astonishingly beautiful child with his blown black curls. "Do you like our place?"

"Is it your place?"

"Oh, yes, it always has been."

"When did you discover it? Did your father bring you here?"

"No, I came by myself. Or sometimes Nanny used to come, while she could still walk. She can't walk much now. She said she used to bring father here, it was a favourite place for small boys. Because of the frogs I expect."

"I must go back now," Sarah said. "Are you coming?"

"We'll stay a bit longer. It's quite safe, truly. Not in the winter, but now, when the pools aren't deep. We won't even get wet feet."

Sarah could almost have sworn that she could see two little boys crouched over the pool where the frog had plopped. Again that tingle of uncanniness swept over her. She was getting caught up in Dolly's fantasy. Or just generally in a fantasy about Maidenshall for, as she returned, she suddenly perceived across the river a faded crimson pagoda. It stuck up above the surrounding willows like an elaborate chimney.

She could scarcely believe it was real until she saw that the humped wooden bridge and an overgrown path on the other side of the river led to it.

She pushed through rhododendrons which shut out the sun, and emerged at the very steps of the pagoda or pavilion, or whatever it was meant to be. A bastardised version of both, she thought. It was a shut-in secret place, obviously never used now, but once it must have had a purpose. As a summer house? For tea parties? Midnight assignations? The floor was rotting, the paint peeling like a burnt out fire, the purpose of the quaint folly outdated, for nobody now particularly wanted secrecy for their flirtations.

Nevertheless, Sarah again experienced her faint not unpleasant frisson of ghostliness. And nearly jumped out of her skin when a twig cracked and a small crooked form dressed in darkish clothes like a shadow appeared on the pathway.

Was it real? Certainly it was, for it started even more violently than Sarah had, and turned to flee, with halting stumbling footsteps.

The old nanny. Old Miss Galloway. Her behaviour was oddly furtive. She seemed to be afraid of something. Sarah followed her, not hurrying, so as not to alarm the old lady even more. She overtook her at the other side of the bridge, and touched her arm gently, making her stop.

She found herself looking into a face like a Japanese netsuke, ivory-coloured and carved into innumerable wrinkles, blurred eyes sunken in hollows. The wary, suspicious and perplexed eyes of a very old woman.

"Why are you frightened of me, Miss Galloway? You are Miss Galloway, aren't you?"

The old lady made a feeble attempt to pull her arm away. She peered at Sarah, the flare of fear in her eyes dying.

"I'm not frightened, miss. I just don't know who you are."

"I'm Sarah Goodwill. Major Storrington's secretary."

"Oh. Oh, that one. Yes, they told me you were coming."

"Then why did you look so alarmed when you saw me? Who did you think I was?"

"Her! Her and the small boy." The old lady was muttering, as if embarrassed by the tricks of senility. "I see them sometimes. But they're ghosts, of course." She looked up with sudden defiance. "All old houses have ghosts. You musn't think I'm feeble-minded, Miss – Mrs –"

"Sarah," said Sarah. "Shall I walk with you back to the house?"

"I can see you're going to whether I say yes or no." A trace of vanished asperity touched her ruined face. "I'm ninety, you know."

"So they tell me."

"Very good to me, the Storringtons. Are you Master Dolly's new governess?"

"No, I'm Major Storrington's secretary. Dolly has a tutor, Mr Crankshaw."

"Oh, yes, him. I forget everything nowadays. It's most tiresome." She peered up at Sarah, her eyes again fearful. "Are you sure you didn't see them?"

"See who?"

"The young woman and the boy."

"No, I really didn't, Miss Galloway. I've been down at the marsh with Dolly and Joseph. I suppose you know about Joseph?"

"Never heard of a Joseph."

Perhaps she hadn't. Or perhaps she was the only one with enough sense not to go along with Dolly's fantasy. Who knew? Senility might be a better defence against this kind of thing than sober sense.

"Well, I hope when my little girl comes, Dolly will get rid of Joseph."

"You have a little girl? Where is she?"

"At boarding school."

"Oh, dear me! How sad for her."

Sarah laughed. "It's not sad at all. She loves it. But she'll love coming to stay here, too. She'll sleep next to me in the nursery wing."

The old lady stood still. Her little shrivelled face seemed alarmed again, full of the strange and unexplained fears lurking in a dim mind.

"Not in that dreadful Miss Knox's room?"

Sarah humoured her. "Who was the dreadful Miss Knox, and what did she do?"

The dim eyes looked up out of their deep pits. "Oh dear, oh me. Oh dear, oh me. You must be careful of Master Dolly. He may be in danger. Oh dear, where does it all end?"

Fascinating, fascinating. The woman old nanny referred to, and who seemed to hold deep alarms for her, must be the new governess Cissie had written about, Miss Knox who was small and neat and quick, like a brown bird. That didn't sound the description of someone who was potentially dangerous. But 'her eyes are big and notice everything' Cissie had written.

Sarah decided that she must examine Cissie's voluminous diaries more closely. And ask for more information from Charles. He must know about the menacing Miss Knox – who was probably only a meek put-upon person who had been driven to commit some misdemeanour.

She encountered Cressida in the hall.

"Oh, there you are, Sarah. For God's sake, get into Charles. He's blowing his top. Wants to know whether he has a secretary or whether he hasn't."

"But I didn't think he came down until ten-thirty."

"He did this morning. Eager to start work, I guess. Do encourage him. It's what you're here for, after all. Bye now. I'm late, too. See you this evening."

She was gone, in a waft of perfume, and the quick clipping of high heels on the tiled floor. The old nanny had disappeared as silently as if she had dissolved. A car was pulling up at the door. Cressida's white Jaguar. Jeremy stepped out and held the door open for Cressida. He was taller than she was, and his fair head bent over her. She looked up at him, said something, laughed, then got into the driving seat and whirled away. She was as sleek and smart as her car. And she had not yet come to terms with having an invalid husband. Her desire to escape was all too evident. She ran out of the house. She didn't run into it in the evening.

Poor Charles.

"Where the devil have you been, Mrs Goodwill?" Not Sarah this morning. A face with brows like drawn swords.

She quickly abandoned her pity. This man didn't want pity. He wanted a fight.

"I'm sorry, Charles. Agnes said you didn't come down till ten-thirty."

"It didn't occur to you to ask me instead of my cook? If I want to start work at ten o'clock I want you here."

"Yes, of course."

"Where have you been, anyway?" Now his voice was querulous. It was very clear that he resented her being up and outdoors on this bright morning.

"Down to the marsh with Dolly. It is a beautiful place, isn't it? Wild and yet peaceful. I can understand how it fascinates small boys."

"I told you he's not supposed to go there alone?"

"Yes, you did tell me. But in Dolly's mind he isn't alone. He has the faithful Joseph with him."

"Damn that crazy apparition, or doppelganger, or whatever it is. The whole thing is getting out of hand. Dolly is old enough to grow out of make-believe. His mother neglects him, that's the trouble. And I'm worth damn all. Agnes merely feeds him, and Nanny's gone senile."

Sarah quickly seized on the change of subject. "I met old nanny. Miss Galloway."

Charles gave a grin that gave him a passing boyishness. "I called her Gallows when I wanted to annoy her. It made her mad. She had a temper like a whirlwind. It sizzled everybody and then it was burnt out in a flash. But you can't talk to her now. She's absolutely potty."

"So I discovered."

"I have to take care of her, whatever my less sympathetic wife may think. She was a double parent to me, and a jolly good one. You can't throw people out like discarded toys, can you? If you can, I'll be following her any day now. I wouldn't be surprised if the idea hasn't gone through Cress's mind."

"Oh, no."

"Sarah, don't be sentimental. We were talking about Nanny. When she got gaga we moved her up another flight of stairs, nearer to heaven, you might say. Agnes sees she doesn't starve. The only thing, I sometimes wonder if she upsets Dolly a bit. He listens to her lunacies, and then can't separate fact from fiction."

"What are her lunacies?"

"Servants' tales, I suppose. There must have been plenty in a house like this."

"She talked of a dreadful Miss Knox."

"A governess who was once here."

"I know. I read about her in your Aunt Cissie's diaries."

"I think there was some trouble and a court trial, I believe, but no one seemed to keep records about it, as if they didn't care for it much. What does my Aunt Cissie say about Miss Knox?"

"Just that she was like a brown bird with big eyes."

"That hardly deserves the epithet of 'dreadful'."

"No, it doesn't. But I've got an awful lot more to read. Your Aunt Cissie must have spent years writing those diaries. It's a wonder she ever did anything else. She seems to have been a terrible prig. But I suppose all good little girls were in those days."

"You're enjoying the diaries?"

"Searching for gold nuggets among all the trivialities? What am I supposed to be looking for?"

"Human interest. That's what most people want to read. I can supply all the facts about the guns. Anyway, through being orphaned so young I know very little about my family myself. So let's discuss what you dig up."

The storm had passed. His face was quiet again. Sarah felt relieved and invigorated. The man hadn't lost his fighting spirit.

"What progress have you made since yesterday afternoon?"

"I've been going through old ledgers and balance sheets. Dated 1857 and 1858. Profits soared after the Crimea. Fascinating. And no income tax to speak of. The old boy had it made. No wonder he could buy those hideous works of art. That's another thing, Sarah. Do you know about art?"

"A little. But like diagnosing illnesses, a little knowledge is dangerous."

"Never mind, I've time now to assess the contents of this

museum and get rid of the worst horrors. We'll have valuers down. We're going to have a busy summer."

His face, when he was enthusiastic, was full of vitality. She imagined how he must have been once, and the knowledge was painful. We'll write a book and sort out your treasures, Charles, but we'll also dig for the lost man and bring him into the light again.

"You said a three months' trial," she murmured.

"Well, do you know," he was smiling now, with genuine and charming friendliness, "I think you've almost passed the test."

"Wait till Jane arrives."

"Ah, yes, Jane, the exorciser of doppelgangers."

"Let's hope so. By the way, Charles —"

"Yes?"

"When are you due for another check-up with your doctor?"

The never far distant anger sparked in his eyes. "My health, my dear Sarah, is not part of your job."

"I think it is. If you're going to work well it's rather important that you should be in the best health possible. I'm a doctor's daughter, remember? You do over-react, don't you?"

"Do I? I suppose I do. Oh, hell, I'm sorry. If you want to touch a raw nerve, talk about my spine."

"But you do have check-ups?"

"Oh, yes, now and again," he admitted grudgingly. "My doctor likes me to keep in touch."

"And Cressida insists?"

"Cress? No, she doesn't insist. Look Sarah, this has been going on for eighteen months. A person's patience wears out."

"But she does go with you to Harley Street, or wherever you go?"

"I prefer to go alone."

"Not even with Jeremy?"

"Jeremy drives me. Come off it, Sarah, what is this? A cross-examination?" He added sulkily, "Cress used to come with me at first, when we both lived on hope. Now she has a lot of deadlines at her office. I don't blame her. Do you?"

"It's not part of my job, is it, to answer that question?" Sarah said evenly. "But on your next hospital visit, I'm coming with you."

"You're doing nothing of the kind!" he exploded. He looked profoundly irritated. "You're not going to be one of those strong-minded women, are you? I'd never have guessed it. You've got a gentle face, a rather nice soft face."

"Misleading."

"Is that why your husband left you?"

"That's below the belt. And he didn't leave me. It was a mutual agreement." She grinned. "Well, now honours are even, perhaps we can do some work."

APART FROM THINKING of Charles, and she realised that it was going to be difficult to stop thinking of him, Sarah reflected a great deal about the mysterious trouble connected with the Edwardian Miss Knox, and the snippets of muddled information given to her by the old nanny, Miss Galloway. Miss Galloway must have heard some version of the story, although everyone who had participated in it was either dead or removed from the scene.

She was longing to get at Cissie's diaries again. She would skim through all the irrelevancies and find the significant lines. Had the dreadful Miss Knox kept a diary, she wondered. Most young women in those days, particularly the spinsters of whom Charles scathingly talked, kept diaries as outlets for repressed emotions. Solitary confessionals.

Were there, by any chance, any fragments of past occupancy hidden in this room? Sarah, although inclined to laugh at herself, began a search that turned out to be rather engrossing. She discovered a hidden drawer in the writing desk, but it was disappointingly empty. She poked about in the back of the deep wardrobe and found a crumpled and faded silk rose, probably off a hat, one of those wide-brimmed picture hats Edwardian ladies had worn to garden parties. In spite of its wilted appearance it looked French, and expensive. Could Miss Knox have afforded a hat of that quality? Although everything found in this room didn't necessarily need to have been Miss Knox's. It was years since she had occupied the room – another age.

Sarah unscrewed the brass knobs of the bed frame, and peered down the hollow tubes, rusted and empty. A marvellous place for hiding small objects, nevertheless. Jane would be intrigued by it.

Then she lifted the hearth rug, and momentarily held her breath. The loose floorboard was so obvious. This was the traditional hiding place. She had only to lift up the board, and find a secret collection of what? Silver teaspoons, pieces of jewellery, perhaps some gold sovereigns? The pickings of a disgruntled and envious servant. Alas, the hollow was as empty as other hiding places, except for a few mouse droppings, a drift of dust. There didn't seem to be anything about Miss Knox that earned the epithet of "dreadful".

So, back to the tiresome Cissie's diaries.

A few days later Jane arrived for a long weekend. Charles had suggested that Jeremy should drive the fifty or so miles across country to Jane's school and pick her up. Dolly had better go, too, and Sarah, if she wished.

Sarah declined, saying the children would get to know each other better if she were not there. They would probably arrive the best of friends.

Unfortunately this was not so. Jane came into the big hall in a state of awe at her surroundings, and bewilderment and outrage regarding Dolly.

"Mummy, is that boy mad?"

"Dolly? No, indeed. He's got a very good brain when he chooses to use it."

"Then why does he talk all the time to someone you can't see?"

"Oh, dear. Joseph?"

"That's what he called him. He wouldn't let me sit in the back with him because he had Joseph. I had to sit with Jeremy in the front, and listen to those boys giggling. I mean, boy," she said, her blue eyes, usually happy and confident, clouded. "But honestly, you'd have believed there were two of them."

"I know what you mean. Joseph eats with us, too, I'm afraid."

"Then Dolly is bonkers."

"That's an inelegant word, and it's not true. In medical terms, he's a fantasist. A not uncommon thing to be if you take an only child and parents with serious problems."

"But that's me, and I'm not a – what you said."

Jane certainly was not a fantasist, Sarah knew thankfully. She was a healthy, sunbrowned, well-adjusted nine-year-old with blonde pigtails and a good, but not uncomfortably high, I.Q. She was compatible and good-humoured and giggled a lot, and appeared not to have any serious hang-ups about a neglectful father.

"No, you're a sensible child, darling. Thank goodness. But Dolly has things in his family history, perhaps rather dark things. And there's another word you won't understand. Heredity."

"What dark things?" Jane asked morbidly.

"I haven't discovered yet. I've only been putting together scraps of information. Dolly's father was orphaned when he was a baby, and no one seems to have told him much about the past. We're trying to reconstruct it and write about it, together with a history of guns. The family was very much involved in guns, which I think might explain some violent things in their past. But I do know there was a son, a great-uncle of Dolly's, who was odd and difficult. They called him Boy."

"Boy! Oh, boy!" Jane giggle at her inadvertent pun. "He must have got teased at school."

"He didn't go to school. He had a governess."

"Ugh! Little Lord Fauntleroy. What happened to him when he grew up?"

"He didn't grow up. He died when he was ten. Not much older than Dolly." The sobering thought had just occurred to her.

"How awful, Mummy!"

"It's all a very long time ago."

Mamma has been petting Boy again, cuddling him on her lap as if he's a baby and not nearly as old as me. Cissie had written resentfully in her diary. *No wonder he had tantrums, Papa says. And he is never punished for them, either.*

"How's Dolly getting on with Jane?" Charles asked.

"They'd get on better if Dolly would discard his inseparable friend. Jane doesn't know what to make of that. I think she's a bit jealous. She's not used to being regarded as second best."

Charles laughed. "She struck me as a young lady who

could stand on her own feet. Congratulations, Sarah. You've done well with her."

Sarah was startled at her pleasure. Compliments, she had discovered, came rarely from her employer.

"Just luck, I think. But she's already getting involved with Maidenshall. Do you mind? She's mad to know more about Boy and Cissie and Adolphus, your father, and their governess, too. Governesses only exist in the world of fiction to her. And she's noticed that Cissie keeps writing about the two major figures in a child's life in those days, Mamma and Papa. You told me your grandfather was killed in the First World War, but what happened to your grandmother? Cissie says frequently, 'Mamma looked so lovely tonight,' or 'All the gentlemen admired Mamma as usual'."

"All too true. I believe there was a scandal. It was hinted that Grandmother ran off with another man. It was hushed up, of course. Do you think that arrogant bastard," Charles gestured towards the painting of his grandfather, ruddy, intolerant, overbearing, "would have put up with an erring wife? I expect he said she'd gone to live abroad for her health. Have you noticed that there are no portraits or photographs of her in the house? That's a pity, because she was supposed to have been a very beautiful woman, though not over-gifted with brains."

Charles's own wife was perhaps more clever than beautiful. A flirtatious wife like Violet Storrington might have been more warm-hearted, even if promiscuous. Cressida was cool and clever, and almost certainly promiscuous as well. Surely it wasn't always work that kept her late in London. Sarah noticed that Charles didn't comment on her occasional absence from dinner. Nor did he seem to notice that she was never home when Jeremy had a night off. So perhaps she didn't dine in London, but in nearby Maidenhead. That was only a supposition on Sarah's part. But on two occasions she had heard their voices late at night. It seemed too much of a coincidence that they should arrive home from separate assignations at precisely the same time.

Jeremy was a handsome fellow, very physical. Under the

circumstances one should forgive Cressida for succumbing to such convenient temptations.

But Sarah could feel nothing but deep indignation and pain for the lonely man sitting in the library or on the terrace after dinner. Cressida had so much, brains, looks, an interesting job, a sumptuous home. Couldn't she have foregone sex? And Jeremy, if he were guilty of adultery with his employer's wife, ought to be sacked, but Charles liked and depended on him. And perhaps shut his eyes to certain possibly inevitable consequences.

If he could do that, then the situation was no business of Sarah's. It was no business of hers, period. But she was a little disturbed that she already felt so fiercely protective towards her employer. An emotional involvement of this kind was the last thing she needed.

"By the way, Sarah," Cressida said that evening, "Charles has an appointment with his specialist next Monday. There's to be a consultation with another specialist. There's the possibility of some new treatment. He's trying not to be too optimistic, poor love. Would it be an awful imposition to ask you to go with him? I usually do, but that day I have people from Paris arriving. I've got to lunch with them. And really there's nothing to do except see that Charles gets there on time, and then sit in the waiting room. Jeremy will drive you, of course."

"Certainly, I'll go. I'd planned to, anyway."

That made Cressida look at her sharply.

"Had you?"

"If you weren't going. I think Charles needs support – whatever he says to the contrary."

Cressida's eyebrows lifted. "The ministering angel? Sorry, Sarah, that was bitchy."

Sarah found it hard to keep her temper. "Yes it is. I'm no angel. Just a human being."

"So am I," Cressida said in a low voice.

Sarah was too honest not to realise that Cressida was more desperate than bitchy. There was a driven look in her eyes which could be interpreted as sheer consternation at the thought of the impossible years ahead. Could she desert an invalid husband and remain a human being? There was her other responsibility too. Dolly. A puzzling small boy who could grow more eccentric if plunged into an unstable background.

There were no easy answers. Really, no answers at all.

"Aren't you hopeful about this treatment?"

"I'm sorry to say I'm not. We've had too many disappointments. And if you're kind, you won't buoy up his hopes too much, either."

"Of course I'll take him," Sarah said, "Jane goes back to school tomorrow. Will Dolly be all right with Agnes and Mr Crankshaw?"

"He often has to be. Did he and Jane hit it off?"

"Jane said no. She said he was rude to her, and if that was what all boys were like she wasn't interested. She hasn't been exposed to the opposite sex very much, I must add. But she wants to come again. And Dolly did play croquet with her, and I believe didn't mention Joseph once."

"Thank goodness for small mercies. I expect he cheated instead."

"I don't think so. Jane wouldn't have allowed it. I'm terribly afraid she's going to be captain of the school hockey team."

Cressida laughed. "She's rather decorative, though. So sunburnt and healthy. Does she look more like her father than you?"

"Perhaps. He's good-looking enough."

Cressida was giving her a searching look. "Sarah, do you mind if I say something to you. And it isn't bitchy."

"Go ahead."

"Well, it's easy to see you're already concerned for my husband. You're kind and sympathetic. But don't get involved."

"I don't quite know what you mean, except that kind and sympathetic women, as you describe me, are always involved."

"You do know what I mean. Serious involvement. Charles is still immensely attractive. What I'm saying is, you have a failed marriage. So you're inevitably a little wary of men.

True? My husband represents no threat in the physical sense, so it could be tempting to use up some of your emotions on him with perfect safety."

Sarah flushed with anger. "My God, Cressida, you're talking about me as if I'm a nervous spinster."

"No, no. Calm down. Just once burnt, twice shy. And you're an emotional girl. Aren't I right?"

"You're saying these things because you're feeling guilty about evading your own responsibilities."

"Perhaps I am, partly. But after eighteen months of living with a man who has completely changed, it's the only way I can cope. You see, I remember what he was. You don't. I have to unload some of what you call my responsibilities. For God's sake, Sarah, don't let's quarrel."

The anger and uneasiness gnawed inside Sarah. She was afraid Cressida might have been speaking the truth. She was a perceptive woman. And an honest one. She could have been a friend. But now the man in the wheelchair was coming between them.

Maidenshall, she thought, was aptly named, and for more than one solitary woman.

Jane, cheerful, noisy and uninhibited, had brought more life to the house than Sarah realised. She was keenly aware of this when Jane had gone. Unexpectedly, Dolly was, too. Sarah found him hanging about in the passage outside her door, looking bored and lonely.

She was just about to leave her room and speak to him when old Nanny appeared.

Dolly shrank against the wall. He seemed frightened, which was not surprising since children often were nervous of and repelled by extreme old age. But this old woman had been around all of his short life and must be very familiar to him.

Nanny was mumbling something that Sarah couldn't catch. Dolly heard, however, and shouted angrily, "Don't call me boy, you silly old woman. It's rude. I have a name. It's Dolly."

Nanny bent forward, peering.

"You must mean Adolphus. But I thought you looked

like –" She suddenly sensed Sarah at her open door and turned. Her mouth gaped open in what seemed to be terror.

"What have you come back for? They took you away. What are you looking for?"

"Come now, it's only me, Nanny. Sarah. We talked in the garden, don't you remember?" She held out her hand to Dolly, who ran to seize it, and to press against her as if for refuge. There was no doubt that old Nanny did alarm him.

"That young woman has taken my things." The old sunken eyes had a look of bewildered anger.

"What things?"

"She doesn't know," whispered Dolly, and indeed the old lady was already shuffling away. "She thinks people steal things. Father says I must be understanding because she's so old. But I wish she would die. So does Joseph." He looked aghast at his wickedness, his eyes wide and strained.

"Do you know, I think Jane would say the same thing," Sarah said comfortable.

"Would she?"

"Well, you enjoyed her visit, didn't you?"

"Not much. At least –"

"At least Joseph didn't?"

"How did you know that?"

"Jane thought he was around a bit too much. She wanted to play with you by herself. But next time perhaps she can."

"Is she coming again?" Dolly asked.

"Yes, in about four weeks."

Dolly sighed. "Then I suppose I had better tell Joseph. He won't like it though. This is his place."

"If it's his place he ought to learn better manners and welcome his guests."

At least that odd conversation had taken Dolly's mind off the creepy old woman. He stayed close to Sarah for the rest of the afternoon, and didn't mention Joseph once. He even inquired if Jane was any good at football.

Sarah believed the experiment was going to work and longed to tell Charles. But Joseph was back for supper, when a lot of foolish and highly irritating giggling went on. That night Dolly had another nightmare. Something about a gun this time.

"You shouldn't fire it. You shouldn't!" Just as he was waking up he screamed. "No, Joseph, don't!"

Then he was trembling and shivering in Sarah's arms, and Cressida was at the door.

"Oh, you're there, Sarah. What has he been dreaming about tonight?"

"Guns."

"Not surprising in this family. Is he all right now?"

"I think so. I'll go down and make him a hot drink if you'll stay with him."

Cressida was still dressed. She wore a long trailing dress, and her usually smooth hair was slightly ruffled. The time was half past one. Charles, assisted by Jeremy, had retired more than two hours ago.

When Sarah went downstairs, she noticed that the lights were on in the drawing room. There was no one in the room. The cushions from the couch, however, had been tossed on the floor as if they had been in the way. There was a lingering aroma of Cressida's rather distinctive perfume.

Sarah had been at Maidenshall for only six weeks, but in that brief time her life had completely changed. For one thing, she could never get Charles's face out of her mind. Me and Hannah Knox, she thought wryly. Cissie's diaries were making it increasingly apparent that meek and quiet little Hannah had fallen in love with her employer. There had been a trip to St. Petersburg, and Cissie had written, *Papa took us to the ballet, Miss Knox looked so pretty, her cheeks pink, her eyes like stars. The next day Papa gave us presents and Miss Knox was overcome at being remembered . . .*

11

Hannah

THEY HAD A suite on the third floor of the hotel, overlooking the grey frozen surface of the river Neva. There were red carpets everywhere, red curtains, brass bedsteads, a great many mirrors and an enormous bath in the bathroom.

"Big enough for bears," Mr Storrington said, to Cissie's renewed enchantment. She had never known Papa to be in such a delightful mood for so long.

Hannah and Cissie shared a bedroom. Adolphus was next to the main bedroom which naturally had been appropriated by Mr Storrington. There was also a sitting room full of heavy mahogany furniture, pot plants and cabinets. Breakfast and the evening meal were taken here, two rather ferocious-looking waiters carrying the trays, but for the midday meal Hannah had Mr Storrington's permission to take the children downstairs into the great gloomy dining room, where they could be diverted by a change of scene.

Hannah had charge of Cissie's and her own baggage. Adolphus importantly shared Beale, Mr Storrington's valet, with his father.

Beale had been allotted one of the rooms kept for gentlemen's servants. He appeared punctually at eight o'clock each morning to attend to Mr Storrington's requirements. He was a solemn young man who occasionally cast a hopeful glance at Hannah. This silent message she ignored. The impertinence of him, she thought. Even Daisy should have higher ideas for her than a valet.

At first they saw very little of Mr Storrington. He was going about his business, and seeing some important officials and army officers. He went on a day's boar hunt in some woods several miles out of the city, and came back in the early hours of the morning. Hannah, who had slept only in snatches, heard his far from silent arrival. He banged doors, dropped things and finally crashed into bed. She heard that because she was standing with her door opened a crack, listening. The brass bed in the big bedroom creaked loudly as it accepted his weight.

She sighed with relief. Mr Storrington might be a little inebriated with the potent Russian vodka, and a little sore and tired from his long day's hunting, but he was safe. That was what she wanted to ascertain. Now she could go back to bed and sleep. That day she and the children had had a sleigh ride, with the snow crunching beneath the horses' hooves, and the sleigh bells ringing merrily. They had driven past the Winter Palace where by great good fortune they had seen a sleigh containing two little girls in hood capes of dazzling white fur being whirled through the gates. Cissie had cried out with delight. They were the two elder Grand Duchesses, she declared. She knew because one of them was the same age as herself. Oh, how she wished they had seen her and smiled at her. But perhaps she would encounter them again. Even that brief glimpse had turned their holiday into a fairy tale.

Then there had been the circus in the afternoon, and after that a supper of thick soup with dumplings, followed by bed. Neither of the children could keep awake for Papa that night. Which was just as well, considering his late return.

But the next evening he came bursting into the sitting room before six o'clock. A very tall gentleman in a long black fur coat, and with a glossy black beard, followed him.

"I want you to meet General Zoubetsky," Mr Storrington said. "This is my daughter, Celia. My son Adolphus. And Miss Knox, our chargée d'affaires," he added in his gently mocking way.

Cissie curtsied, Adolphus bowed in his well-mannered way. Hannah gave the smallest bob. She had hoped Mr Storrington would be alone and eat with them that evening, and she didn't much care for the frankly assessing glance the stranger had given her. In ten seconds he had decided she was not to his taste, and had turned to Mr Storrington to accept the brimming glass of vodka he was offered.

He tossed it down in one accomplished swallow, and allowed his glass to be refilled.

"Won't you take off your coat, General, and sit down?"

"No, thank you. I won't stay. I'll leave you to your family. Very cosy and nice." He addressed himself to Adolphus, speaking his excellent English. "I hope they are treating you well in this hotel."

"Yes, thank you, sir."

"Splendid. Then Mr Storrington, we may expect a visit from you and your beautiful wife in the spring."

"Myself, certainly. My wife is a less than enthusiastic traveller."

"Then if you are alone you must be the guest of the Countess and myself. You can expect Grigorei and Andrei to inspect the Storrington works early in January. They will have full authorisation to finalise our deal if they are satisfied with the performance of your machine gun." He turned to the children, "You have a clever father – no?"

"Yes!" cried Cissie loyally, liking the jovial stranger.

A third glass of vodka was following its predecessors. The General laughed loudly.

"So you have two female admirers, lucky fellow." He slapped Mr Storrington heavily on the back and was gone, banging the door resoundingly.

"Is he a Cossack, Papa?" Adolphus asked in some awe.

"No, he's one of the Czar's most trusted advisers. He can ride like the devil, though. Most of these chaps can."

"As well as the Light Brigade?"

"Ah, you're thinking of the Valley of Death in the Crimea. Well done, my boy. No, not even the Cossacks could outdo our Lancers. Or if they can, we can't admit to it, eh? Well then, who are my two female admirers?"

There was that bright teasing look that Cissie loved in her father's eyes. On the few occasions that she had seen it, Hannah had known that she was not averse to it herself.

"Don't be blind, Papa, it's Miss Knox and me."

"I don't think I am blind," said Mr Storrington quietly.

"Papa, could that General not have stayed and told us something about the Grand Duchesses? We saw two of them today. At least we are sure we did, aren't we, Miss Knox? They were very pretty."

"And who is going to ring for our dinner before I starve?" Mr Storrington cried. "Come Cissie, your first lesson in being a woman of the world. You may give the order. Caviare, bortsch, which is red cabbage soup, grilled mullet, roast venison, a plate of hot pancakes, another bottle of vodka – that Cossack has knocked this one about – and a bottle of red wine. What else can you think of?"

"Oh, papa, we'll all burst."

"So we very well may, my treasure. Come and give Papa a kiss."

"I wish you could be with us every evening, Papa."

"Perhaps I may be. We'll see what happens after the ballet tomorrow."

"Papa!"

"Miss Knox, can't you stop the child from screeching? It's a very unattractive sound. I was simply announcing that I have tickets for the ballet. There's a new young dancer called Nijinsky who is supposed to be remarkable, they tell me. Not that ballet is my line of country. I'd rather go boar hunting and get another million pound order from these crafty army officers. Don't know whether they'll ever be able to honour their payments, though. I fancy their exchequer isn't as sound as ours."

Cissie and Adolphus almost fell asleep over the lavish meal. Hannah's eyes met Mr Storrington's across the loaded table. Like parents, she thought.

"Yes, I'll get them to bed," she said.

When she returned someone had been to clear away the meal, and Mr Storrington was sitting in one of the armchairs smoking a cigar. He looked sleepy, too. His eyes were half closed.

"All is well, Miss Knox?"

"Very well, thank you, sir."

"Splendid. Then tomorrow night you ladies may wear your finery, eh?"

There was the merest glint beneath the heavy eyelids. It was not possible to read any meaning into it.

What sort of meaning did she expect?

Cissie crouched in the front of the opera box, too excited to be able to sit on her chair, and longing to be nearer the fairy-tale world on the stage. Presently Adolphus joined her, although he was not quite so star-struck. He would have preferred a military parade with bands and horses and flashing swords. He had said as much as he grumblingly changed into the dark suit and stiff white collar that made him a smaller replica of his father. Ballet was for girls. But the sparkling stage set of snowy forest and castle, and the brilliantly dressed dancers leaping and spinning began to engross him almost as much as it did his sister.

Neither of them were aware of the detachment of their father and Hannah, who sat back from the lights, Mr Storrington sprawling in a bored fashion, Hannah prim and upright and feigning an interest she did not feel.

The spectacle was superb, of course, and she was so fortunate to have the opportunity to be there. When the lights were up she had looked with the greatest interest at the occupants of other boxes, seeing the splendid toilettes and the glitter of jewels. The modest sparkle of her garnets was lost among all that brilliance. At first she had shrunk back so that her richly attired neighbours could not look with curiosity at the plain little Englishwoman whose husband apparently did not bother to deck her with jewels.

But presently her head lifted proudly, the way she would have carried it had she really been Mr Storrington's wife. She began to indulge in a fantasy as compelling as that taking place on the stage.

Mr Storrington's voice in her ear made her jump. "Why do you look like a mouse?" he whispered.

"Oh no! Surely not!" Stung by his unkind remark she retorted hastily and angrily. She had thought, before leaving the hotel, that she had triumphed over the sober grey dress, her neck stretched long, her hair done in the most elaborate fashion she could devise. Certainly Cissie had admired her.

But one should not have taken the admiration of a child seriously.

She knew Mr Storrington was giving that lazy bland smile and could not look at him.

"It's the dress your wife chose for me," she said, not bothering to conceal her resentment.

"Oh, Violet. Bitch."

Had she heard those words correctly? Perhaps she had, for, as the music from the orchestra pit grew louder, fingers, warm and caressing, nibbled at her neck. A tendril of her hair was tugged gently.

"Mr. Storrington!"

She lifted the hand off, only to have it return.

"Hush! Must I sit through three more acts of this nonsense? I can only do so if you allow me to amuse myself. Would you have Cissie disappointed by my leaving early?"

The whispering voice was part of the sensuous music. She must submit to it and the liberties being taken because she couldn't make a scene here. Didn't want to, to be honest. And not just for Cissie's sake. Judging by her quickened heartbeat, the mouse he likened her to was a warm-blooded creature.

What was to happen when they returned home? Was he intending to pursue this activity, or behave as if it had never happened? She remembered the hints and suggestions about the athletic and flirtatious Miss Shepherd, and her neck stiffened in rejection. But the wandering fingers relaxed her muscles, and her token opposition faded.

It was cold enough in the snowy streets to freeze the warmest blood. Although wrapped in their fur cloaks everyone was shivering when they reached the hotel, Hannah the most violently of all. Neither hot drinks brought in by a rosy-cheeked chambermaid who made solicitous but unintelligible clucks, nor the glowing stove in her and Cissie's bedroom could stop her trembling.

She tried to say that she was not cold, but how otherwise could she explain her fit of shaking?

Mr Storrington had brushed off Cissie's rapturous thanks, and Adolphus's polite ones, and said bluntly that the ballet wasn't much to his liking. Tomorrow, by courtesy of his friend General Zoubetsky, he would take Adolphus to the army barracks.

"What, sir?"

"Listen, can't you, boy! I thought you wanted to see the cavalry. Now I'm off to bed. This gay life is more exhausting than a day in my factory at home."

So Hannah lay in her own bed, still shivering, and wondering why suddenly she felt so flat and grey and inclined to weep.

The next evening, however, some of the gaiety returned. Adolphus came bursting in saying excitedly that he had been allowed to mount the General's charger and walk it round the yard, and adding that if Cissie and Miss Knox had had a dull day their reward was coming.

"Papa has presents for you."

"Trust Dolly to give away secrets," grumbled Mr Storrington good-humouredly, throwing off his fur hat and overcoat, and taking small packages from his pockets.

There was a fat pink quartz piglet with ruby eyes for Cissie, a cossack with red enamelled uniform and a jewelled sword on an ebony horse for Adolphus, and an amethyst mouse with green eyes – surely emeralds – for Hannah.

She met his eyes in a sharp, aware glance. Holding the cool object in her hands she didn't know whether to be delighted or affronted.

"These must have cost a great deal," she said uneasily.

"Yes. I got them from that famous jeweller's workshop. What was his name, Dolly?"

"Fabergé, sir," Adolphus said. "He makes jewels and things for the Czarina, Miss Knox. We saw an egg that opened, and inside was a beautiful clock that struck the hour. You'd have liked that, Cissie."

"I like my little pig. It's perfectly sweet. Thank you so much, Papa. Oh, what's that? You have another parcel."

Mr Storrington was sliding a long slender box into his pocket. "That's for your mother, and no, you may not see it."

(*Violet, bitch*, Hannah thought. No, she could not have heard those words.)

"You are the most inquisitive child I have ever known," Mr Storrington was saying. "If you had your way you would know all my secrets. I believe Miss Knox is looking insulted."

Cissie was not only inquisitive but aggravating. "Why, Miss Knox? Because Papa gave you that darling little mouse? But you're so lucky."

She could not escape his eyes. He was worse than Cissie with his probing.

"Yes, I am lucky. Thank you, Mr Storrington, you're too generous."

"Not in the least. It's just a memento to remind you of St. Petersburg." His gaze abruptly moved away, as if he were bored. He sat down, stretching his long legs. "Well, what have you and Cissie been doing? Not reading all day, I hope." He picked up the book Hannah had left lying on the table. In the last hour she had been reading aloud because Cissie had seemed, not surprisingly, over-tired and fretful.

"Keats' poems," he said. "Ah! The perfect travelling companion, I'm sure." For people like her, his ironic voice suggested. Really she was growing over-sensitive, ready to prickle at the slightest innuendo.

He had opened the book at random and was reading, *"Thou still unravish'd bride of quietness, Thou foster-child of silence and slow time . . ."* He paused for a moment, and when he began to read again Hannah was aware that his voice had changed and become deep and sensuous, *". . . What maidens loth? What mad pursuit? What struggle to escape? What pipes and timbrels? What wild ecstasy?"*

His eyes lifted to look at Hannah with a kind of glad surprise, as if something had just been made clear to him, some decision made.

She had to turn away as the warm colour mounted in her cheeks.

"My education seems to have been neglected," he said thoughtfully.

A little later, at his suggestion, the children were sent to bed.

"Off with you!" he roared when they protested. Then,

"You, too, Miss Knox. You look as if the brats have thoroughly worn you out."

"Oh, no, they haven't. I'm not at all tired."

"Looks speak louder than words. Here!" He tossed the book of poems to her. "You'll want to take your Keats with you."

"Will you read to me in bed, Miss Knox?" Cissie asked in their bedroom.

"No, I will not," Hannah said crossly. You're too tired and so am I – at least, I am told so. So let us have a good night's sleep."

She had actually fallen asleep, in spite of her conviction that rest was impossible in her disturbed state of mind, when she was woken by a loud exclamation and Mr Storrington calling urgently, "Miss Knox! Can you come?"

She was out of bed in a moment. Cissie had not stirred.

"What is it? Where are you?"

"Here, in my room." The door of the big bedroom was open and Mr Storrington was standing in his brocade dressing gown wrapping a handkerchief round his forefinger. There were bloodstains on the white linen. "I've nearly cut off the top of my finger. Are you good at first aid?"

"I think so. Let me see."

She unfolded the handkerchief and studied the injured finger. The cut was not serious. The blood was already ceasing to flow. She smiled a little, thinking of the fuss.

"I think it will be all right. I'll just bathe it in the basin. How did you do it?"

"On that damned fruit knife. I was peeling an apple. What about tetanus?"

"Oh, I don't think so. The knife looks clean."

"Yes, well, a foreign country, you know. You ought to see inside some of the peasants' huts, and the peasants themselves, ragged and filthy. Starving too, poor devils."

"Where are the apple peelings?" Hannah asked.

"What?"

"Weren't you peeling an apple?"

"Oh? I was just about to do so. You are very observant, Miss Knox."

"Observant enough to suspect this is a deliberately self-inflicted wound," she said levelly.

His brows arched.

"Why would I do that?"

"I have no idea, except that you wanted to make a fuss."

He was laughing softly. "I'm observant, too. I like your nightgown. The little edging of lace here." He touched her neck.

Hannah was blushing violently. "I came in such a hurry. I forgot my wrap. You did this intentionally."

"Of course."

Now was the time to ask him to take his hands off her, to retreat. He was a gentleman, after all. He would not rape her.

She stood quite still saying in a barely audible voice, "Why do you want me here? You said I was a mouse."

"But a unique mouse. You play Chopin very well indeed, you like poetry, and yet guns excite you. An intriguing mixture. You aren't pretty but your eyes can be magnificent. They burn up your face. Glow in the dark, too, I shouldn't be surprised."

"You wanted to see me at a disadvantage without clothes," she accused, angrily.

"To see you aroused, my dear. I think there's a lot of passion in that cool little body."

She picked fastidiously at the front of her nightgown. "You have put a spot of blood on me here."

He peered at the almost invisible smear. "So I have. Then you must take the offending garment off. Allow me."

He began to undo the buttons, at the same time letting his dressing gown fall open. He was naked underneath.

Before the shock of that fact could register he was holding her in his arms, and he was no longer smiling. His face had taken on a grim starved look, like the Russian peasants of whom he had spoken.

"Come." There was an edge of roughness in his voice. "Come to bed."

"If I – refuse –"

"You're not going to. I've seen you looking at me. You've been setting traps."

"Me!"

"Did you pretend it was only me doing that? Shame on you, an intelligent woman."

Somehow her nightgown had fallen about her feet. She could only whisper, "The door."

"Leave it. Children that age don't wake in the night. Anyway —"

Anyway, the element of danger gave an added excitement that was making her burn and shiver.

"You're cold. This is a very warm, very wide bed. Ideal for our purpose."

"Ours?"

"Stop playing with words, you little school mistress." He swooped her up out of the white lake of her nightgown, and laid her quite gently on the bed. In the next moment, as if pinning down a butterfly before it escaped, his heavy body lay across her, his great head blotted out the light.

There was no time for ignorance. Was there ever ignorance when instinct was so strong?

She was momentarily suffocated and swept into darkness by that massive face pressing down on hers. She could not even cry out. Then there was an instant of sharp pain followed, most felicitously, by an astonishing pleasure.

And it was over.

Or not quite, for he remained close to her, caressing, nibbling at her breasts, stroking and soothing her, whispering, "Was your first love nice? My charming little rodent, no longer unravished. Just ripe to be caught. Ah, you're a lovely small thing. Like those Fabergé toys. Narrow little limbs. Shall you remember this?"

Remember? That had a final sound.

"Is it over?"

"Don't sound so tragic. Of course it isn't over. It's scarcely begun. If you were to curl up close against me, like this, we will see, shortly . . ."

The clock in the sitting room struck two, an ominous sound.

Hannah stirred. "Charlie, I must go."

"Why?" He mumbled, blurred with sleep.

"Cissie may wake."

"She'll be all right. Sleep for hours still." He stretched, the movement of his body against hers sending delight coursing through her veins. "All the same – you're probably right. Better be careful"

"This isn't the only night?" she murmured hopefully.

"We have six more."

"And then the ship."

"Ship berths aren't made for lovers. No privacy, anyway."

"Oh. Then –"

He didn't answer her half-spoken question. He didn't say Maidenshall. How could he, with Violet there, and the servants, and Boy who slept lightly, and winter coming so that no outside nooks could be found.

But surely it wouldn't – couldn't – be over. He didn't love his wife. How could he, after this night?

He slapped her gently on her thigh.

"Off you go. Don't forget your nightgown."

She was being dismissed!

"Let's give Cissie and Adolphus a strenuous day so they'll sleep well tomorrow night, how is that?"

"Oh Charlie!" She was nearly in tears. He noticed and said with a touch of impatience, "Why do women always have to weep, bless them? I don't care for damp tears and melancholy. Can't stand them, to tell the truth."

"I'm not weeping."

He stroked her arm gently, but his voice was unmistakably curt, "Then don't, if you want to please me."

And she did want to please him, as he knew very well. Always, always.

12

HANNAH HAD THREE souvenirs to take home, the amethyst mouse, a theatre programme in the curious spiked Russian lettering, and one of the fat cosy Russian dolls that when opened produced numerous offspring, this a present from Cissie to her "dear Miss Knox".

She herself would not be producing any offspring, fortunately. At least not yet. She was both relieved and disappointed to make that discovery during the journey home. In spite of the enormous complications that would have ensued, she would have dearly liked to experience the pride of conceiving a child for her lover.

Mr Storrington. Her lover. Charlie.

On the last day of their visit to St. Petersburg something shocking had happened. A madman had flung himself beneath the Czar's carriage. He was probably one of those starving peasants Mr Storrington had talked about. There was blood on the snow, and a bundle of rags, and Cissie, deeply shocked, had wanted to go home. It was no use to tell her that this sort of thing had happened in England, too, even to Queen Victoria. There were always madmen who would tilt against impossible odds. Cissie wept and said that now everything was spoiled. It was such a pity, because she had never known Papa to be in such a happy mood for so long.

"Perhaps he will be the same when he gets home," Hannah said. (I will be there to nourish his happy mood.)

"No, he won't. He'll have worries at business and he'll lose his temper with Boy, and with Mamma, too, and probably Dolly and me. Probably with you, too, Miss Knox. It will be the same as it always was."

It can never be the same again, Hannah thought. Although she couldn't think what shape the different life was to take. She only knew she would never be content to sit in the schoolroom directing the children's studies, keeping out of sight when there were guests, and being generally modest and reticent and tactful and subservient.

But Charlie would solve the difficult situation. He was bold and resourceful. She had complete faith in him.

Back in her room, with its sober brown walls, she could not resume familiar habits, and knew that she would never be able to do so again. Too much had changed.

In their absence the days had shortened into winter, and the chestnuts and willows, the creeping wisteria and the espaliered peaches and apricots were leafless. Their knobbed bones were exposed. So was the dark glimmer of the river, and the faded red, like a tall glowing fire, of the Chinese pagoda. She wondered what the marsh was like in its winter desolation, and whether Boy sought its loneliness in this damp and chilly weather.

Barker had thoughtfully laid the fire in her room. When she had changed for dinner she sat beside it to warm her frozen limbs. It was curious that she should feel this damp cold so much after the freezing Russian temperatures. Or perhaps it wasn't the cold that was making her give spasmodic shivers. Perhaps it was because she was listening for a certain tap at her door.

But that was ridiculous. Whatever arrangements Mr Storrington (it slightly chilled her to find that she was automatically thinking of him as Mr Storrington again) made for the future, he would hardly be so rash as to come directly to her room. Perhaps at midnight, but not at this time when the servants were about. He had been extremely discreet on the ship, scarcely glancing her way, and addressing all his remarks to Cissie and Adolphus, as if their fellow passengers would begin gossiping if he paid Hannah too much attention.

But now they were home, and Violet's welcome had been casual rather than rapturous, Boy's positively hostile. Boy had enjoyed escaping lessons and having his mother to himself. He has been an angel, Violet said wistfully. There hadn't been an occasion when Max had been required.

Hannah had noticed the beginnings of a scowl on Mr Storrington's forehead. Jubilation filled her. Already it was apparent that only she could bring back his happy St.

Petersburg mood. But privacy was essential. He would find a way.

When there was a brisk tap at her door Hannah started up so nervously that she tipped over her chair.

"Goodness, miss, you a bit tipsy," joked Elsie, carrying in a tray. "Or have you still got your sea legs?"

She set the tray, its contents covered with a napkin, on the table.

"What's that?" Hannah asked.

"Your supper, miss. Mistress's orders. She thought you might like it quietly in your room after your long day."

"But – the children – aren't we all to dine downstairs?"

"Barker's taking care of the children. The master and mistress want to be alone. Understandable, isn't it?"

"But she – I mean –" Hannah realised she was staring at Elsie in disbelief, and quickly shifted her gaze.

"You thought she acted a bit cool? They're not the sort who mess about in public."

"What do you mean, mess about?" Hannah asked icily.

It was Elsie's turn to stare. "Blimey, you got a lot to learn, miss. Didn't you hang over the ship's rail in the moonlight? Didn't that Beale give you a bit of a cuddle? He's a nice-looking young fellow."

"Thank you for carrying up the tray, Elsie. You may go."

"Blimey, travelling gives some people airs," Elsie said under her breath, but quite obviously intending Hannah to hear. She had never regarded Hannah as her superior.

Left alone, Hannah took the cloth off the tray, and looked at the perfectly agreeable, indeed tasty, meal. It should have been pleasant to eat English food again, the slices of roast beef and gravy, the hot potatoes and buttered carrots, and the liberal helping of plum pudding to follow. But her appetite had vanished.

In the dining room, Mr and Mrs Storrington would be dining by candlelight, no doubt, and drinking a bottle of Mr Storrington's best burgundy. Candlelight, Hannah had observed at other times, caught marvellous lights in Mrs Storrington's hair and made her face young and soft and very beautiful.

It was bitterly humiliating to be confined to her room, as if she were sentenced to solitary imprisonment, on her first night home. Something steely was developing in Hannah. She was not going to tolerate this kind of treatment, nor would Mr Storrington when he became aware of it. Though must he not be aware of it now?

In the morning, although she joined the children at breakfast at the usual time, Mr Storrington had already left for business.

"Papa has a great deal to do," Cissie said blithely. "He wanted to get to his office by eight-thirty. I was just down in time to say goodbye to him."

At least he hadn't lingered late with his wife, Hannah told herself. Had he spent the night in her bed? The uncertainty was driving her mad, already. She reasoned with herself that since she had got herself into this position she must accept its drawbacks as well as its ecstasies.

Just now on a cold rainy morning the drawbacks seemed too great – loneliness, uncertainties, an intense feeling of being slighted, and an acute and corroding jealousy of that beautiful, lazy, voluptuous woman lounging so late in bed, as if the night had given her little sleep. But this was fantasy. Mrs Storrington usually stayed in her room until midday. It did not mean that one had to view her bed to see if the other pillow had been used.

All the same, Mr Storrington might have lingered to say good morning. Was she expected to rush downstairs, like Cissie, to catch a glimpse of him?

"In the schoolroom at nine-thirty, Cissie and Boy," she said crisply.

"Oh, Miss Knox –"

"Holidays are over. Boy, I shall expect to see what work you have done while we've been away."

"Mamma said I needn't," Boy said, staring at her. She had forgotten how glassy and brilliant his eyes could be.

"That really is fair, Miss Knox," Cissie said in her aggravatingly earnest manner. "After all, we've had holidays."

"Don't interfere, Cissie. Adolphus, the dogcart has been at

128

the door for ten minutes. You'll have a great deal to catch up with Mr Beard."

"What did you say, Miss Knox?"

Now Adolphus was using his deafness as a weapon. This was too much.

"I think you know what I said. Get on your outdoor things and be off with you."

Cissie was still docile enough and followed Hannah to the schoolroom. But Boy had disappeared.

Now Hannah had a subject on which to vent her anger and hurt. She set Cissie an essay to write, "A Journey to St. Petersburg", and went off in search of her will-o'-the-wisp pupil who had vanished as effectively as a bird flying out of the window. She intended to track him down, even if it meant a long wet trudge to the marsh.

She thought she heard a faint sound of laughter coming from Mrs Storrington's room. The little wretch was in there! She would have to be forgiven for intruding, but she could not allow her authority to be flouted.

A quick tap at the door and she was in the room. "Excuse me, Mrs Storrington."

Mrs Storrington was in the centre of the bed, propped up by several pillows. The covers had been smoothed so that there was no visible sign of whether or not she had spent the night alone. She was certainly alone now. Her hair was tumbling in attractive disorder, her cheeks were flushed from sleep. She was no grey mouse, this woman, but rather one of those ripe plums that had fallen into the long grass at the end of summer, fruit so rosy and irresistible that it surely demanded instant consumption.

"What is it, Miss Knox? Is something wrong?"

"I'm looking for Boy."

"He's not here."

"I thought I heard someone laughing."

"Not in here. I'm alone and about to have my breakfast. Must I get up and help you look for him? Call Max first. And Miss Knox, don't scold the boy. He's going to find discipline a little difficult after a month's freedom. He does so hate authority."

"Nevertheless he must learn to accept it," Hannah said curtly.

"Oh dear, Miss Knox, you sound very stern this morning. But I do advise you to use velvet gloves with Boy. Anyone who can handle him is above price in this household. Remember that."

Was there an underlying significance in that remark? Mrs Storrington's turquoise eyes were lazy and bland.

"And, Miss Knox – you were extremely fortunate to have had such an interesting trip. I'm sure not many young women in your position would have had such an opportunity. But don't let it spoil you, don't imagine that these pleasures can be repeated."

Hannah's lips were stiff. Was she hinting that she *knew*? But how could she know, and still look amused rather than angry? No, she was guessing at something quite mild and predictable, a little flirtation, perhaps a kiss. She would know her husband and be prepared to overlook modest indiscretions. But Hannah must not attach any significance to them. That was the warning. Young women in her position were dangerously vulnerable, was what she was really saying.

There was a telephone on the table by her bed, and Hannah, much more intimately aware now of flirtatious behaviour, suddenly knew the explanation for the overheard laughter. Mrs Storrington had been talking to someone, a good morning call after her husband had left the house. Marriages like hers needed a little titillation, a little forbidden amusement. But there were certain rules to be kept, and appearances must be respected.

"It was a very enjoyable trip, Mrs Storrington, and I am grateful for it," Hannah said stiffly. "But now if you'll excuse me I must find Boy." At the door she said quietly, "I don't think you need have any worries about my not being able to handle him."

And that was a bold lie if ever there was one. She was far from certain about her influence on that wild strange child. But in that few minutes in Mrs Storrington's bedroom she had recognised that she must become indispensable in this household, not just invaluable as Mrs Storrington had suggested, but truly indispensable. If she wanted to remain here.

For she sensed a crisis approaching. Shortly she might be expected to go the way of previous governesses. At least she was sure that that was what Mrs Storrington was privately reflecting. However, Hannah was confident she could deceive her by a mild obedient manner, and keep her unaware of her inflexibility and her interior of steel. She could keep Mr Storrington unaware, too. She would remain his charming little mouse for as long as he wanted her. Soft and acquiescent and uncomplaining. Even forever.

There was a gleam of excitement in Hannah's eyes. She found that she was enjoying the challenge. Although she had an underlying apprehension that the excitement might become desperation.

Max, the quiet, rather sinister young man who half the time seemed to be invisible, knew where Boy was.

"In his dark room, miss."

"His dark room?" Was this a new form of imprisonment?

"Where he develops his photographs, miss. Thank goodness for that camera. It keeps him out of a power of trouble."

"Do you think he would mind me going in?" Hannah asked, mindful of her new plan to placate Boy. She intended to exercise her authority gently and persuasively.

"Not if he's wrapped up in his work. He's as gentle as a lamb then."

"But isn't he very young to be so scientific, developing plates from a camera?"

"He's a sort of genius in some ways, miss. I don't think his parents realise it. His mother likes him to be happy, and his father –"

"Yes?"

"Between you and me, he doesn't care a button, miss."

The dark room, Max told Hannah, was next to the still room, down a back staircase leading into the cool dim recesses of the lower ground floor.

Hannah pushed open the door without knocking, and went in. The slender shape of the child moved in the dim light.

131

"Shut the door!" the imperious voice rang out. And then, "Who's that?"

"It's only me, Miss Knox," Hannah said mildly.

"Miss Knox! You have no right to be here. I didn't invite you. Are you spying?"

"I suppose I am. But I do have a right to be here since you're supposed to be in my schoolroom. However —" She wished that it was light enough for Boy to see that she was smiling. "I daresay this could be called schoolwork of a different kind. Are you developing pictures you've taken? I wish you would show me how it's done. You be the teacher."

There was a long moment while Boy hesitated between sulkiness and accepting her presence. Finally his absorption in what he had been doing swayed the balance. He went back to his bench which was equipped with bottles of chemicals, glass plates, printing paper and a sink filled with some dark liquid. There were also cameras, a tripod, and a long box in which Hannah guessed he kept the developed photographs he had taken during the summer.

He was like a youthful alchemist.

"Show me what you're doing," Hannah said again.

"I've finished now. I have to hang up these prints to dry."

"Oh?"

"They've been in a solution," he explained magnanimously.

"I wish you'd show me some of the pictures that are dry. Ones you've taken lately."

"It's too dark in here."

"Can't we put the light on?"

"Oh, very well. I'll show you my best one of Mamma. She was playing croquet and she had just knocked Uncle Reggie's ball into the shrubbery. She's laughing. Look."

Violet's hat was tipped back, and the sun shining on her lively face. It was a beautiful shot of arrested mirth, laughter caught in her bright eyes forever. Reggie Mainwaring was not in sight. He had obviously gone to retrieve his ball from the rosebed. But in the next picture Hannah picked up he was very much in sight. He was lying on the riverbank down the slope which would be out of sight of the house, and Violet was beside him, leaning on her elbow and looking down on him with a half smile, seductive and caressing. There was no one else in sight.

"Oh, that," Boy said, snatching the photograph from her. "You're not supposed to see that. Mamma doesn't like me taking pictures when she doesn't know. She says I stalk people, like a tiger."

"Do you?"

"It's fun. They look so jolly put out when they see me. I don't do it to Papa, though. He gets too angry. He calls me a voyeur. I don't know what that is."

A voyeur was a nasty prying person looking for salacious scenes, Hannah could have explained. She began to wonder what pictures Boy had in his cabinet. He was too precocious, and knew very well that these stolen images were far more interesting than formally posed scenes.

He was looking at Hannah sideways and saying, "Don't touch those."

"Why not? They're so good. Can't I see more?"

"No. Mamma would be angry. I'm going to shut up my workroom now."

"Very well. Thank you for showing it to me. I think you're a very clever young man, but there are still a great many things you don't know. So come upstairs and we'll get on with a reading lesson. Cissie must think we're lost."

To her relief Boy came without argument. She noticed that he didn't lock the door of the dark room. It would be perfectly easy to slip down some time and go through his collection of photographs. Had Boy caught his father in some compromising position, and that was why he had been so angry?

If this were so it would be much better not to see the evidence. But she knew she would be driven to seek it, to take a fearful satisfaction in her pain.

Later, when Hannah knew she would be uninterrupted – Boy and Cissie were by the fire in the drawing room keeping their mother company, as ordered – she examined the contents of the long box on the bench.

So many pictures of Violet, of Mr Storrington innocently

mounting a horse, or loading a gun, of Cissie and Adolphus playing tennis, of the servants posing in their Sunday clothes, of visitors arriving.

And then one at the bottom, as if deliberately hidden. Technically it was a beauty. Violet and Reggie Mainwaring, lying on the cushions in the Chinese pagoda. Reggie's tie unloosened, Violet's blouse half off her shoulders and his hand slipped inside. The sunlight dappling them with shadow, the colours sharply black and white. They must have been very engrossed not to see Boy setting up his camera. But then he could move like a cat. And he had probably lain in wait for a long time, with all the patience required by his craft.

There was no similarly compromising picture of Mr Storrington. Hannah felt deeply thankful for that, as some instinct made her slide the incriminating picture of the lovers – surely unmistakably lovers – inside her blouse.

Now so much was made clear. This was why Violet had refused to go on the journey to Russia, and had gladly let Hannah take her place. It must have suited her very well to have the two elder children, old enough to be awkwardly observant, out of the house, and Hannah, too. There were still the servants, of course, but perhaps she could count on their loyalty. She was a generous mistress. And what was it to them if she amused herself while the master was away? Many of the women of her class, too idle and too bored, did so. Husbands were frequently complacent, though one doubted Mr Storrington being complacent about any filching of his property – no matter what his own behaviour might be.

So Hannah, growing devious herself, stole the photograph, knowing that it could provide a weapon for her in the future, should circumstances require it. And she had a sharply prescient feeling that they would.

Maidenshall, with its charming innocent name, was no longer in the least innocent, and probably, in all its long history, never had been. Human beings were not perfect. They were devious and greedy, and desirous and lustful, and immensely susceptible to physical beauty.

She was thinking entirely of Charlie Storrington. But the same characteristics could be applied to his wife. And, if she were to be honest, to herself . . .

Crack! The explosion echoed through the house. Adolphus pressed his hands to his ears. Cissie cried, "Darling Papa! I must go and welcome him."

"Without my permission?" Hannah said, controlling her voice though her stomach was tightening with a spiral of excitement.

"May I, Miss Knox?" But Cissie was off without waiting for an answer.

"At least Papa must be in a good mood," Adolphus grumbled, still wincing. "I suppose that is something."

"Yes, that is something," Hannah replied calmly.

Boy, absorbed over his paintbox, hadn't bothered to look up. He seemed to be able to shut himself completely in his private world. He really was an unusually artistic child, for Hannah had discovered that paints and brushes could occupy him almost as contentedly as his photography could. She intended to devise a scheme of teaching him by these visual means. If nothing more was achieved, it kept him quiet. Fortunately he had not shown his face of hate to her again. Perhaps his anger that day down at the marsh had been because she had intruded on his private landscape. He was a Jekyll and Hyde child, with two distinct personalities. He was a conundrum and a stimulating challenge. Her dislike had vanished in her interest. At least for the moment.

But Boy had a much stronger rival for her interest tonight. Mr Storrington was home for the evening. Surely he would at least contrive a way that they could be alone.

Cissie returned upstairs.

"We are to go down to dinner," she announced happily.

Hannah's heart lurched with pleasure. Since the children were going down, dinner would be early and not lingered over. Afterwards there would be the long evening until midnight. Plenty of opportunity for whispered messages, and surely for an assignation.

That revealing photograph of Violet and Reggie Mainwaring had removed all feelings of guilt. Though guilt was an emotion over which Hannah had never wasted much time. Now, any slight remorse she might have felt was completely overshadowed by recklessness and desire.

"How pink your cheeks are, Miss Knox,' Cissie said, with her irritating artlessness. "Have you a fever?"

"Not even a ghost of one," Hannah said merrily, "I just think it's rather nice to be home again."

Boy looked up with his shining glassy gaze. "But this isn't your home, Miss Knox."

"Boy, that's rude," Cissie reprimanded him. "It's Miss Knox's home for as long as she wants it to be."

"For as long as Mamma and Papa want," quiet Adolphus was always logical. "That's the truth, isn't it, Miss Knox?"

"The unpleasant truth, which we won't dwell on at present," Hannah said lightly.

"Don't worry, dear Miss Knox. I would never let you go," Cissie said.

"And you're so all-powerful?" Hannah was finding Cissie's ardent championship a little tiresome. But she must cultivate it, all the same. She might need it in future. "Thank you, my dear, but we'll hope your powers won't be put to the test. At least not for some time. Now, who's going to be first to be dressed?"

Cissie shrugged. "Papa said not to fuss. It's only Mr Sharpe."

"Mr Sharpe?"

"Who's coming to dinner. Papa's manager at the factory. They have a lot of business to discuss, so we're not to spend too long at the table."

"It will be about the Russian deal," Adolphus said. "Papa would rather talk about guns than anything. I think it's jolly boring. Come on, you two, I'll race you."

Hannah stood in the empty schoolroom. So after dinner Mr Storrington and his manager would retire to the library and she would not see Mr Storrington again that night.

Mechanically she began tidying up. She should have made the children do this. Boy was very messy with his paints. Cissie left her books spread about untidily.

Mrs Storrington would be bored, too, if the conversation were to be all business. One could hardly imagine Mr Sharpe being an amusing raconteur or even a flatterer. Not with a name like that.

So Mrs Storrington would go upstairs to her room soon after the children did, perhaps to make one of her private telephone calls to Reggie Mainwaring. And she, Hannah, could linger in the drawing room. Playing the piano, or doing a little quiet reading, curled up in a corner of the couch. Eventually Mr Sharpe would leave, and Mr Storrington would come in to see if any one were still up. And she would be there, a little sleepy-eyed and flushed. Limp and yielding when he picked her up in his arms . . .

When at last, two hours after dinner, Mr Storrington came into the drawing room he didn't see Hannah, or pretended not to. He had shown Mr Sharpe out himself, then apparently imagining the drawing room empty – although Hannah had thought herself quite visible – he turned to go upstairs.

She had to spring up and call, "Charlie!"

He stopped, turning slowly, as if against his better judgment. He said in a stiff voice, so unbelievably stiff for someone who could speak in the warm deep tones of love, "Yes, Miss Knox? Aren't you very late? Is something the matter?"

"Only that I wanted to see you," Hannah answered.

"About something in particular?"

Hannah could hardly believe her ears. "But of course about something in particular," she cried, running to him. "Oh, Charlie, it's been so long since you even looked at me, let alone –"

"Not in this house," he interrupted harshly. "Haven't you any common sense?"

"Not about you," she looked at him boldly and he stared back, his eyes hard.

"Then you must acquire some, or it won't work."

"What won't work?"

"Your remaining here. I don't want the children upset by another change."

Hannah's sense of shock made her insist loudly, "They would be upset if I left. Especially Cissie."

He looked at her thoughtfully. The disturbing thing was that he wasn't even drunk. That might have excused him a little for treating her like a recalcitrant servant. But he was sober, cool-headed and objective as he assessed what seemed to be, to him, merely an awkward problem.

"Yes, I've noticed that my daughter is fond of you."

"I thought you were, too?" The words flew out of Hannah's mouth. She felt her eyes filling with tears. He hated tears.

His expression softened a little. He looked half-regretful. "That's perfectly true. I am fond of you." His eyebrows twitched. Oh, thank heaven, he was going to make a joke. "But what are you expecting me to do? Come up to your bed in this house? Or invite you into mine, next door to my wife? Come, Miss Knox —"Miss Knox, he dared to call her! —"I thought you were more sophisticated than that."

"Then can't we meet somewhere? Can't you arrange something?" She almost hated him, in that moment for leaving her so little dignity. "I love you, Charlie. I thought —"

"Yes, yes, I should have anticipated thoughts. They're always inconvenient."

"What are?" She didn't know what he was talking about.

"Female thoughts. They're too emotional, too impractical for everyday life. In other words, for a man who has a wife and family and wants no trouble in his house," he finished brutally.

Hannah was clutching her hands together to stop them trembling. "But — you should have told me this. In St. Petersburg, when you thought I should be loved." She attempted a wan riposte. "Or should I say ravished?"

He gave a half laugh, a little embarrassed. "You may be unsophisticated, but you're clever enough, aren't you? So how can you be so naïve?" He sighed in exasperation, "Look, you can't stand here crying. Come into the library and have a shot of brandy. I thought I made it clear, since leaving St. Petersburg, on the ship —"

Hannah sat at the library table, her tears spilling through

her fingers. "You – only said the berths – were too narrow."

He gave a sudden sputter of laughter. "And so they were, and so are the beds in this house. Here, drink this, don't spill it."

She choked over the brandy and he said more gently, as if that moment of involuntary laughter had melted some of his coldness, "Look, Hannah, a liaison in a man's own home, with the governess of his children, is impossible. It is risky, and uncomfortable, and in abominable taste. It would have to be somewhere else. In Maidenhead, in London –"

She was thinking suddenly of the expensive and charming hat he had perched on her head when she had inconveniently walked into the milliner's shop.

"I could do – what you wish." She hated herself for her willingness, her lack of pride, but could not help it. Fear of losing him, and deprivation of that startling pleasure he had taught her in St. Petersburg, and for which her body had been hungry ever since, were making her desperate.

"Then I'll see what I can do. But really, you must learn to be a little more worldly –"

Like your wife? Hannah almost said, thinking of the photograph hidden in her writing desk.

"– because this was never meant to last. You must have realised that."

She had stopped crying. She stared at him with half comprehension, half disbelief. But now, bewilderingly, his voice had changed and taken on its deep sexual quality.

"When you bend your head the back of your neck is very appealing. Soft and childish. You have a lock of hair falling down. Perhaps one day in a week or so you could have a day off to visit your sister."

The treacherous joy stirred in her.

"I won't beg you –"

"I should hope not. Now off to bed. And practise some common sense, will you? Treat this situation practically, otherwise it won't work. Your staying in this house, I mean, and teaching my children."

No kisses, no endearments. Just that cool detached voice giving her the unwanted advice. And, following her up the stairs, the low injunction, "And Miss Knox, no more lurking, please!"

"And yet I can't shut his image out of my head," Hannah wrote in her room, her pen stabbing despairingly at the paper. "Standing there so tall, so masterful, so annihilating. I should hate and despise him. I will, too, in time. For he is a coward, and false as well. But now I can only long for his arms around me. Oh, God, it *can't* be over. It is like a summer finished in a day. Did I mean so little to him? Did I only interest him because I was still a virgin? Is it always this way with men, so soon as they have captured a woman they are tired of her? No, of course they can't all be like that. Daisy's husband wouldn't dream of even glancing amorously at another woman. Anyway, if he did she wouldn't respond! But men like Mr Storrington only have to beckon with one finger and silly women like myself think the world well lost for love.

"I have just been burning that hat which by mischance he gave me. It has made a lot of smoke and a rather unpleasant odour. I hope Barker or anyone else doesn't smell it and come prying. But I enjoyed the sparks and the flames while they lasted. I felt I was burning away some of my own foolishness and weakness. It was another woman's hat, and now perhaps he will give yet another woman something intended for me. Oh Charlie, Charlie. Let me be with you again."

Hannah paused a moment, and then, her face twisted, she wrote very firmly, her nib splashing small blots of ink, "Even if you don't, I promise you you haven't got rid of me. And you never will."

13

Sarah

SARAH SAT IN the spartan waiting room trying to concentrate on the latest copy of *Country Life* magazine. Charles had been with the two doctors for three-quarters of an hour. He must be very tired by now, Sarah thought, and tried to stop experiencing his pain in her own back. An uncanny sensation, that, and proof of far too much of the forbidden involvement.

Jeremy was waiting in the car outside. He had been very efficient in his transportation of an invalid on a warm summer day. And Charles had been in good spirits.

"What is this about human beings, Sarah, that makes hope rise eternal? For the last three months, since I got signed off with the 'no further treatment possible' label, I've been adjusting myself to a negative existence. I don't know what the doctors have got their heads together about. I don't suppose it's anything but some more bloody physiotherapy for my jailer here to administer." He nodded good-humouredly towards Jeremy. "However, it gives us an excuse to have a change from Agnes's cooking. I've booked a table for lunch at Claridge's. I hope you'll join me, Sarah. We'll let Jeremy go off to a pub of his own choice."

"Thank you, sir," said Jeremy formally. He had been very thoughtful about Charles's comfort on the journey. Perhaps he had been remembering those tumbled cushions in the drawing room, and the rapid exit when Dolly had cried out in his nightmare. He seemed to be fairly amoral, but in a strange way he made adequate amends by his skill and kindness. If Charles were aware of the situation he gave no sign at all.

The mild Hannah Knox might have got out of her depth with her ebullient formidable employer, but no more than she, Sarah, was now doing with her vastly different but no less complicated one.

How long had Charles now been with the doctors? Nearly an hour. Whatever were they doing to him?

A nurse put her head round the door.

"Major Storrington is ready now. Can you manage the lift?"

"Yes. Yes, I can. I'll get him."

Sarah's heart was beating as rapidly as if it were her own future at stake. Charles was being brought out of the consulting room by a cheery-looking man in a white coat.

"Cressida with you?" he was asking.

"No, my secretary volunteered – Mrs Goodwill." Charles indicated Sarah. "Doctor Phillipson, Sarah. We've been having an interesting chat."

The doctor gave Sarah a friendly smile.

"We've kept you waiting, Mrs Goodwill. We had a lot to talk about. Well, goodbye, Charles. Think it over carefully. Don't make a hasty decision. Discuss it with Cressida."

"I rather think Sarah and I will discuss it over lunch. Goodbye Bill. Thanks."

"What is it, Charles?" Sarah demanded in the lift. "You look as if you've been reprieved from hanging, or something."

"That's not a bad analogy. I'll tell you at lunch. I need a drink first. You do, too. Why do you worry about me so much, Sarah?"

"Me? Worry? How can you tell?"

"You have a very transparent face."

"Well, your own, at this minute," Sarah retorted, "looks about to take part in the Charge of the Light Brigade."

"You've said it. Now, no more. Until drinks."

At Claridge's they were given a quiet table in a corner. There was some discreet fussing by waiters, and warm greetings from the *maître d'hôtel*.

"It's good to see you, sir. I hope you are well."

"I could be a lot better. And I promise you I will be. Have

you got some decent oysters? Fresh salmon? But we'll have martini cocktails first. Double and very dry."

"This wouldn't be a celebration, would it?" Sarah asked tentatively.

"No. That would be a bit premature. But in a way, yes. Bill Phillipson told me not to make a hasty decision, but I believe I made it before I left his room."

"What was it?"

"Now, Sarah, you're looking as white as that tablecloth. It's I who, as you so aptly said, will be riding into the valley of death. Sorry. Melodrama."

Sarah lost her patience and her temper. "For God's sake, tell me. All this dithering."

"I was waiting for the drinks. And here they are. Take a good swallow, Sarah, and listen. There's an operation I can have, but it's a bit tricky. It takes seven to eight hours, and there's no certainty of success."

The alcohol burned Sarah's throat.

"But there is a chance?"

"A reasonable one. Forty to fifty per cent, they tell me. That's reasonable to me."

"You could walk again?"

"If it's a success."

"Oh, Charles!"

"For God's sake, Sarah, don't cry."

She took another long swallow and was able to blink back her sudden rush of tears.

"Tell me about it," she said more calmly.

"So you're with me?"

"But of course. If there's a chance, you've got to take the risk. Haven't you?"

"Even of not coming through?"

She nodded stubbornly. "No question." She fell silent, thinking. "At least, that's what I would do if it were me."

He put down his drink, took hers from her and set it down, then held both her hands in a grip that made her wince, and say shakily, "There's nothing wrong with those muscles, anyway."

"I'll never forget you for this, Sarah. I believe you've been there with me, haven't you? You've understood."

She nodded. "As much as a fully mobile person can. What I do understand is that you'd choose to have this operation and perhaps lose your life rather than sit in a wheelchair forever. I do understand that, Charles. Even if the operation fails and you have to go back to the wheelchair, well, you've tried, haven't you? That can be nothing but good."

"Splendid girl." He was perfectly composed, though his eyes glittered in a way she had never seen them do. Just now he looked, she imagined, rather like his dynamic determined grandfather. And under the present circumstances that could be nothing but good, either.

The martini was beginning to make her head swim.

"Why are the risks so high?"

"Well, it's a very new procedure. And after eighteen months of immobility I'm not in the best physical shape for a lengthy operation and all that it entails. It's what the ortho-paedic surgeon calls heroic surgery. I'd be something of a guinea pig, as well. I don't mind. I'm willing to take on the whole thing. I'll tell Cress tonight. Now, shall we have some food? Oysters, steak, a bottle of Chateau Margaux?"

"Perfect." She sighed with strange pleasure. Surely it was inappropriate to feel pleasure at this moment. The drink really was going to her head. "Let's do this again when you can walk in here on your own two legs."

"Mario will fall backwards with surprise."

"And delight. Cressida, too." She hadn't wanted to mention Cressida. Something had forced her to.

"I'll tell her tonight," he said again, and then gave one of his familiar scowls. This, it appeared, had nothing to do with his wife, but with her. "Don't you assume, my girl, that you're going to get a long holiday while I'm in hospital, or that when I'm recovered I'll abandon my project. I've got hooked on Grandfather Charlie and his machinations."

Sarah felt a great relief. So she wasn't going to be banished from Maidenshall when its owner was active again.

"So have I," she said eagerly. "Do you know, I believe that little governess, Hannah Knox, fell in love with him."

"If she did, I bet she got mauled. I've found one of his

private account books with some fascinating entries. 'Trip to St. Petersburg. Presents for children. Gift to General for assisting in sale to Russian army. Jewel to take home for Violet.' And a little later, 'H.K. Twenty pounds.' Was he buying the little governess off, do you think? Or paying for an abortion?"

"Poor girl. The pill would have been a blessing for her."

"That old scoundrel Charlie Storrington didn't deserve blessings of that nature. I'm glad he seems to have had to pay something."

"I'll go on digging out material while you're in hospital."

"Bring it in to me. I'll be lying flat on my back for three months, so I'll need some diversion."

"As long as that!" Sarah quickly concealed her dismay and said cheerfully, "We'll think of plenty of diversions. Dolly and —"

"Dolly musn't be told. He's a nervous little brat. Besides, he might bring the horrible Joseph. Old Nanny musn't be told, either. She was marvellous once. But now she'd be confused and go into some sort of trauma. Sometimes I wonder if it isn't time she was confined to her room. For her own safety."

"Cressida, I was going to say," Sarah said, at last interrupting the animated flow.

"Cress hates hospitals. Has to put on a terribly brave face. Illness, disability, wounds, repel her. Some people are like that. More people than you would think."

"Then isn't she going to be delighted when you're well again?" Sarah said determinedly.

"I expect so. Perhaps. I gain my freedom, and she loses hers." He gave Sarah a quick, cynical look. "See what I mean?"

Dolly was hanging over the big gates at the end of the long drive. When the car turned in he waved madly and leaped down.

"Don't you know that's not allowed?" his father shouted.

Jeremy opened the front door and Dolly slid in and sat very still.

"Don't you?" Charles insisted.

"We were lonely," Dolly said in a defensive tone. "Mr Crankshaw's gone and Agnes said to keep out of her way, and then Nanny kept following us about."

"Why did she do that?"

"I don't know. She always follows Joseph."

That made a certain mad sense, Sarah supposed. Nanny, if anyone, could be expected to see invisible people.

"Mother home?" Charles asked. Sarah fancied Jeremy stiffened slightly.

"No. She said she'd be in in time to say goodnight to me."

Hardly the picture of an anxious wife waiting for the doctor's report on her husband. Or unable to stay away from her lover. But Cressida seemed to have several lives, all of them conducted with aplomb. The question that had nagged Sarah ever since Charles had given her his news loomed large again. How was Cressida going to feel about having her husband restored to her? Would the image of Charles as a helpless invalid always be superimposed on her mind, had she enjoyed straying too much, had they both dug too deeply inside themselves and found people other than they had supposed themselves to be?

Agnes was just calling in her strident voice that dinner was ready when Cressida's white Jaguar swept down the drive. A few moments later she rushed in, trailing scarf and shoulder bag.

"Sorry, everyone. Hell of a traffic jam in Maidenhead. I'll be down in five minutes. Don't wait for me." Over her shoulder she said, "Charles? Okay? Don't tell me now. Tell me when I come down. Jeremy, fix me a vodka and tonic. Long and very cold. Has Dolly gone to bed?"

"Hours ago," answered Agnes from the passage. The briefness of her answer made her disapproval plain. Sarah was surprised that she hadn't been aware of this sooner. Agnes, the dour countrywoman, and Cressida, the scented whirlwind who could not restrict her life to the needs of her husband and son. Dolly had gone upstairs only ten minutes ago.

"Promised I'd say goodnight to him." Cressida's voice,

breathless now, drifted down. It occurred to Sarah that she had made herself deliberately late, either because she was postponing a confrontation with Charles and what she imagined would be another hopeless medical report, or because her lunch with the Paris connection – male or female? singular or plural? – had been so absorbing that she was covering up her excitement with this flurry of activity.

Jeremy was looking more poker-faced than ever, his handsome face aloof and unreadable. But, when told Charles's news he had shown what seemed to be genuine pleasure, and had said that they must start a muscle toning-up routine immediately.

Cressida, to him, was probably just a sophisticated slut who had not unexpectedly seduced him. But what about Charles who might get well and stop being tolerant?

"You're miles away, Sarah. What are you thinking?" That was Charles's composed voice, apparently not at all upset by his wife's late arrival.

Sarah didn't dare to look at him, afraid of what her eyes might express. He had told her that she had a transparent face.

"I was thinking that after that marvellous lunch I'm not a bit hungry. But shouldn't we go in, or Agnes's dinner will spoil."

Cressida joined them ten minutes later. She had made a quick change into a ruffled housegown, very becoming in a rather old-fashioned Edwardian way. Sarah was suddenly thinking of Grandfather Charlie's wife who must have sat in that very chair, smiling brilliantly at her husband while hoping that none of her afternoon's dalliance showed. Did these women think their husbands were blind, or too sunk in self-absorption to notice a wife's happiness or unhappiness?

"Now, Charles," Cressida said, "Tell me everything. How was Bill Phillipson? I suppose he told you the usual. Poor darling. Thank you, Jeremy, this drink is delicious."

"Perhaps you'd better drink it all," Charles suggested in the same way that he had told Sarah to drink her Martini.

"Why? Why, darling? Have you got something to tell me?" Eagerness. Deep interest. A hint of alarm?

"Actually, I have. Sarah and Jeremy know, so I'd better tell you. I'm going to have another operation."

Cressida's throat moved convulsively. "Oh, no! You remember the last one. Surely they're not putting you through that agony again. And uselessly."

"Probably not uselessly this time, Cress. There's a real chance for me. I may walk – no, dammit, I will walk."

"Oh, Charles, my darling, no! Don't do it." Cressida jumped up and went behind Charles to throw her arms round him, pressing her cheek against his. "You're not strong enough. I won't allow it. Really, surgeons, they grasp at every straw."

"So do I," Charles said.

"No, but they want to learn. Fair enough. Only I won't have them learning any more on your poor body."

Charles pushed Cressida away. "It's not a poor body, it's in good shape, thanks to Jeremy's care. Bill Phillipson said so. Congratulated you, Jeremy."

"It's your own efforts, sir," said Jeremy.

Cressida, standing back from the table, her face in shadow, said in disbelief, "Jeremy, are you encouraging him to go through all that again? You know what spinal operations are. You really must be pretty cold-blooded."

"Just realistic, Mrs Storrington," Jeremy said stolidly.

"But he may die. Charles you may die. You know the last one –"

"Shut up, Cressida!" Charles interrupted angrily. "I've agreed to this. Sarah and Jeremy, who are both sensible people, think I have made the right decision. So why aren't you with me?"

Cressida covered her face with her hands. "Because I am a coward," she wailed. "I can't go through all that again, even if you can. I want you here, safely."

"A stuffed toy?"

"Not a stuffed toy, you idiot. A lovely brilliant man. Alive. No matter how."

Charles wheeled his chair away from the table.

"To keep the status quo?" he asked, very quietly. "Isn't that what you're saying?" He gave Cressida a long look, searching her face with some emotion that seemed to wither him. "I don't want to eat tonight. Apologise to Agnes, will you, Sarah." He began to roll the chair out of the room. "Sarah and I had a rather too good lunch at Claridge's, Cress. I hope yours was equally good."

"At the Savoy Grill," Cressida gasped, and burst into tears.

Charles didn't turn back. She went on sniffling into a handkerchief for a minute or so. Her tears were real enough. Sarah could see the dampness on her cheeks. But she guessed they were from bewilderment and apprehension rather than sorrow.

"I'm not a bitch. I'm really not." She was talking to no one in particular. "But I can't bear to see Charles mutilated again. And I hate illnesses and hospitals. I thought we had adjusted pretty well – as well as possible –"

"Shall I bring the coffee on to the terrace, Mrs Storrington?" Jeremy asked in his suddenly too formal voice. Sarah's lips twitched. There, if it was what she wanted, was Cressida's real stuffed toy. But an animated one, of course.

"Yes. Do that, Jeremy. None of us seem to want to eat tonight."

So they sat on the terrace in the moth-haunted dusk, the scent of Jeremy's well-nurtured roses filling the air. Cressida sat by Charles, holding his hand. He allowed her to do so for a short time, then said in a voice that was as audible to Sarah as it was to Cressida, "You smell of him. The man you had lunch with. I could tolerate this while I was helpless. Only fair, I told myself. But after – after –" His voice had become incoherent. "Never."

"You don't even know if you'll get well," Cressida burst out.

Charles was in control of himself again. "You have to have faith, my love."

Cressida abruptly got up and went indoors. Jeremy brought out the coffee tray.

"Is Mrs Storrington not staying down for coffee, sir?"

"No, she's a bit upset. I did rather spring it on her."

"She had to know, sir."

By which cryptic comment Sarah realised that Jeremy was now on their side. Charles's and hers. The day had produced more than one traumatic result.

And the traumas were not yet over. When Sarah went up to her room, praying that Dolly would not have a nightmare because she was afraid she would be too tired to go to him, she saw the shape on her bed.

At first she thought it was an animal. Her weary eyes were playing tricks, because on going closer she found it was nothing but a very crumpled paper bag. Curious though, she thought dazedly.

On investigating she found a note pinned to it. The writing, scrawled and feeble, was almost illegible.

"I found these things unaccountably in my possession. I believe they are yours. I do apologise. Henrietta Galloway."

The spelling was impeccable.

The packet contained a shabby volume of Keats' poems, a diary with short, cryptic entries obviously made under stress, a small leather bag containing ten golden sovereigns, minted in 1910, and a beautiful little amethyst mouse with emerald eyes, a treasure. It might conceivably be Fabergé. The gift bought in St. Petersburg, surely. The entry in Charlie Storrington's account book had noted "H.K. Twenty pounds." H.K. must have spent some of them. There were only ten here.

Boy has had to be locked up again.

As Sarah opened the diary the words sprang to her eyes. She crept into bed in a daze of excitement. She didn't put her light out until long after midnight. Then she was saying to herself the beautiful words underlined in the volume of Keats. *Thou still unravished bride of quietness*.

Hannah Knox. Poor lost Hannah. And confused old Nanny thought she had returned to her old room. In the form of Sarah Goodwill, late twentieth-century secretary, and far from being unravished.

"Old Nanny! The secretive old devil!" Charles exclaimed in the morning. "I wonder where she found these things, and why she's been hiding them."

"There's a loose floorboard in my room. I was disappointed not to find a cache under it. But Nanny had been there before me. She's awfully confused, though. She was accusing me the other day of stealing things."

"Well, you sort it out, Sarah. I haven't the time or the inclination just now."

Sarah looked at him sharply. "Something's happened."

"A call from Bill Phillipson. Seems there has to be a quick decision after all. He can get me a bed in a couple of days. Mr Ormond will operate at the beginning of the week. Well – the sooner the better."

Sarah reached for his hand. "Oh, Charles. Yes, I agree. The sooner the better. Can I pack for you?"

"Jeremy will do that, I imagine. Don't let Dolly know."

"He'll know you're going away."

"To stay at Claridge's for a few days, as I often do. Keep an eye on him while I'm away, will you, Sarah?"

That afternoon Sarah was roused from her work by the sound of the piano in the drawing room. She had never heard it played before. She went in quietly and saw Charles at the keyboard, his head bent, his expression peaceful and absorbed. Someone was curled up on the couch out of sight. Dolly.

Charles saw her come in and stopped playing.

"I didn't know you could play."

"Nanny taught me. She was surprisingly good."

"Charles!" Sarah whispered, indicating the couch. "Dolly is here."

"The little fox."

"No, no, he's quiet. He's loving it. Go on playing."

So that was how she would remember them both, Sarah thought, after Charles had gone into hospital. The absorbed pianist playing romantic music, and the similarly absorbed small boy.

The scene had surprised her, and yet it had seemed so natural, as if something of this kind had frequently happened in this room.

14

Hannah

WHEN HANNAH WOKE that morning, drained and tired from a restless night, she realised that it was the first day of December and that Christmas was almost on them.

Cissie had realised it, too. She was the kind of impulsive generous child who wanted to give presents to everyone, Hannah, Barker, the other servants, as well as her family. She had been saving her money for weeks, she said, and Miss Knox was to take her to Maidenhead to have a wonderful day searching for gifts.

"Am I?" said Hannah.

"Of course. We'll ask Papa's permission at breakfast. I know he won't refuse. Perhaps he may spare some time from his office and take us to luncheon. You would like that, wouldn't you, Miss Knox?"

Alone, she certainly would, but with Cissie prattling artlessly she feared for her patience.

"Really, Cissie, you're a very spoiled child. You think you can have everything for the asking. You must learn that life isn't like that."

"Why are you cross, Miss Knox? We're talking about Christmas. You should be full of peace and goodwill."

"I will be. If everyone else will be."

Cissie, who thought she was referring to Boy, said, "Don't worry, Boy loves Christmas. He gets very excited about the Christmas tree, and lighting candles and pulling crackers. Poor Dolly hates pulling crackers, they remind him of Papa's gun going off. What would you like for a present, dear Miss Knox?"

Your beautiful, false and cruel Papa, said Hannah to herself.

"Miss Knox, what are you thinking? You suddenly look very fierce."

The child was like an interrogator, her pretty brown eyes perpetually on Hannah. But this was something one had to endure. Cissie must not be antagonised or made suspicious in any way.

"Well, first we must establish if we can go to Maidenhead." Life coursed through her again. "So come along, let's go down to breakfast and ask your Papa."

However, Mr Storrington had already left the house. It was a grey December morning with a chill in the air that suggested early snow. The dining room was cheerful, with a fire blazing, the electric lights turned on, and the air full of delicious odours of hot coffee, fried bacon and freshly made toast. But Mr Storrington's place at the table was cleared away and the room, to Hannah, had become a desert. He was being deliberately elusive. She was sure of it. He had not wanted to encounter her secret and hopeful gaze at breakfast, so he had made himself scarce.

Then, since she had no wish to visit Violet again in her bedroom, she would authorise the trip to Maidenhead herself.

"We will go in the dogcart with Adolphus, as we did the other time," she said to Cissie. "Since your Papa isn't here, I am sure he would expect me to use my own common sense." Cissie had no idea what a double-edged remark that was. She was simply listening admiringly to her clever and resourceful Miss Knox.

"We will do our shopping and have some hot chocolate and then be ready to bring Adolphus home. Boy may have a holiday from lessons this morning. There, how does that please you, sir?"

Boy, with tousled curls and limpid eyes, was looking cherubic. One wondered how long this good phase would last. Perhaps it would be for a long time, now that he seemed to trust her more.

"I shall enjoy it, thank you, Miss Knox. I intend working in my dark room."

"On Christmas Day Boy makes us all arrange ourselves on

153

chairs outdoors in the simply perishing cold, to be photographed," Cissie said. "This year I will wear my Russian fur hat. You can do the same, Dolly, and you, Miss Knox, and Papa."

"You'll all look like polar bears," said Boy delightedly. "Oh, that will be jolly."

"Yes, won't it," said Hannah, thinking that she could keep the picture for a memento, standing beside Mr Storrington. She would make sure that she did stand beside him, and the picture would be a purely personal treasure, not a weapon like the other one.

She had never before seen Violet angry. But in the early afternoon, on their triumphant return from Maidenhead, Cissie highly excited by the extravagance of spending all her accumulated money, and pleased with Miss Knox's clever ideas as to suitable gifts, and Adolphus glad to have been able to escape an extra half hour with old Beard and French verbs, Violet met them, tight-lipped and frowning.

"Miss Knox, I am extremely displeased."

"Why?" Hannah opened her eyes wide. "Have I done wrong?"

"Of course you've done wrong. Surely you must know that. Taking Cissie off without a word to anybody, leaving Boy on his own."

"Isn't Boy all right?"

"He's all right, but no thanks to you. I thought you understood that someone must *always* know where he is and what he is doing. I imagined you were all in the schoolroom until Barker told me that you'd gone off. Really, you young women all begin to take too much on yourselves."

"I am just one woman," Hannah said, not caring to be associated with previously and obviously unsatisfactory governesses. "And I had fully intended to ask Mr Storrington's permission for this expedition, but he had left early. I didn't want to disturb you, Mrs Storrington."

"But what was the sudden urgency? It's nearly four weeks to Christmas."

Cissie flung herself at her mother. "Mamma, please don't be angry. It wasn't Miss Knox's fault, it was mine.

I know Papa would have let us go if we had been able to ask him."

"You think you can persuade your father into anything," Violet said sharply. "I must talk to him about indulging you too much. Spoiled young girls aren't very popular. I think you're beginning to do the same, Miss Knox, and not only with Cissie."

"I thought the children were happy," Hannah said softly.

"You're here to teach them, not to worry about their personal happiness. Their father and I are quite capable of taking care of that. Cissie, what are all those packages? I hope you haven't been too extravagant. And why did you have to be so premature? The next thing, I'll hear you've been gathering holly for the tree."

But Mrs Storrington's anger was dying. It was too energetic an emotion for her to sustain for long. She had suddenly become a jealous mother, but Hannah suspected the real cause of her anger was something else, something that had put her out. Perhaps Reggie Mainwaring hadn't telephoned, or wasn't riding over to see her. Perhaps she had heard Hannah and Mr Storrington talking on the stairs last night, and had become suspicious.

"I am out of favour," Hannah murmured regretfully to Cissie. "We had better make amends by all doing a hard afternoon's work. And then being dressed and ready for your Papa this evening."

"Papa won't be angry with me," Cissie said confidently. "I don't care if he does spoil me. I very much like it, to tell the truth. I'm his favourite."

"Well, don't boast about it," Hannah said tartly.

She herself didn't know how to wait until the evening, and Mr Storrington's return. He *must* speak to her privately, or slip her a note. He couldn't ignore her again. If he did . . . She hadn't formulated her plan of action, but she would have one. That was certain. After all, he had an unfaithful wife. So what need was there for compunction?

Barker came to the schoolroom with a message just as Hannah had given permission for books to be closed, and the table tidied.

"You're to eat up here tonight, miss. The master isn't coming home, and the mistress is out visiting."

"Oh, Barker!" Cissie had burst into tears. "Oh, I did so want Papa to be home tonight. He's almost never home now. It isn't fair."

"Oh, yes, you're neglected children, I can see," Barker said, her long face ironic. "You've only taken half the day as a holiday to shop."

"I didn't," said Adolphus.

"And I didn't," said Boy.

"But you had a nice morning in your dark room, didn't you, Master Boy? And Master Adolphus, you know you've a lot to catch up on after all that time away in Russia. Neglected children, indeed!"

He *was* avoiding her, Hannah brooded. Had she scared him away, after the scene she had made last night? Mr Storrington scared? Oh, no. He would be back, he would have news for her. He was in London making arrangements for a meeting place. He would come home to tell her what day she was to pretend to be visiting Daisy. Surely. Surely.

But Elsie, grumbling at having to carry heavy trays upstairs, said did Hannah know that Mr Storrington would be away all the week. He was attending an important conference in London.

The mistress would be absent a bit, too, no doubt, she said under her breath to Hannah. The mistress didn't like a house without men in it.

"So you can get Miss Cissie to practise her piano lessons," she added for all to hear. "There'll be nobody to object to the cacophony."

"That's a nice word," Boy said to himself. And kept on repeating it, cacophony, cacophony . . . It had a harsh sound that seemed to please him, as it pleased him to carry broken glass in his hands. But fortunately he wasn't being too strange. One of his attacks now, Hannah thought, would be the last straw.

Worse was to come. Two days later Mrs Storrington, who seemed to have got over her displeasure, announced that she had had a telephone call from London from her husband.

"About you, Miss Knox," she said.

It was impossible to prevent the startled blood from staining her cheeks.

"What is it, Mrs Storrington?"

"It's so thoughtful of Charles. He suggests that you have a week off at Christmas so that you can spend it with your sister."

In reality to meet him in London, to have seven idyllic days? The pleasure must have shown in her face.

"I thought you would be pleased," Mrs Storrington said. "Charlie's bringing some friends down to spend Christmas with us. Political friends. I have never been able to talk to politicians." She smiled. "We're going to be madly busy. You'll be lucky to escape the chaos."

Gullible little fool that she was . . . Hannah tried to ignore her sinking heart and said calmly, "If there's going to be so much to do you won't be able to spare me."

Violet gave her a quick scrutiny, her eyes narrowed. "These are Mr Storrington's orders, not mine. I don't think we should argue, Miss Knox."

"I'm not arguing, Mrs Storrington. I'm only suggesting that you will need me to keep the children amused and happy and not underfoot all the time. I hardly think Mr Storrington's political friends would be entertained by noisy children. You know how over-excited Boy gets."

Mrs Storrington spoke curtly, "I can look after Boy, Miss Knox. And Cissie and Adolphus are quite old enough to know how to behave with adults. I'm sure your sister will need you much more than we will. Besides, families should be together at Christmas. So please go and write to your sister and make plans. My husband does insist on being obeyed. Haven't you discovered that? And I really can't risk having him in a bad temper over the holiday."

"Because I'm here!" The words sprang out of her mouth in incredulity.

Mrs Storrington gave her a surprised look. "Nothing of the kind, you silly creature. You over-estimate your importance. Now don't look offended. Go and do as I ask."

"But aren't we your family, Miss Knox?" Cissie

demanded, when she heard the devastating news.

"I had been optimistic enough to think so."

"Of course we are. I shall tell Papa so as soon as he comes home. He can't mean what he said."

"I believe he had misunderstood about Daisy needing me. I would really be about as welcome there as snow in June." Hannah gave a light artificial laugh. "Because her husband's parents are coming to stay and she has only one spare room."

"Poor thing," Cissie exclaimed. "What a small house she must have. You must be careful who you marry, Miss Knox. You wouldn't like a tiny house like that."

"And I shall see that I don't get it," Hannah said lightly. She added more soberly, "It's very kind of you to offer to speak to your Papa. I would so like to spend Christmas with you, my favourite children. But do thank him for his generous offer to me."

Thank him for his deliberate cruelty, his contempt for promises, his determination to keep her out of sight to spare himself embarrassment? Would the next thing be her dismissal on some pretext?

Hannah's throat tightened, making her feel that she was choking. She couldn't cry. She would never cry. She would simply turn all her desperately wounded feelings into anger. Charlie Storrington had thought he had been coupling with a mouse, but he was going to find out that it had been a tigress with dangerous claws. He was going to get savaged. Unless he would come back to her . . .

That night Hannah took care once again to be the last to go upstairs. After much thought she had written a note.

"Was I under a wrong impression that we had an appointment? I don't want to be forced to call you out, Charlie."

She signed it with a tiny sketch of a mouse, and slid it into the case which held his treasured duelling pistols. She guessed that he frequently looked at them when he was alone. Even if he opened them in company of a guest, the note was too anonymous to embarrass him. She hoped it would amuse him. He had enjoyed her quiet wit in St. Petersburg. She had thought to prove to him that a woman had other attributes, as well as a neat small body. Now, that awakened body scarcely ever let her forget its hunger.

He would eventually find the note, and the order that she spend Christmas away from Maidenshall would be rescinded. If he showed her tenderness, and loved her, even in the Chinese pavilion wrapped in rugs and chilly river mist, she would be willing to wash out of her mind all the hurt and bitterness of the last days.

If not . . . Hannah's lips were pinched together. Men made the rules in this society, but clever women could manipulate them. Violet did, and very successfully. She could do so, too, and even more effectively than Violet because she had a superior brain. She could be quite clever at blackmail.

Mr Storrington came home on Saturday. He was in an affable mood, greeting Cissie and Adolphus noisily, but as always being wary of Boy. He seemed a little afraid of his youngest son, perhaps being the kind of man who feared what he could not understand. Once Hannah would have fiercely denied that he could be a coward. Now she was discovering painfully disturbing facets of his character.

However, he was amiable enough to her, too, and when Adolphus and Boy had rather too hastily slipped out of the library he said with great heartiness. "Well, Miss Knox, have you kept my three rascals hard at work?"

"I think so, Mr Storrington. For a change from school lessons I'm teaching them the songs from a little musical fantasy, Humperdinck's 'Hansel and Gretel'. Cissie particularly is enjoying it."

Cissie gave a predictable simper. "I have a true singing voice, Miss Knox says. We thought we would sing to everyone on Christmas Eve."

"Capital. I hope this operetta or whatever it is, isn't too serious."

"No, it's quite funny in parts. It's a bit scary too. Miss Knox is going to dress us in costume."

Hannah felt a quiver through her whole body as she intercepted his glance. It shattered her with its hostility. How could he hate her so much, without cause?

"But Miss Knox is spending Christmas with her sister. Hasn't she told you?"

"Yes, but Papa –"

He swooped Cissie into his arms, nibbling at her hair and her nose. "Beloved little girl, don't argue with me."

"But, Papa, we have so many plans!" Cissie, again predictably, began to cry. "I will die with disappointment if Miss Knox isn't allowed to stay. Dolly and Boy will, too."

Mr Storrington's eyebrows twitched. It was a sign Hannah had come to recognise as a prelude to a display of temper.

"I sniff a conspiracy. Come now, clever Miss Knox has put you up to this."

"No, no, Papa. You don't understand. She has to stay. We need her. We love her. Even Boy does."

"Don't keep on dragging Boy's name in. The child doesn't know what love is. He simply knows how to use people. And you do, too, I'm sorry to say."

"Papa, you're being cruel! I never believed you could be cruel." Cissie was scarlet, and drenched with tears. "I don't want to be with you. I'm going to my room."

"Do so. And stay there until I send for you."

Cissie gave a wail of pure disbelief.

"Papa –"

"Off with you. Upstairs. Miss Knox will stay. I want to talk to her."

Together they watched Cissie's forlorn and tear-stained departure.

The moment they were alone Hannah had an unplanned but overpowering urge to fling herself into his arms. *I will forgive you, truly I will forgive you . . .*

"Well, Miss Knox, you seem to have done a very good job of corrupting my children."

"Corrupting!" Hannah's moment of warmth and longing vanished. "What do you mean, sir?" She laid heavy emphasis on the formal "sir".

"Shall I put it more bluntly? You have been attempting to steal their affections."

"If I have done that," said Hannah steadily, "their affections were available. Just as mine were."

To cover what seemed to be a slight, but only slight embarrassment, he put his hand in his breast pocket and took out the note she had written and hidden in the gun case.

"And this!" he declared, working up his displeasure, "I suppose you think it clever."

"You've found it already! Do you always look at your guns before you look at your women?"

Somehow she didn't wince before the fury of his gaze. Her flippancy had turned his annoyance into anger.

"This isn't funny, Miss Knox. Especially that ridiculous signature. I want you to stop your jokes. I want you to be out of this house for Christmas. If you're not careful I may want you to be out of it forever. I've only refrained from dismissing you because Cissie would be rather unduly upset, and I didn't want the child to be unhappy. But she would get over it." He came towards her, making his expression persuasive. "Come along, Hannah, be an adult woman. What is over is over. It was pleasant for us both, but you must understand these things are – temporary."

Thou still unravished bride of quietness . . . Do you particularly like virgins, Charlie?

"I shall be here for Christmas," said Hannah.

"I don't think so."

"But you and your Cabinet Ministers and other guests have to hear the songs the children have been practising." Hannah tilted her head, and sang softly, "*Naughty little mousie, Nibbling at my housie* . . . What's the matter Charlie? Don't you think that's very apt?"

"Miss Knox, if you are going to go on being impertinent like this I will personally escort you to the railway station tonight."

"Oh, dear," said Hannah, with a shrug. "Then I'm afraid I'll be forced to tell."

"Violet?" he said, too hastily. He gave a short laugh. "I think I can guarantee she's not unaccustomed –"

"No, not Violet," Hannah interrupted. "And I'm sure she's not unaccustomed, as you say. Actually I was thinking of your daughter. And I believe she is unaccustomed to hearing the sort of thing her adored Papa gets up to."

He had begun to breathe heavily, his nostrils pinched.

"You little bitch!"

"No, only a mouse. Quite a small one. Don't you remember? She intrigued you. For a very short time. Much too callously short a time. And she really does want some sort of amends."

After a long pause he asked, "What sort?"

"Well, since you're so concerned for my sister at Christmas, what she actually would appreciate is not me, but some extra money. Say twenty pounds to begin with. Though I would keep a little of it for myself to buy suitable gifts for Cissie and Adolphus and Boy. I would enjoy that. I assure you your money would not be spent on myself."

She paused and looked at him fully, making her eyes wide and persuasive, as if she were as benevolent as her intentions. "I don't think that's too much to pay for preserving your daughter's innocence and happiness, and her affection for her Papa. Do you?"

"By God, I don't believe my ears!"

"You just misjudged me, Charlie. You men. You never like to be proved wrong."

"My wife will deal with you."

Hannah shook her head, as if in regret. "Truthfully, sir, I don't think she will dare to. I wish you would understand that I wouldn't have done this unless you had driven me to it. But people who have secrets are vulnerable. I think your wife will understand that just as well as you do."

His face had gone dark. The very pigment of his skin seemed to be altered. He lifted half closed hands, and for a moment Hannah thought he was going to put them round her neck.

She lifted her chin higher, deliberately exposing soft, unprotected skin. For a full thirty seconds she stood like that, in defiance.

Then his arms slowly fell to his sides. This was not one of his seductive bedroom scenes, and therefore he wasn't sure how to cope with it. For the first time in the forced humility of her life Hannah experienced the heady sensation of power. It was almost as alluring as love.

Although the aftermath would be bitter. But so was the aftermath of her ill-judged love.

Even now, if he were to put out his arms in remorse . . .

Hannah was never to know how much forgiveness of which she was capable, for he had abruptly gone to his desk and taken out his cheque book.

"Oh no, Charlie," she said quickly. "Not a cheque. People like me don't have bank accounts. I want payment in sovereigns. Besides, I'm sure you don't want any awkward records. Leave the sovereigns in here on Monday evening before dinner." She lifted the lid of the gun case and ran her fingers over the beautifully chased stocks of the guns. "You know, Charlie, if I were you I'd stick to guns. You're a better judge of them than of women."

"Be careful, those are loaded."

She snatched her fingers away, startled.

"You keep them loaded?"

"Naturally. I like things to be in working order."

"But the children . . ."

"The children know better than to touch my valuables."

Hannah subsided. "Well, I'm glad of that. So. May I take it that I'll be producing the children's little musical fairy tale at Christmas?"

He was in command of himself again. She knew that he would never now give up searching for a way to get rid of her, but in the meantime he would have to be civil to her in front of his family and the servants. She was well aware that she had drawn swords – or pistols – with an enemy who could be formidable. The knowledge gave her a flash of terrible and irresistible excitement.

"If it amuses them," he said offhandedly, answering her question. "And if my wife approves. She may not think it the most sophisticated entertainment for our guests." He gave her a deliberate sidelong glance. "I hope Violet will be wearing the little trinket I bought for her in St. Petersburg. I don't think you saw that, Miss Knox. It's a rather superb pigeon's blood ruby. Violet was delighted with it."

The slim box he had slipped in his pocket after giving her and the children the Fabergé toys. Even then, while taking

her into his bed and professing enchantment with her, he had
been buying his wife the superior gift. He had told her this
now not only to hurt her but so that she would know her
oblique references to his wife mattered little to him. Although
she didn't believe that for one minute. It was his prerogative,
not his wife's, to be unfaithful.

Powerful Charlie Storrington with eyes that had gone as
cold as winter. Yes, he was going to be a dangerous
adversary.

But she would have time to gather some money together
before the ultimate crash came. This was the only form of
revenge she had.

On Monday evening, just before dinner, when she had
brought her charges to the drawing room and noted that both
Mr and Mrs Storrington were there, Hannah made a pretext
to return to her room for a handkerchief.

Instead, she slipped quietly into the library and made for
the gun case, standing in its usual place on a side table. The
wash leather bag of sovereigns nestled in the hollowed lid.
She transferred it to the silver mesh evening bag hanging on
her wrist. It felt solidly heavy. She would count the money
later, though she knew that in this respect Mr Storrington
would not cheat.

"What are you doing, Miss Knox?"

Hannah spun round, her breath held.

Boy, in his neat white-collared jacket, with his hair
brushed, his face a well-scrubbed pink. He looked a picture of
innocence, yet Hannah knew how quickly his expression
could change to sidelong craftiness.

"Do you keep your handkerchiefs in Papa's gun case?" he
asked, giggling.

"No. I was just having another look at these beautiful
objects." (Loaded, Mr Storrington had said.) "They do
fascinate me. Just as they do your Papa." She closed the lid
with a snap. "But they're not children's toys, and I think
Papa might be angry if he found us here. So off you go, back
to the others while I do what I set out to do and get my
handkerchief."

164

"Your eyes look very big, Miss Knox. Are you going to cry?"

"Far from it."

Which was indeed the truth, Hannah reflected. Her tears had dried up several days ago. In her room she found a hiding place for the small bag of sovereigns. They kept company with the Fabergé mouse, the incriminating photograph of Reggie Mainwaring and Violet, and her book of Keats' poems, the lines *Thou still unravished bride of quietness* heavily underscored. She hardly knew why she had underlined them. A vague thought that if there were trouble in the future, some clever investigator might pick up a clue in her favour had come into her mind. But that was so shadowy, so improbable. Who was going to care about the activities of someone so unimportant as a governess? She supposed she had been a little hysterical, a little romantic. From now on she would be severely practical. Those sovereigns represented triumphant reality. And she intended their number to grow.

15

CHRISTMAS AT MAIDENSHALL was going to be lavish, gay and colourful, judging by the preparations now being made.

Lessons were out of the question. None of the children would concentrate. They wanted to gather holly and mistletoe to decorate the curving banisters of the stairs, the front door knocker, and the lofty Christmas tree that stood in the hall. There were red ribbons and tinsel everywhere, and an infinite number of parcels to be wrapped. Tradesmen kept arriving with supplies of food and drink. The maids were cleaning the spare bedrooms and making up beds. Mrs Storrington, who had accepted without particular curiosity her husband's change of mind about Hannah's presence in the house, spent most of the time on the telephone, arranging for an orchestra, carol singers, times of arrival of guests, fittings with her dressmaker and all the manifold preparations of a busy hostess.

She was perpetually dishevelled and flushed, she laughed a lot and seemed as excited as a child. Her coolness towards Hannah was temporarily forgotten. She had too much else to occupy her. But Hannah took no chances, and unobtrusively made herself so useful that she could be thought indispensable.

Imagine spending Christmas in Daisy's dreary household when she could be a part of this warm and colourful scene.

She wanted a new low-cut dress and a cashmere shawl to drape over shoulders which were not accustomed to being bared. She refused to wear anything that she had worn in St. Petersburg.

She would like a piece of jewellery, too. Her garnets were too modest, especially compared with Violet's pigeons' blood ruby. But jewellery was expensive and would eat up her supply of money. She needed more money.

This thought had occurred to her when she had hidden the little bag of sovereigns. It came back to her sharply the afternoon Reggie Mainwaring arrived unannounced, and she personally witnessed the flood of colour in Violet's cheeks, and the delight she didn't or couldn't conceal. Why should she bother to hide it from Hannah, that tiresome but useful governess, whom Charlie had suddenly decided to dislike?

Hannah had come to recognise the swift burning excitement that preceded further daring action. It was as vivid and addictive and almost as pleasurable as the act of love. After noting the length of time that Violet and Reggie were shut in the drawing room, she decided the time had come to carry out her next plan.

No sooner had the sound of Reggie's motor died away she went into the drawing room without knocking and asked permission to speak to Violet privately.

"What is it, Miss Knox? There's no one here but us."

The sofa cushions were crushed in all the wrong places. The fire had been allowed to die down to embers and no one had rung the bell to have it replenished. The room was almost dark.

"This is rather an awkward matter, Mrs Storrington. My sister – you know, my sister Daisy –"

"I know you refused to spend Christmas with her."

"That's true, but it doesn't mean I'm not fond of her. I care about her very much. It worries me that she's in pretty straitened circumstances, with her husband on a miserable salary and with doctor's bills, and everything. So I would dearly like to send her a generous Christmas present."

"Are you asking my advice as to what the present should be?"

"No, I know what it must be. Money is the only practical and useful thing for Daisy. I want to send her ten sovereigns."

"Well, I must say that is generous of you. Can you afford it? Have you a secret hoard?" Violet said lazily.

"Now where would I get that, Mrs Storrington?" Hannah gave her recently learned gay artificial laugh. "No, I was hoping you might be good enough to give me the money."

Mrs Storrington lost her languid air. She sat up straight. "Give it to you! Why ever should I do that? Have you lost your senses?"

"To speak candidly, Mrs Storrington, I've only just found them. I think, for certain reasons, you will give me the money."

Mrs Storrington's colour had heightened, as if she were too near the fire. "Miss Knox, are you by any chance threatening me?"

Blackmailing is the word, Hannah said to herself. It isn't a nice word, but it's full of unholy excitement. And I'm going to be very good at it.

"I won't threaten you if you will be generous, as I suggest. If not –"

"Yes? If not?"

"Well, your youngest son is very clever indeed with his camera. You know that already. After all you encouraged him, didn't you?"

In the gloom Mrs Storrington had a still, listening air.

"So – what are you about to tell me that I don't know?"

"Only that Boy has shown me some photographs he took last summer. They're astonishingly good, but rather – compromising. One in particular. Which I have in safe keeping." Again Hannah gave her brittle laugh. "I know married people in yours and Mr Storrington's circumstances, I mean rich and gay and a little bored, don't entirely live by the rules. On the other hand I don't think they ever want to be found out for breaking them. I really think Mr Storrington would be very upset if he were to see this photograph that I have."

Violet had sprung up in a rustle of taffeta and a cloud of perfume.

"You little wretch, would you mind telling me what you're up to?"

"I'm only asking for ten sovereigns," Hannah said in her soft voice. "It really isn't much to you, with your larder downstairs stuffed with rich food and champagne and everything. Daisy and her husband can't afford a turkey, or a lot of gifts, or any of the nuts and bonbons and sugared fruits that all of us will be gorging ourselves with. There is so much in this house, it makes me feel –"

"Don't tell me it gives you a bad conscience! Oh, no, you're just jealous, Miss Knox! So eaten up with envy that your sneaking little mind is searching for ways of revenge!" Violet's voice rang out furiously. "Where are these photographs? That one in particular?"

"I have them safely."

"I don't believe they exist. I'll ask Boy."

"I wouldn't do that, Mrs Storrington. He doesn't care much for them himself. They worry him. You'll only precipitate one of his attacks if you upset him. You don't want that at Christmas with the house full of guests. Although I might add," Hannah went on primly, "that that will be when you're grateful to have me here. Don't you remember how I calmed Boy the last time? I think I have won his confidence."

"Miss Knox, I am dismissing you on the spot. You'll pack your bags and leave this evening."

"But how would you explain that to Mr Storrington and the children? Would you compel me to tell them the real reason? Don't be foolish. Ten sovereigns really aren't much to you, especially when you consider that they're buying your peace of mind."

"Miss Knox, I simply don't understand you. Ever since you returned from St. Petersburg you've changed. It was my fault for allowing you to go. It has been a great mistake. It seems to have given you very unpleasant ideas."

"But it suited you very well, I fancy?" Hannah's eyebrows were raised archly. "Shall we go into that?"

Violet made a swishing movement with her skirts, as if she were sweeping up dirt.

"Get out of here, you evil creature! Get out!"

"Certainly, Mrs Storrington." Hannah couldn't resist making an ironic bob. "Shall we say that I have the money tomorrow morning? Or in the afternoon. I don't want to inconvenience you. And then I would like a day to visit my sister. I had thought of taking Cissie with me."

"I'll never allow it."

"But I've suggested the outing to Cissie already and she

would be very disappointed if she isn't to go. I'm afraid she would be bound to appeal to her father, who as you know doesn't refuse her anything."

Mrs Storrington gave a strangled sob. "Are you trying to ruin me?"

Hannah put her small hand on Violet's shoulder, gently. "Hush now. Don't be upset. This is a mere trifle. You can go on having your happiness. As if I would dare to interfere. Or even to criticise. Hush now. I declare you're as excitable as Boy. I always knew he didn't get his nature from Mr Storrington."

There was an abrupt silence. Violet seemed to have stopped breathing.

Then she said in a passionate whisper, "People like you, Miss Knox, get killed, and not accidentally."

Hannah's light laugh fluttered. "Oh, goodness me, no. I'm not nearly important enough."

However galling it might be for Mr and Mrs Storrington, Hannah knew that a great many admiring eyes were on her, on Christmas Eve, when she accompanied the children in their modest songs.

Cissie sang very well in her light pure voice, Adolphus, embarrassed and reluctant, strove to keep in tune, and Boy, the third in the trio, scarcely needed to open his mouth. He would still be admired for he looked so beautiful with his tumbled curls and his porcelain skin.

But Hannah had the entirely unaccustomed sensation that it was she who took the attention of the men. Her new Indian shawl had slipped off her shoulders, and, finally deciding not to wear any jewellery (for who could compete with Violet's magnificent ruby pendant?), her tender white throat looked innocent and young.

She would be twenty-six years old in January, and her life had taken a very strange turn.

It was ironic that now, too late, she had gained the interest of men and of one man in particular. A person whom Daisy would have greeted as a very acceptable suitor for her sister. It was Doctor Peters, the local physician who attended the family. He was unmarried though in his mid-forties. He had a plain but attractive bearded face, and shrewd eyes. He was a little inclined to plumpness. There were small pouches on the backs of his hands which he kept mostly clasped over his stomach. He didn't appear to have much in common with the other guests, such as the Cabinet Minister's wife who was intimidatingly elegant and brilliant, and kept most of her attention for Mr Storrington.

But it was clearly Hannah who interested Doctor Peters, and she, who had been cured forever of romance, knew that he would have made a tolerable match. Since he was in his mid-forties and still unmarried, she guessed that he would not be a demanding husband, and this would be very much to her taste. For after Charlie Storrington, she knew she would never welcome another man's intimacy. Apart from that revulsion in her, she was well aware that she could not deceive Doctor Peters, a physician, about her virginity. And she would never explain her condition, nor apologise.

However, the final argument against any thought of matrimony was that she had embarked on something much more exciting than sex. She was quite the cleverest and most devious woman in this room tonight. The knowledge made her eyes burn and sparkle, and she no longer kept her eyelids modestly lowered.

Cissie had enjoyed accompanying Hannah on her visit to Daisy. The whole outing had been entertaining, the train journey, giving the babies the toys she had brought and playing with them, talking to Daisy in a grown-up way and politely eating cottage pie, which she disliked, for luncheon. Daisy had been full of admiration and had said, "What a charming young lady, Hannah. You must be very fond of her." And Cissie, on the homeward journey, had taken Hannah's hand, and asked, "Are you fond of me, Miss Knox? Because if you are, you're much better off with us than getting married and living as your sister does. I found that house quite stifling. Oh, am I being rude?"

"Yes, you are, but you're also speaking the truth. In every particular." Hannah squeezed the smooth young hand in hers. "And I truly am very fond of you, my dear."

Somehow that little incident removed any guilt she might have had. She was only making Cissie's parents pay for their own private guilt, and giving them excellent service in return.

For no one could say the three Storrington children were unhappy or ill-taught, and that was her function in the household.

As the music came to an end, people began congratulating Mrs Storrington on her good fortune.

"You've struck lucky this time, Violet. Your Miss Knox seems to be a paragon."

Violet nodded but said nothing. Mr Storrington was absently patting Cissie's head, since she had run to his side for approbation. Reggie Mainwaring was looking over Hannah's head, and Blanche, his wife, an unobtrusive narrow figure, sat quietly in the background, not talking to anybody, but watching beneath her long pale eyelashes. Someone else was saying, "Absolutely tophole, Vi, your three songsters, but when are we going to start a game of whist?"

Doctor Peters stood beside Hannah.

"You play the piano beautifully, Miss Knox. The children were charmingly amateurish, but you are quite professional."

"Thank you, Doctor Peters." Since he stood hopefully waiting for more conversation, she went on, "I find music, as well as poetry read aloud, has a soothing effect on Boy. He really is a very highly strung child. How would you diagnose his trouble? You may speak freely to me since I am almost entirely in charge of him."

Doctor Peters pursed his lips and looked pompous. "He suffers from a disorder of his personality. Not too common but not exactly rare either. It's a form of dementia. At times he becomes, literally, another person."

"A very violent one."

"Yes, unhappily. And I mean unhappily for him because he has to find his way through these very puzzling and frightening nightmares."

"Is this an hereditary disease? If one can call it a disease."

"Oh yes, it is a disease. Hereditary? We're not entirely sure. Certainly neither of his parents shows any trace of it. But some mental disorders can follow a family pattern. You know the rather horrifying stories of an elderly relative shut in an attic, or even tied to a bed. If the house were not big enough to keep the patient at home, he, or she, would be sent to Bedlam. Where Charles Lamb's sister, poor creature, suffering the same trouble, had to be kept at intervals."

"Boy isn't as bad as that!"

"Not at present. One hopes he will always be able to be kept at home. Fortunately, there are his loving parents, and plenty of servants. And you, my dear young woman. They're extremely fortunate to have you."

Hannah found his soft admiring gaze a balm to her battered spirit. Then, unluckily for the mildly amorous Doctor Peters, she heard Mr Storrington's ringing jovial laugh across the room, and his strong heavy-browed face superimposed itself on the gentle bearded one facing her. Who wanted balm? Rather this burning emotion of revenge, jagged and sharp like the pieces of broken glass Boy carried about. She now understood Boy's desire to hurt himself, for the dark pain blotted out the grief.

She had been over-confident about Boy's improvement. The stress of the evening proved too much for him. Before dawn he had plunged into one of his nightmares, the worst one Hannah had yet witnessed.

She had been half aware of his screams in her sleep before Max knocked at the door and begged her to come.

"No one can quiet him, miss. Neither the doctor nor the mistress. It's a bad one."

Hannah dragged on her dressing gown and ran to the door.

"How long has it been going on?"

"An hour or more. The mistress said you weren't to be woken, but the doctor disagreed. He thought you might be able to get him to swallow his medicine since he's come to trust you. Well, as much as he trusts anybody."

"We'll see," said Hannah grimly, hurrying along the passage.

The scene had become familiar, Boy crouched on a dishevelled bed, his face as wild and hostile as a cornered animal's. He was quiet at that moment in that he wasn't screaming or gabbling, but his eyes were the most unquiet Hannah had ever seen. They seemed to be looking into dark shadows and one couldn't begin to guess what they saw to give them such a look of fright. She wanted to rush and take the slight rigid body into her arms, but her first movement made the child stiffen and shrink away.

"Don't go near him!" Mrs Storrington hissed. "He thinks everyone is – oh, God, his enemy."

Mrs Storrington looked much older, wan and distraught, her swansdown-trimmed robe unsuitably frivolous in this situation. She looked almost as frightened as Boy did, which was not the wisest way to behave, Hannah decided. She was sure that infinite calm was needed.

"Do you think, Miss Knox, you could keep him still while I give him his medicine?" Doctor Peters whispered.

"What is it you're giving him?"

"Just a sleeping draught. One hopes, when he wakes up, the fit will have passed. It's usually effective."

"If not –"

"Then he will have to be restrained before he gets destructive. Max knows how."

Hannah saw Mrs Storrington shudder violently. She was shivering inwardly herself, distressed beyond words. *And cast out evil spirits*, she was thinking. Oh, give me power, please God.

She went towards the bed, moving quietly, and began instinctively to sing the song Boy himself had sung so sweetly earlier that night. "*Now I lay me down to sleep, I pray this night my soul to keep . . .*"

Did the little boy relax slightly? She couldn't be sure. She could only see the damp tousled hair, the staring eyes, the dribble from a corner of his mouth. His hands were clenched round the rumpled sheets, his body pressed against the brass bedstead as against the bars of a cage.

Still singing the same words over and over, not hurrying them, knowing that repetition was soothing, she managed to sit on the edge of the bed without Boy starting away from her. She reached her arm backwards for the glass Doctor Peters was holding.

"Give it to me. He'll take it presently. I'll sing to him a little more. And recite some poetry. *Where are the songs of spring? Aye, where are they? Think not of them — thou hast thy music, too . . . The redbreast whistles from a garden-croft, And gathering swallows twitter in the skies . . .*"

Boy stirred and seemed to listen. Keats. This strange young wandering soul and I love Keats.

"Drink this, Boy. Then I'll lay you down to sleep the way the song says. You'll have sweet dreams. Listen." A quick transition from Keats to Tennyson. "*Now folds the lily all her sweetness up, And slips into the bosom of the lake, So fold thyself, my dearest . . .*"

Never moving his lost eyes from her face, Boy at last allowed her to put the glass against his lips. Then he drank in gulps, thirstily. If the mixture tasted nauseating he didn't appear to notice. When he had finished Hannah beckoned for some water. This too, he drank greedily.

"He's used so much energy. Does he get dehydrated, Doctor?"

"Yes, he must do so. He'll settle in a few minutes now. Well done, Miss Knox."

"I'll stay with him."

"There's no need once he's asleep. Max will be here."

"It's better that I should be here when he wakes."

"Miss Knox, I don't think — " Mrs Storrington began, but her voice held only a shadow of its familiar imperiousness.

"She's right, Mrs Storrington," Doctor Peters interrupted. "She has a remarkable power over the wee boy. It's hypnosis to a point, unconscious of course, but it's effective."

Hannah felt very strong and elated.

"I can doze in this chair. No need to spoil your Christmas Day, Mrs Storrington. It's almost begun. I'll take full responsibility for the patient."

It was too soon to reflect on the possibilities of this new development. At the moment she was only surprised at the depth of her concern for the now sleeping child. She felt drained and tired and full of that curious elation. She would sit beside her charge until he woke.

It was a long drawn-out attack, not completely passing until Christmas was over and the house empty of guests. Boy kept slipping in and out of his strange terrors, at one moment passive and sane, the next shrinking away from his private fearful visions.

At last, when he had been quiet for a whole morning, Hannah said that she was taking him out for some fresh air. It was time he got away from the confines of his room which must now represent a prison to him. Mrs Storrington, who still looked worn and curiously haunted, her voluptuousness shrunken, expressed doubt.

"You'll take Max with you, Miss Knox."

"No. Let everything seem normal. If Max follows us Boy will get suspicious."

"You won't be able to control him if he gets difficult."

"I'll take a risk," Hannah said cheerfully.

They went down to the marsh, Boy wrapped in an overcoat and muffler, herself in her buttoned boots, her old grey cloak and a woollen cap.

The air was marvellously fresh, the sky a dim far-off blue with ragged clouds. The marsh, flooded by recent rains, had become a lake, all its familiar hillocks drowned beneath glassy water. Coots and tern waded at the edges, twittering and fussing. Their legs were reflected in the dark water like wavering red tapers. Boy hung over the bank, fascinated.

"Look, Miss Knox. That's a grey gull come in from the sea. And there's a mallard. But there aren't any tadpoles or frogs. And no dragonflies, no butterflies."

"They'll all be here in the summer."

"I can't wait that long," Boy said in a curiously mourning voice. Then he lifted his pure young face, looking at Hannah. "But I like it quite well this way."

"So do I."

And it was true that the desolation had a washed sweetness, sharply clean and invigorating. Indeed, Boy ran all the way home like an ordinary, energetic healthy child.

That night, without any prompting, depriving Hannah the chance of enjoying once more her new found power, Mrs Storrington gave her an envelope containing five sovereigns.

"I know that you value money, Miss Knox." Her voice was only slightly scathing. "This is to show my appreciation of what you have done for Boy. You seem to have a knack of managing him. Thank heaven. I'm really very grateful. However," she added, fixing Hannah with an uneasy glance, "it doesn't mean that I condone other aspects of your behaviour. I would still like you out of my house. To be quite truthful, I believe you frighten me."

"Me!"

"You can look so deceptively innocent. And you're not innocent at all, are you?"

"Who is?" Hannah asked.

"Ah! Well, if we're forced to live together, let it at least be in peace."

"You're very wise, Mrs Storrington."

And I hope your husband will be as wise when I remind him that it's time he replenished the gun case with another bag of sovereigns. Thirty this time. Would she dare?

16

A WEEK LATER Hannah, in a state of acute distress, wrote in her diary:

"I am not the sort of person who listens at doors, though in this house I might well be forgiven for doing so. I was merely passing Mrs Storrington's bedroom door late tonight – I had been downstairs to get a book to read to Boy because he was having one of his sleepless nights, this is a new symptom that disturbs the doctor, when I heard Mr Storrington saying in a loud angry voice, as if at the end of a quarrel, 'I have two sons, one is deaf and one is mad. So I want another, and you're my wife, aren't you?' I could have told him that that hectoring voice was no way to woo a woman. One should hate, hate, a man like that. Instead, the overheard remark and my immediate vivid imagination of what was about to happen in Violet's scented tumbled bed has made me realise that I can still be stricken to the heart, and made half mad with jealousy.

"I won't hesitate any longer to demand more money.

"But first I must strengthen my position. Boy is now entirely under my influence. I have had to spend so much time with him that Cissie has been feeling a little left out, but she is a sweet-natured child and I can soon make amends. Adolphus, I intend taking to London to see an ear specialist. He is soon to go to Eton, and he will be miserable there if his hearing doesn't improve. I had been going to speak about this. Now I will do so tomorrow morning, at breakfast. One son is deaf . . . How dare that brute be so callous when the poor boy's deafness is his father's fault.

"At breakfast, if he has had a night of love, he will be relaxed and amenable. Damn him, damn him, damn him."

She put the diary in its hiding place, along with her increasing store of sovereigns, the incriminating photograph of Violet and Reggie Mainwaring, and the amethyst mouse which she only kept because she suspected it would become an object of some value.

She was almost certain that on more than one occasion her room had been searched. But Violet hadn't the time, or the craftiness, to think of examining the floorboards beneath the hearthrug. Long ago Hannah had found that one of them was loose and easily pried up. Had this hollowed space been a hiding place for previous governesses' treasures over the last century? Ill-treated, poorly paid creatures who may have done a little justified thieving from a careless mistress.

None of that former regiment of lonely women would have had the secrets she had, Hannah thought with forlorn pride.

Once Cissie had caught her with the hearthrug raised. She had said she thought she had seen a mouse, then scolded Cissie for coming in without knocking.

Oh, she was clever, and more than a match for Charlie Storrington who wanted another son by an unfaithful wife.

When she caught sight of her face in the mirror she saw that her eyes were huge and lambent, sucking up all the colour from her cheeks and lips, so that she looked like some night creature that only saw and hunted in the dark. It was a good analogy. She was in the dark permanently.

At breakfast, Mr Storrington was certainly relaxed and affable, as she guessed he would be. He had looked like this on St. Petersburg mornings.

When she made her quiet suggestion that it would be a good idea for Adolphus to see a Harley Street specialist since she didn't believe his troublesome ear had been looked at for some years, Mr Storrington looked only mildly provoked. He knew that this suggestion should have come from his wife or himself.

"Yes, we must arrange that. Since you'll be off to school soon, won't you, Dolly old man? You'll need all your senses about you then. How's the Latin coming on?"

"Tolerably, sir. At least that's what old – I mean Mr Beard says."

"Good. Good. And by the way Miss Knox, since we're discussing the children's welfare – which I know, is near your heart – Mrs Storrington and I have decided that Cissie might benefit from going to school, too."

Cissie gave an indignant and predictable wail, which made her father lift his hand placatingly.

"Be quiet, my pet, until you hear what I have to say. You're a bit old for your years, you know. Mighty pretty, but a little, shall I say, too serious. This is only because you have no female companions of your own age. You need a best friend and all the sort of things girls talk about. So we intend looking for a suitable school. You wouldn't begin until Adolphus goes to Eton, of course, so until then things will stay as they are." He was directing his words to Cissie, but looking beyond her to Hannah. "Now, please, no tears, Cissie. You know, with my soft old heart, I can't stand tears."

Cissie's eyes were streaming with instant and copious tears.

"But Papa, what shall you do without me? What shall Miss Knox do?"

"I shall die of a broken heart, of course. Miss Knox . . ." His quickly significant gaze was on Hannah again and she knew that this was a far worse threat than being sent to Daisy's for Christmas, it was meant to undermine her very existence. "Miss Knox will have to accept the fact that pupils grow up."

Her mouth was dry. "Boy?" she managed to say. Boy had finished his breakfast and had wandered off a little while ago.

"Yes, I admit that's a problem, now that you seem to have made yourself indispensable to him. But Mrs Storrington and I have discussed this. Eventually, if the boy goes on getting more unmanageable, as Doctor Peters seems to think he will, we'll have to make other plans for him."

One son is mad . . .

There must have been quite a lot of talk in the marital bed last night, as well as other activities. Hannah felt a squeeze of fear. Had there been a complete reconciliation, each of them confessing to the other their misdemeanours? So that her fascinating blackmail plans would now be ineffective? She hardly thought this was likely.

"I can manage Boy," she said tightly.

"Yes, and we're grateful to you. But he is growing bigger and stronger and you're not the most outstanding physical specimen, are you? If you should be alone with him and he became violent, what could you do?"

"It may never happen," she cried. "If it does happen, I can quieten him. I really can. Doctor Peters will tell you. It would be cruel to send him away. He's so young and vulnerable. As for Cissie," she went on with some force, "she's making such advances with her music and her literature. And she's so happy at home. Would you upset that?"

"I appreciate your concern for my children, Miss Knox, but Cissie is growing up, too. Rapidly. Hadn't you noticed?"

Fool she had been to allow Cissie to put up her hair on Christmas Eve, and to wear that rather grown-up dress. Now Cissie had stopped her tears long enough to look gratified at her father's remarks. And also just faintly intrigued at the thought of boarding school, best friends, games, midnight feasts, and all the things she had read about. Hannah knew exactly what she was thinking, and her feeling of apprehension grew.

But had Mr Storrington overlooked her trump card? Even with school and best friends, Cissie would still be shattered to hear of her beloved Papa's perfidy.

"I don't agree at all with your suggestion, Mr Storrington. I think Cissie is growing up charmingly at home. Do you really want her to become a rough hockey-playing school-girl?"

Mr Storrington gave a humorous wince. "Not possible. But I understand your reasons for exaggeration. You will be sad to lose these two pupils. However, you must think about it. Cissie must too. In the meantime you have my permission to take Adolphus to an ear specialist. I'll find who the best man is and make an appointment." He smiled genially. He was looking his most attractive. And as the devoted family man, infinitely far out of her reach. In that bitter moment she at last accepted that she had lost him forever.

"Now I must be off to business. There's going to be a war in Europe before long. Did you know that, Adolphus? Has your Mr Beard lifted his head from Latin texts to give you his opinion? I am urging the Government to re-arm. Sleepy devils, politicians. Heads in the sand. Stupid too. And complacent. I'm sure you don't agree with complacency, Miss Knox? Discretion is preferable. Eh?"

Giving his loud jolly laugh, he was gone. She knew exactly what he had been doing. Calling her bluff. But she wasn't bluffing. As he would shortly discover.

Adolphus was fairly philosophic about the doctor's opinion. His hearing was unlikely to improve. There had been irreversible damage to his right ear drum. It might grow worse, but with luck not before middle age. School could be coped with well enough, and there was no reason to doubt that he could have a successful career.

"But not in the army. Had you any thoughts in that direction, young man?"

"No, sir. But my father says there's going to be a war so perhaps I'll have to fight even if I am deaf."

"Does he say that, by Jove? No, I hardly think you'll be in the front line if gunshot did this to your ear."

"So Papa may have saved my life by deafening me," Adolphus said on the train on the way home. "Don't you find that strange, Miss Knox?"

"Very strange. I suppose there are compensations in everything."

Her own compensations had to take the limited form of money. And soon. She missed her customary feeling of elation, and instead felt tired and dejected.

This feeling of weariness increased when they arrived home and a rather subdued Cissie met them. She made sympathetic sounds when she heard the verdict on Adolphus, then tucked her arm in Hannah's and held her closely as they went upstairs.

"Well, what is it, what are you feeling guilty about?" Hannah asked.

"Guilty, Miss Knox?"

"It's very plain to see. You're not good at secrecy, are you?"

Cissie flushed and looked about to weep.

"I do love you, Miss Knox. Truly. You're the very nicest governess we ever had. But —"

"But what?" Hannah asked evenly.

"But today I've been alone since you and Dolly went to London and I've been bored and bad-tempered. Even Mamma said so."

"Didn't you do the work I left you? The essay . . ."

"Miss Knox, I hate working alone. Even Boy wouldn't stay in the schoolroom. So I kept thinking that it would be rather nice if I had some friends of my own age. And not boys. I'm tired of boys."

"You mean at boarding school?"

"Yes, that's what I mean," Cissie exclaimed in a rush, clearly glad to be rid of her guilty secret.

"How long have you been thinking this way? Since Papa mentioned the idea?"

"Yes, precisely. And Mamma has talked about it, too. They do plays and operas at school and I would dearly love to act — and sing —" Cissie's voice faltered. "Miss Knox, are you angry?"

"No. Just a little hurt. After all, it was I who taught you to enjoy music."

"I know. And I do love you. I shall miss you awfully."

But you refuse to be sacrificed for my sake, Hannah thought. Although you don't even know you were meant to be a sacrifice. Ranks of imaginary schoolgirl faces, friendly and laughing, rose up in front of her, and she hated them bitterly.

"Don't look so upset, Miss Knox, please. It won't be yet. We'll have all the summer, you and Dolly and Boy and me."

Boy! Yes, there was her ultimate weapon. She had become indispensable to that flawed child. She could make herself so for a long time to come, and accumulate, perhaps a little more rapidly, her hoard of money, her comfortable nest egg for what looked like a bleak future. While Boy remained here she must remain, too.

But it would not be the same. She would feel as lonely as Cissie had done today. She was genuinely fond of the child. It was difficult not to return affection so spontaneously given.

Quiet grave Adolphus, too, shared in her affections. And for that strange imp of brilliance and wildness, Boy, she had developed a strong protective instinct.

Let no one say she was entirely wicked.

But she must make haste in gathering in her golden harvest, before the winter storms that seemed inevitable.

Two nights later she wrote in her diary:

"It is done. I have fifty more sovereigns. Fifty. Mr Storrington was unexpectedly generous because he swears this is my last payment. When Cissie is out of the house, and rapidly growing up, my threats will be empty, for she will no longer be broken-hearted over what I could tell her. Anyway, Mr Storrington said I overrate my worth. He can do better with a lady in Maidenhead, with dinner at Skindles thrown in. He laughed evilly as he said this. I would never have guessed he could be so vulgar."

"But what about you, Hannah Knox," she wrote in a sudden mood of self-awareness. "What has happened to your character? Sometimes I don't like living in your skin."

Daisy seemed to sense something of Hannah's mental and physical torment when next she made a visit to her sister's household.

"Hannah, are you quite well? You look awfully peaky."

"Yes, I'm well. Who doesn't look peaky at the end of the winter? We've been shut in the schoolroom too much. Adolphus is fretting about Eton, although he doesn't say so, and Cissie – she may be going to school, too. So I'll be left with Boy."

"Hannah, you didn't tell me this about Cissie. Are you sure they'll want you to stay?"

"Of course. They couldn't possibly manage without me."

"They managed before you went there," Daisy said shrewdly.

"Muddled along would be the better way of putting it. Poor Mrs Storrington used to be a nervous wreck when Boy was bad."

"It's you who looks a nervous wreck now. It's taking too much out of you, Hannah. I think you should leave and find another position."

"I'll never leave!" Hannah said vehemently.

Daisy looked puzzled and worried.

"I've never heard you talk like that before. What's bothering you? Cissie going to school? Or is that boy getting too crazy? Or have you met someone among the guests? Some man? Come on, tell me."

"Oh, you and your everlasting matchmaking!" Hannah burst out. "Is going to bed with a man all you can think of?"

"Hannah!" Daisy was deeply shocked and offended. "How can you say such things?"

(Why can't I say them since it's true of me almost all the time?)

"Sorry, Daisy. That was a bit rude. It's only that your matchmaking gets on my nerves."

"More than your nerves, I should think. You looked terrible just then. Fierce and angry. Has someone hurt you, or deceived you?"

"No, no, I'm loved by the whole world," Hannah said airily. "Just forget I was bad-tempered. I am a bit tired. It's the end of a long winter. Boy's been the same. I can hardly keep him indoors now that spring's coming. He's so restless. He's really a handful, Daisy, I admit it. But no one except me can manage him, so I must stay. Mr and Mrs Storrington would be lost without me."

All the same she was beginning to have secret fears that Boy was getting too much for her. He had grown quite a lot. His thin wiry body was surprisingly strong, as she had discovered when she had tried to restrain him without the help of Max. He was sometimes charmingly disobedient, shaking his head regretfully and giving his ravishing smile, and sometimes sullenly and stubbornly so. But almost always disobedient. Any lessons he did were at his own whim, not at her request.

His reading had improved, however, and his paintings were immensely clever. He hadn't been using his camera lately because he said the winter light was not good enough. That might have accounted for some of his restlessness.

But Hannah was privately deeply uneasy about the future, and could only hope that spring and outdoor pursuits would make him happier and therefore more amenable.

Another thing was on her mind. How long would it be until Violet announced her pregnancy – if at all. She had been morose lately, not at all her ebullient self. Her looks had suffered, she looked overblown and her untidiness was careless rather than picturesque. Nor did those regular visitors, Reggie and Blanche Mainwaring, call as frequently, not even Reggie alone. He had been told to stay away, Hannah guessed, but whether from caution or because Violet found herself pregnant, or even because she was enjoying having her husband as a lover again, Hannah could not decide. She only knew that the prospect of Violet bearing another child for Mr Storrington haunted her. Violet might make a reluctant mother, but Hannah herself was afraid that if a baby were born and she still here, she would resent it enough to suffocate it.

"I should go away from here," she wrote in her diary. "I am so afraid that something dreadful will happen. I am a fool to stay, to be tortured daily. Loving is hard enough, but hating is worse. I see my pinched face in the mirror, and wonder what I am becoming. The witch in the gingerbread house?"

A late spring storm had blown up, but the rain was over by mid-morning, when such fresh and golden sunlight came out that it was a crime to stay indoors.

In any case Boy had departed in his wilful way half an hour ago, and Cissie and Adolphus had only half their attention on their books. What did it matter now whether Cissie became inculcated with a love of poetry, and Adolphus for the dazzling exploits of Dumas heroes? Hannah was dejected. She was never going to see the fruits of her labours when these children had grown up to be literate and cultivated. If she could have remained a close friend of the family – but that was out of the question . . .

"Let's shut our books," she said suddenly. "If Boy can enjoy the sunshine why should we be deprived?"

The children obeyed with alacrity. Adolphus, saying he must exercise the mongrel puppy one of the gardeners had given him, was off down the stairs. Cissie followed more slowly, grumbling that brothers were the worst company. When she went to school she could bring friends home for the holidays, and you can teach us all, dear Miss Knox.

However, Hannah had scarcely tidied the schoolroom before Cissie was back, exclaiming breathlessly, "Miss Knox, Boy has done something terrible. He has been in the library and opened Papa's gun case and taken one of the guns. You know, Papa's specially treasured ones."

Hannah felt a quick jerk of apprehension. Those guns were loaded. "How do you know it was Boy?"

"Who else could it be? You know Dolly hates guns."

"Then I'd better find him," Hannah said as calmly as possible.

"I'll come with you."

"No, I think not. If Boy should be in one of his moods it's better I be alone. I expect he's gone to the marsh. And if he should get upset and throw the gun in the water I really don't think your Papa will ever forgive him."

She hastily changed her shoes – it was still swampy down at the marsh after the winter and spring rains – lifted up her skirts and ran out of the house, careless of who saw her undignified exit.

A terrible sense of precognition possessed her. It was as if she had always known a moment like this was going to happen, Boy alone on the marsh with a dangerous weapon.

As long as he was not in one of his crazy moods, as long as he would listen to her and allow her to approach him, and quietly give up the gun . . .

She was out of breath by the time she reached the end of the river path and came out into the open.

She had been right in her assumption. Boy was there, in his lonely and beautiful retreat, the marsh water gleaming in the sun, the white wings of seabirds making the sky alive.

He was standing on a small hummock that had emerged green and dry from the surrounding water. He hadn't seen her coming, but stood waving the gun about dangerously, his head thrown back in an imperious way, his voice raised in one of his unintelligible chants.

Was he imagining himself some young warrior defying

enemies with his all too real and deadly weapon? He had a strange look of exaltation, his face lifted to the sky, the sun glinting on his tumbled curls.

Then he heard her calling and turned to look in her direction. She knew him well enough to realise that he was furious at being woken from his dream. Or else he remained in it and she was the enemy, for she saw that he was raising both arms to steady and point the pistol.

"No, Boy, no. Don't do that. The gun's loaded."

The seagulls' crying drowned her words, the wind carried them away. Her innocent executioner gave her his steady exalted stare, and took slightly wavering but still dangerous aim.

"Don't move or you're dead!"

A low-flying gull screeched, and distracted him for a second. Hannah seized the advantage and leaped forward, splashing through shallow water.

"Give me the gun, Boy. Give it to me, please."

She was almost at his side and reaching out. He wouldn't know how to work that ancient trigger. But he would. He had a diabolical cleverness. She didn't dare risk the slow process of persuasion. She must knock the gun out of his hand. Two more yards, one more, and she lunged and slipped on the grassy turf, and fell against Boy. She heard his eerie scream as he too lost his balance and went backwards, gun and all, into the reedy pool.

In one horrifying instant, struggling wildly, he had sunk out of sight. The water bubbled. A pair of browsing ducks fled with clattering wings.

"Boy!" Hannah shrieked.

She lay flat on the edge of the hummock, reaching out her arms, expecting him to come threshing to the surface and splashing to safety.

But it must be a very deep pool for it seemed to take minutes before a vague impression of a form and a blurred white face appeared, too far off for her to reach.

Panic-stricken, she began to slide feet first into the water. She couldn't swim. She only hoped to be able to touch the bottom and wade to his rescue. Clutching strong reeds, she groped, her skirt dragging her down. There was nothing for her feet to rest on. Nothing. She was not tall enough, or the pool was very deep indeed. If she persevered she was merely going to follow Boy to a similar death.

Frantically she dug her fingers into the reeds and clumps of grass, clawing her way back to firm ground.

Of Boy, clutching his father's prized pistol, there was no sign. The water was black glass, and opaque.

With appalled horror, she waited. Presently the ducks came back, quacking in mildly reproachful voices.

"What is it, Miss Knox? Speak up, for goodness sake!"

Violet was shaking her as if that would bring out an explanation as to why she was so distraught, and soaked through. Her mouth opened and closed soundlessly. No words would come.

Mrs Storrington cried with fearful intuition, "Where is Boy? What have you done with Boy?"

Something angry and indignant was loosened in her, bringing back her speech. "I haven't done anything to him. He slipped and fell. I was trying to get the gun."

"Where?" Mrs Storrington demanded. "Where, for God's sake? The river?"

"The marsh. The marsh, of course. You know how he loves it. And now – it's d-drowned him. I tried to reach him!" she called despairingly. "It was too deep."

But Mrs Storrington, shouting to someone to telephone Mr Storrington, and Doctor Peters, was running across the lawn to the river. Followed by Max and one of the gardeners, she was already out of hearing.

Then Hannah sank to her knees in the hall, careless of the mess made by her wet muddy clothes, and sobbed.

What have you done with Boy? The accusing words echoed in her ears. This was the doom she had always anticipated. But it had come too soon. On this lovely spring day, with bird-song and catkins and flying clouds. She didn't know how she was going to bear it.

Someone pulled her to her feet. Barker, her long face aged and yellowed with shock, but not accusing as Violet's had been. Not even surprised.

"I knew this day would come," she muttered cryptically. "I don't suppose it was your fault, Miss Knox. Unless you were driven to it."

"Driven to it!" Hannah's hysterical tears were drying. She didn't think she would ever cry again. She couldn't afford to, for she would have to remain composed in order to refute all these suspicions.

"I tried to save him, Barker. He fell over backwards. But perhaps he isn't dead. Perhaps they will bring him back alive."

"Beneath the water you said? Not much chance of it. Well, he was a poor, queer young thing always. He was bound to come to a violent end." There was no difficulty for Barker in keeping her emotions under control. In a lifetime of servitude they had been so habitually repressed that they had probably withered away. "You'd better come upstairs and change your clothes before the master gets here."

"Is he coming?" Hannah asked stupidly.

"He's been sent for, and Doctor Peters, too."

Nice Doctor Peters who admired her. He would be on her side.

What have you done with Boy? There were no witnesses. And Mr and Mrs Storrington would both want revenge for her small acts of blackmail. Would they seize this opportunity? Hannah's heart was a stone, heavy and cold. People who had secrets were vulnerable, she had once said smugly. She had secrets that could never be told, even in a courtroom.

A courtroom? How could her mind be leaping ahead like this when Boy's blanched face had not yet been lifted from the water. Perhaps he was still breathing. Please God let it be so.

"And we'll have to be careful how we tell Miss Cissie and Master Adolphus," Barker was saying. "Such a shock for them. It's as well they'll soon be going to school. Well, come on, Miss Knox, I declare you're as vapourish as a real lady."

That stiffened Hannah. She lifted her white mud-streaked face haughtily. Real lady or not, she would show them how she could fight all their innuendos and suspicions and accusations. She would not be defeated by what lay ahead.

What did lie ahead was far more dreadful in reality than in

imagination. Boy's limp body being carried home by Max and laid on his bed, the curtains drawn, and the door closed so that the little boy who had been the victim of so many fears was truly alone.

Doctor Peters arrived and disappeared into the hushed room and shortly came out, gravely pronouncing that life was extinct.

By mid-afternoon the police had been sent for. Someone had dived into the reedy depths of the marsh pool and retrieved the gun. It lay on a cloth on the library table when, later, Hannah was brought in.

A police officer stood at one side of the table, Mr Storrington at the other.

The officer's face was serious but impersonal. Mr Storrington, in contrast, looked at Hannah with a cold ferocious anger that chilled her to the bone. She began to shiver as violently as if she were still in her wet clothes, and could scarcely answer when the policeman spoke.

"Miss Knox, we would like you to tell us exactly what happened this morning. You followed your pupil, the dead boy, down to the marsh, I believe?"

"Yes, sir. When we found the gun was gone."

The anger flickered across Mr Storrington's face, almost as if the outrage to his precious gun offended him more than his son's death. After all, the weapon was perfect, and Boy was flawed.

"You knew Boy had taken it, and you wanted to retrieve it?"

"Yes, sir."

"But how did this involve endangering his life? Couldn't you have persuaded him to give it up?"

"I tried to, sir, but he was pointing the gun at me, and shouting that he would shoot me."

"Shoot you, Miss Knox? With an ancient pistol that can't have been fired for a century or more?"

"It was loaded, sir."

"Loaded!" Mr Storrington interrupted in a greatly surprised voice. "Wherever did you get that idea, Miss Knox?"

"Because you told me so, sir. Some weeks ago when I was

in here and we were looking at the pair of pistols. I wondered at the time what sort of gunshot you would put in them, but I supposed you knew."

Mr Storrington put his hand out towards the gun.

"May I, officer?"

Mr Storrington snapped back the breech and exhibited the empty chamber. "Not loaded," he said. "A figment of your imagination, Miss Knox."

"But you told me they were both loaded. I swear you did."

"Your romantic imagination, I fancy. The gun was harmless, as you must have known, so there was no need to attack my son and push him into water so deep –"

"Mr Storrington, sir –" the inspector protested.

"So deep that he would be sure to drown." Mr Storrington finished implacably.

"But I didn't," Hannah cried, all her calm gone. "I only attempted to get the gun from him and he slipped backwards. It was an accident. It was in self-defence, too. Wasn't it self-defence, officer?"

"Do you really believe that, had the gun been loaded, the boy would have shot you?" the inspector asked.

"Oh, yes. Oh, yes. He was – unreliable. Often violent. Anyone will tell you. Doctor Peters, Max who often had to restrain him, his mother –"

"But he was merely playing with an old gun that you can't possibly believe was loaded," Mr Storrington said. "Speak the truth and admit what really happened – that he had run away from his lessons this morning and you lost your temper and deliberately pushed him. Deliberately."

Hannah was shaking all over. "Oh, sir!" was all she could whisper. "Oh, sir!"

The dreadful picture of coming events was all too clear. Mr Storrington was lying, and he would persuade others to lie. He would never admit he had pretended, for sheer devilment, that the guns were loaded, and had had her believe him. He was a powerful and feared man, and she was friendless and of little importance. Indeed, of no importance at all, for Cissie and Adolphus would be whisked away and no one else would speak for her.

And poor tragic beautiful Boy lay dead.

She wanted to go and kneel at his bedside, but this was not allowed. After the police officer had finished asking his questions she was ordered to go to her room and stay there. Indeed, she was locked in, for she heard the key turn in the lock.

By evening there were clouds blowing up from the west. The lovely spring day was over.

Once Hannah heard a scratching at her door and Cissie's awed whisper, "Miss Knox! Miss Knox, are you all right?" When she didn't answer, Cissie, her voice breaking into sobs, said that she and Adolphus were being sent to stay with their Aunt Adelaide. "We hate her!" she said passionately.

Just after dark Barker came with her supper on a tray. It was she who carried the key of the door. "Orders, miss, I'm sorry."

"I don't blame you, Barker. But it's all such a terrible mistake. You believe that, don't you?"

"It isn't for me to say, miss. I wasn't there."

"That's the trouble. No one was there. Except Boy and me. That marsh – that's where I saw him for the first time, and the last time. As if it was fate."

"Don't brood too much, miss. Get some rest."

"What will they charge me with? Murder?"

"Murder!" Barker gave a muted screech.

"If not murder, it will be manslaughter. If Mr Storrington gets his way. And he always does."

"You didn't ought to think those things. The master's hard, but fair."

"Fair, did you say? Now see what you've done, Barker. You've made me laugh."

Twenty-four hours wasn't a lifetime, although it seemed like it. Especially since the clouds hung low all the next day, and there seemed to be almost no light.

At five o'clock Hannah wrote in her diary:

"It has been raining all day and I have sat at my window watching the dripping trees and the spilling petals of the magnolias and the flowering plums. And waiting for them to come and take me away. Because they will come. Of that I am sure."

17

Sarah

THERE HAD BEEN no need to tell Sarah to keep an eye on Dolly. She could not have avoided it since Dolly seemed determined to keep an eye on her. After the car, with Jeremy driving, and Charles and Cressida in the back, had gone she would have liked to shut herself in her room and indulge in the luxury of tears.

Mostly from anxiety, but also from the most acute jealousy. She had hoped Cressida would have evaded what she regarded as a painful duty, and asked Sarah to take her place. Or she had expected Charles to irritably refuse all female companionship, and opt for Jeremy alone to accompany him to the hospital.

But Cressida had presented herself downstairs and said jauntily that of course she was going, hospitals scared her sick, but she would probably survive. After all, she had done so often enough in the past. Jeremy wouldn't need to wait for her afterwards . . . She would go on to the office and catch a train home.

"I take your point, darling," Charles said, equally jauntily. "You have important work to do."

"But of course. You don't think I'd go to London on a hot day just for you."

This was a game they had played before, Sarah guessed, light-hearted badinage to cover Charles's tension and Cressida's aversion to the whole episode. Cressida wouldn't allow herself to be labelled as a heartless wife. She would play her part. It was Sarah, acknowledging Charles's casual wave to her, who was struggling with agonising emotions.

It hadn't needed the trauma of the last few days to tell her that she loved him. Sick or well, invalid or whole man, she wanted to be at his side. She wanted to be as necessary to him as he was to her. She loved him for his worn face, for the complicated emotions and philosophies in his head, for his hands that had been laid on her intimately, for his sudden eruptions of temper and then his heartbreaking resignation to his disablement. Charles Adolphus Storrington. He was as much a man as his rampaging self-indulgent grandfather, more even, for he had the courtesy and distinction of his own patient and gentle father.

Heredity was fascinating. She had been able to observe it in Charles, and also in his son, highly-strung, over-imaginative and sensitive Dolly. The little boy marked by the preceding generations.

She thought that she would have given all the rest of her life, save ten years, to bear another Storrington son.

She and Hannah Knox. Two generations apart, but both too emotional, too devoted, too reckless. Certainly Hannah had proved her recklessness in attaching herself to a man like Grandfather Charles Storrington, a man who indulged in passing whims, in less tolerant times than now.

On this summer day, sixty odd years later, Sarah was facing her own difficulties with a Storrington male. But her Charles would survive. By the very force of her thoughts she would make him.

And now there was Dolly demanding her attention.

"Sarah, since there's just us –"

"Where's Joseph?"

"Joseph's here. He thinks it would be nice if we all went down to the marsh."

Out of reach of telephones, away from the empty library.

"So do I," she said. "Let's go."

In the loneliness of the marsh, sun-drenched and subtly stirring with its many forms of life, Dolly laughed and sang and was as carefree as the most extrovert of small boys. In this small oasis of calm, Sarah gained her own feeling of deep peacefulness and confidence. She sat on a grassy hummock, letting the sun bathe her face, breathing in the clean air.

Before too long Charles would be able to come here again. Perhaps she would be with him. Perhaps not. But so long as he was well . . .

Dolly was screaming. He hadn't fallen in a pool, he was standing upright, but screaming. What was it? A grasssnake? A water rat?

"It's Nanny!" Dolly shouted. "She's here. She gave me such a fright."

Nanny drowned? Dead? Sarah ran towards Dolly, a brown duck with her brood of ducklings fussing out of her way. Something stirred in a hollow, a ghostly bundle of old clothes.

"Nanny, what are you doing here?"

The old eyes blinked against the sun. "Sitting. Thinking." She pointed a chicken-bone finger. "That's where he drowned."

"Drowned? Who?"

"Boy, of course."

"Did he drown? I didn't know." Sarah had a vision of the pale dripping body being lifted out of the dark water. Had it been a sunny day like this, or the steel-grey of winter? She felt suddenly cold, as if plunged back into winter.

"But, Nanny, isn't it morbid sitting here alone?"

"I'm not alone. She's here."

"Who?"

"The woman who pushed him." The old eyes peered in confusion, the trembling skeleton finger pointed at Sarah uncertainly. "Aren't you her?"

"I certainly am not." Sarah shook herself out of her own shock and confusion. She remembered Dolly. This wasn't the kind of thing for his ears. But fortunately he had stayed out of earshot, full of dislike for the tattered old woman.

What Charles had feared was coming true. It was time Nanny was confined to her room, permanently.

Cressida was home in time to have two vodkas before dinner. She poured them herself, concealing the quantity. She needed them, no doubt. It must have been a gruelling day for her.

It had been for everyone. Sarah couldn't criticise because

she had been fairly lavish with her own pre-dinner drink. Jeremy only came into the drawing room on invitation. No one invited him tonight.

But he was at dinner, naturally. The three of them sat uneasily at one end of the long table. It was a very warm evening, dark and humid with lowering thunder clouds.

Cressida, on being questioned, told Sarah that she had left Charles in a cheerful optimistic frame of mind.

"He was welcomed like royalty, I might say. After all, he's been a patient there often enough. If all the tests are okay they'll operate tomorrow."

She had seemed quite calm when she had said that, but suddenly at dinner she exclaimed, "How I hate this house!"

"Do you?" said Sarah in surprise.

"It oppresses me. It didn't at first, when Charles was well and we were away a lot, and Dolly was a baby. A rather darling baby, not a bit neurotic as he is now." She leaned forward, her face intense. "I really do blame this house for that. He's over-sensitive and he picks up its past in some way. He almost makes me imagine I can see other people, too."

"I feel the same," Sarah admitted. "I could swear I sometimes see two little boys."

"And creepy old Nanny doesn't help. She was fine at the beginning when we were first married. Just an elderly rather superior servant whom Charles was devoted to. But over the last year or so she's really gone round the bend."

"I know. She was down at the marsh today. She gave Dolly a fright."

"Good God! If she's wandering like that she'll have to be put in a home. I've thought that for some time. I'll have to talk to Charles when he's well enough."

Cressida swallowed her wine and indicated to Jeremy to refill her glass. She had scarcely touched her food.

"I have to go to Paris immediately Charles is out of danger. I really have to if I'm to keep my job. They won't keep on giving me time off. The world goes on, as they say."

The fashion world, Sarah thought silently. Was it so important? Or was it the people Cressida worked with who were important? The Frenchman she had lunched with the other day?

She didn't want Charles to die, she wasn't as inhuman as that. But an invalid husband, and a background like Maidenshall (although she had declared she hated the house) were very convenient to her. She was an attractive, completely modern, highly-sexed lady who, to give her her due, carried her own secret burden of guilt.

Jeremy had scarcely spoken during dinner. He had obviously come to some private decision of his own, and loyalty, no matter how belated, to his employer was one of them. He said, "Will you be taking coffee on the terrace, Mrs Storrington?"

"Not tonight. It's going to rain at any moment. It's so dark."

As if to confirm her remarks there was a flash of lightning, followed by a clap of thunder. Cressida put her hands to her ears.

"Hate that," she said. "It's too doom-like. Draw the curtains and put the lights on in the drawing room, Jeremy. We'll sit in state among the Storrington art collection. If I had my way I'd send most of it to an auction room. What appalling taste the Victorians had. The Storringtons in particular. Rubens and guns. What do you think that means? A sign of virility?"

At ten o'clock the telephone rang. Jeremy answered it in the hall. He spoke for a minute, then came in. "It's Major Storrington."

Cressida sprang up.

"Sorry madam." He really had grown extremely formal with Cressida. "He's asked for Mrs Goodwill."

Cressida was put out. "Then you'd better go, Sarah. I expect it's something he wants you to do."

"Hullo, Charles."

"Sarah."

"How are you feeling?"

"How anyone feels on the edge of a precipice, I suppose."

"I have the same feeling."

"I've been lying here thinking. I seem to remember being

told something about a trial that took place just before the First World War. Something to do with a devious servant."

"Hannah Knox!" Sarah exclaimed.

"You knew?"

"I've guessed something disastrous happened, but she was an infuriatingly cautious lady. She didn't even risk total confession in her diaries. They're just bits of spilled over emotions. But the last line does say 'They're coming for me' or something like that."

"Could you look up court records in Reading?"

"I intend to. But not for a few days, Charles. I wouldn't be concentrating very well."

"Why not? You've plenty of time. You can regale me with bits of information."

"I will, of course. When you're ready to hear them. Right now it's not Hannah Knox but you who is occupying my mind."

There was a short silence.

"Is that true? Nice girl."

"Of course, it's true. Shall I say it again?"

"Just talk to me."

She searched for something to interest him, longing to keep him there.

"We're in the middle of a thunderstorm. Dolly's in bed. Asleep, I hope. We couldn't have coffee on the terrace. None of us wanted to eat much at dinner."

"Because of me?"

"No, you egotist. Because it was too hot."

He laughed a little and sounded more relaxed. "Bless you, Sarah. I like to think of you down there. You've changed the place."

"How do you mean?"

"Well, you're straightening Dolly out, you've removed some of the gloom. Now, if we can lay the formidable Hannah's ghost we might be normal people again."

"You feel something, too?"

"Ever since I was a child. But the shadows are lifting, as they'd say in the sort of books Hannah read to her small charges."

"She read Keats' poems."

"Nice," he said. "Night, Sarah." His voice faded. He murmured another word she couldn't catch. She thought it sounded like "love" but she wasn't sure. Anyway, she didn't know in what context he was using it. However, it was a good word, for whatever reason.

Complete exhaustion made her fall asleep quickly. Sometime in the night there was a mouse-like scratching at her door. It aroused her to something like panic. Old Nanny, she thought. She couldn't cope with a demented old woman now.

But a small thud on the floor made her leap out of bed. When she opened the door a body half rolled inside.

It was Dolly, falling asleep, literally falling against the closed door. More than half asleep he had stumbled instinctively to her. In search of comfort, warmth, reassurance? He must have guessed more about his father than they had known.

She pulled him to his feet and guided him to her bed. "Hop in, old chap. We'll comfort each other."

It seemed that there was nothing like sleeping with a male, no matter what age, to bring about a closeness in one's relationship. In the morning Dolly sat up and surveyed her with a proprietary air.

"I dreamed you were here, and so you are."

"Is Joseph here, too?" Sarah asked cautiously.

Dolly was shocked. "Oh no, he wouldn't get in your bed."

"You did."

"Joseph's bigger than me. He'd think it was rude."

"Thank goodness he has some principles. What shall we do today?"

"Us?" said Dolly eagerly.

It would be late afternoon or evening before any news of Charles would come.

"Who else were you thinking of? Oh, yes, Joseph, of course. Do you know, I've never been to the village church."

"Church!" said Dolly in disgust.

"All right, if you don't care about it I'll go while you're having your lessons. Then we can do something else this afternoon. Near the house, in case the telephone rings."

"Agnes will answer it."

"I know. But near the house, all the same."

Cressida surprised Sarah and Dolly, and Agnes less agreeably, by joining them for breakfast in the kitchen.

"I haven't set for you, madam."

"Never mind, Agnes. I only want a cup of coffee. I'm going to London, Sarah. Can you cope?"

"Why not?"

"Yes. Why not? That's what Charles would say, too. I really meant for you to keep an eye on the young heir."

The choice of words didn't seem to be the most propitious under the circumstances. But Cressida was very tense, almost on the edge of hysteria. She drank her coffee standing up, ruffled Dolly's hair, hitched up her smart shoulder bag, and said she was off.

"I'll call at the – " she stopped abruptly, remembering Charles's instructions about Dolly. "You know where. If you need to get in touch with me, my office number is in the telephone book in the hall. But I'm sure there'll be no news before evening. It's better to keep busy. Charles agrees."

When she had gone Dolly said, "What did mother mean about the young hair? My hair?"

At the sink Anges gave a snuffle of laughter. "She well might. You've got plenty of it, young sir."

Joseph, Sarah realised, hadn't been mentioned once at breakfast.

Sarah's purpose in paying a quick visit to the parish church was to investigate the graveyard. There surely would be a Storrington family vault. She remembered what Charles had said about court records, but churchyards sometimes told unexpected tales.

It was as attractive as any churchyard could be, with mossy crooked headstones, trailing ivy, the golden gleam of sun between branches of a superb spreading oak tree.

The Storrington vault was impossible to miss because it towered over all its neighbours. It should have been orna-mented with crossed rifles, Sarah thought ironically, or replicas of that pair of beautiful duelling pistols in the library, or even a small cannon such as those supplied by Adolphus Charles Storrington to the British armies in the Crimea.

Instead, there was the obligatory urn and the bowed female figure presiding over the record of the Storrington deceased. Sarah had to pull strands of ivy away to read the inscriptions which began with the founder of Maidenshall.

Adolphus Charles Storrington 1818–1901

And more humbly, beneath him,

Maud Charlotte, faithful and beloved wife of the above 1843–1902

There was the death of an infant,

Caroline Maud Storrington, born 1 May 1862, died November 6, 1862
Asleep in Jesus.

Then came Grandfather Charlie.

Charles Adolphus Storrington 1872–1916 Fell at Arras, France.

Poor Charlie, at the height of his virility and success. Killed by one of his own guns exploding, perhaps?

And then, more sadly,

Celia Maud Storrington, 1899–1919 Died in the influenza plague.

Prim good Cissie who had truly been the last maiden at Maidenshall.

Lastly came Charles's own parents,

Helen Louise, dearly loved wife of Adolphus Charles Storrington
1916–1941 Killed by enemy bombs

and

Adolphus Charles Storrington 1901–1941 War Correspondent, killed
in Tunisia.

But where was Boy? Where was the drowned Boy?

So engrossed was Sarah that she started violently when footsteps crunched on the gravel.

"You're interested in our most famous monument?" said a rotund man wearing a tweed jacket, and under it a clerical collar. The vicar, no less. A twinkling person who looked as if he might have an addiction for graveyards, his eyes were so merry.

Sarah explained who she was, and the reason for her interest in the Storrington vault.

"Ah, you're not being gloomy because of Major Storrington, are you? I heard he was to undergo more surgery, poor fellow."

"He'll recover," Sarah said quickly.

"Of course. You have faith, I see."

"Yes, I have faith. He and I are working on a family history. But I confess I'm puzzled. Everything is recorded here except a memorial to a youngest son, Boy."

"Boy?"

"A child who was drowned in the marsh. You hadn't heard of him?"

"Not anyone called Boy. There's only one other Storrington grave in this churchyard and that's the small one over there." He pointed to the privet hedge. "I've not been here for too long, but I've wondered about that grave, seeing that the name is Storrington. It seems an ostracised position to choose. If he was a member of the family why wasn't he put in the vault?"

"What does it say on the headstone?"

"It says it's the grave of a ten-year-old child, a Storrington. Joseph."

For a moment the green and grey landscape tipped, like the tilting gravestones. The shock and the illumination were shattering. Joseph, Dolly's permanent companion, must be the ghost of a dead boy, possessing him. Not unpleasantly, not even frighteningly, but destructively, nevertheless. Retarding his development, removing him partially to another world. If this were true, it was eerie and disturbing.

The grave was badly overgrown. Sarah had to pull ivy and brambles off the simple inscription.

Joseph Storrington aged ten years and seven months. Tragically drowned 8 April 1912

and at the bottom, barely decipherable after she had removed the ivy, the simple word "*Boy*".

There was no mention of whom his parents were. He might have dropped from the sky, Sarah thought. An anonymous child, not willingly owned by anybody.

"*Boy had to be locked up.*" Hannah Knox had written. Had his parents wanted to disown a subnormal child?

"He was probably illegitimate," the vicar was saying to Sarah. "There were plenty of children like this in those times. If the family was important enough the husband covered up the wife's peccadillos to avoid a scandal. Gave the boy a name and brought him up."

"I'm surprised Grandfather Charlie was so tolerant," Sarah said.

"Grandfather Charlie?"

"The Edwardian Storrington. A dynamic man, by all accounts. But his tolerance didn't extend to putting that poor little boy in the family vault."

So he escapes from his grassy grave and comes back searching for company . . . Was it a case for exorcism? Sarah longed for Charles's advice. As soon as he was well enough, he would find this story rivetting. But it was only half complete. She had to search for the records of a trial some time after April 1912. The cold month, the stormy month of spring and Boy drowning in the icy water of the marsh.

It was as if everyone in that period was coming to life, for when she returned home Dolly was waiting for her, waving a handful of old brown photographs.

"Look, Sarah. We found these in the dark room."

"You and Joseph? The dark room?"

"It's where they developed photos," Dolly said patiently. "Look, Agnes says these must be my great-grandparents. And that would be Great-aunt Cissie in the funny hat, and here's Grandfather. Those pants are called knickerbockers, Agnes says."

"And who is this?" Sarah asked, taking another photograph. She found that her hands were shaking as she stared fascinatedly at the image of the small woman in the hard-brimmed boater and the high-necked blouse and neat dark skirt.

Hannah Knox, of course. The woman at the centre of the puzzle. The grey mouse. The photograph, remarkable for its period, was still exasperatingly dim. The blurred face would have looked prim and quite ordinary except for the enormous dark eyes. When sparkling and luminous they must inevitably have drawn the attention of men. Especially of lusty men like Charlie Storrington.

"Poor Hannah," Sarah said to herself. "You don't look at all wicked, whatever it was that you did."

The family was grouped in a tight cluster, Violet bosomy but elegant, a large picture hat casting a shadow over a handsome face, Charlie, thumbs in his waistcoat pockets, displaying his heavy gold watch chain, a fine figure of a prosperous gentleman. Cissie, the good child, in a muslin dress and sash and sailor hat, knickerbockered Adolphus slender and young, and wearing the slightly anxious expression of the deaf.

To Sarah's acute disappointment Boy was not there. Then the explanation occurred to her. Cissie had written in her voluminous diaries, *After lunch Boy made us line up outdoors so that he could take pictures with his new camera. Mamma has given it to him. She spoils him dreadfully*.

There was no mention of Papa spoiling him. Indeed, he must have found that little cuckoo hard to tolerate.

18

Hannah

THE ORIGINAL CHARGE of murder had been reduced to manslaughter. The manslaughter of the child aged ten years and seven months, known as Boy Storrington.

Mr and Mrs Storrington were not in court at the commencement of the trial. They were waiting to be called as witnesses. But there was one familiar face in the public gallery, the handsome but uncharacteristically sombre face of Reggie Mainwaring.

Boy's natural father? Yes, she was certain this was so. It had been Violet's secret. Hannah guessed that Charlie Storrington had always known but had made it his secret, too, in the all-important face-saving operation that was frequent enough among the upper classes.

But then Charlie Storrington had many secrets and she, who had not betrayed him, could not do so now. Not because she wanted to protect him, but because she had no intention of facing an additional charge of blackmail, a nasty crime and heavily punished. What Charlie Storrington had done to her had no connection with the present case. Rich and powerful men like him, with friends in high places, would not, in any case, be brought down by a small inconspicuous nobody, a governess, a mouse.

Naughty little mousie, nibbling at my housie . . . As advised by her counsel, she must stick to her one line of defence, that she had genuinely believed the gun to be loaded, that she had acted only in self-defence, that she had loved Boy and had been deeply grieved by his death. In prison, where she had been kept on remand for unending weeks, she had suffered a nervous and debilitating illness. She was still ill. The courtroom kept blurring and tilting, and her mind flashed away to inconsequential things like the recurring lines of the Hansel and Gretel operetta.

She had had to ask for a glass of water, and for permission to sit down in the dock.

She had on the simple bonnet and cloak she had worn to her first interview at Maidenshall. She looked grey and shrinking, her eyes so dulled that no one would believe how they had once blazed and shone. Nor that they had had a hypnotic power. At least that was what someone was saying.

"She seemed to have an hypnotic power over the dead boy. Her eyes could glow like – like jewels." That was nice kind Doctor Peters who had once admired her. Was he being kind now, or was he too intimidated by his rich patrons? "But may I point out her hypnotic powers were all to the good in this case. She would calm the boy when he was suffering from his delusions. Everyone, I particularly, encouraged this."

"But I suggest she didn't attempt to calm him on the fatal morning. I suggest that instead she lost her patience with him and behaved in a highly dangerous manner." That was prosecuting counsel again.

It was an accident, it was an accident!

Barker was in the stand. Poor Barker who would not be able to afford to lose her place. As the elderly nanny to the Storrington children from infancy she was entitled to her humble corner of the family hearth until her death.

"As the children's nurse, Miss Barker, did you observe that the accused had gained a good deal of influence over her charges?"

"They were fond of her, sir, if that's what you mean."

"Do you believe she sought to gain power in this way?"

"My lord, I object." That was Hannah's counsel's voice. He was a small earnest man, no great advocate. But she was still surprised that someone appeared to be speaking for her. "This is an irrelevant question and has nothing to do with the crime of which the accused stands charged."

"I was only seeking to establish, my lord, that if the accused had such power over her charges, the dead boy would have obeyed her that morning on the marsh, and relinquished the gun and there would have been no need for a physical attack."

He never obeyed, my lord, he was always disobedient. Ask his mother . . . Ask Violet, that self-indulgent woman who only loved her flawed youngest son because he was fathered by Reggie Mainwaring. Ask her that.

"Objection sustained. Keep to the facts, Mr Thompson."

"As your lordship pleases. Then I would like to ask the witness again, because she had the most occasion to notice these things, if the accused had acquired a more extensive wardrobe than her salary was likely to afford?"

"There was a nice Cashmere shawl," that was Barker's perplexed voice. "And a new gown. But she did have to go down to dinner with the family quite often."

"My lord, I object."

"Yes, Mr Thompson, I told you to keep to relevant facts."

"I was trying to establish the facts of the accused's character, my lord. Vanity, extravagance –"

"Objection sustained."

There was a very expensive hat once, my lord, but I burnt it because the circumstances under which I came to possess it offended me . . .

"Then may I be permitted, my lord" this was said with heavy sarcasm, "to ask the witness if she ever saw evidence of the accused having a violent temper?"

And Barker's reluctant answer, "Once, she – Miss Knox – found Boy in her room and she said he was prying and she shouted at him. She told him her secrets were no business of his."

But everyone has secrets . . .

"I believe she used to read poetry to the child to calm him. Is that correct? Poems of Keats?"

Thou still unravished bride of quietness . . . You little fool, it was your fault as much as Charlie's. You wanted him. Admit it.

"But I imagine she didn't have her volume of Keats down at the marsh on that fatal morning?" Again the sarcasm, and laughter somewhere. Who could laugh?

"Mr Thompson, I don't want to have to warn you again about making suppositions. Have you finished with this witness?"

"Yes, my lord."

"Very well, stand down, please."

"Call Mr Charles Storrington . . ."

Don't let him give evidence! Please! It will all be biased. He only wants me jailed for life, so that I am safely out of his way. Like a bit of dust swept out of his house. Violet does, too, so she can go back to her lover. She isn't pregnant, that I know. She hasn't the look. Daisy has it, though. Poor Daisy, dying of shame because I am her sister.

"Mr Storrington, did you ever tell the accused that your pair of antique duelling pistols were loaded?"

"No."

"Would it be possible to load and fire them?"

"Oh, yes. I could make the kind of shot required."

"But you didn't?"

"No, I did not."

"Would it not be a temptation to you, a gun maker, I could say a gun lover, to see how this particular pair of pistols fired?"

"A temptation, yes, but I never succumbed to it. Frankly, I'm a busy man and hadn't the time."

"Isn't it true that you frequently discharge a gun on your return home in the evenings?"

"My lord, I object."

"Objection overruled. The witness will answer the question."

"I do discharge a modern revolver occasionally. One of my own make. Not an antique pistol."

"Would you say that the accused had exceptionally good treatment in your house?"

"I would."

"And that she even had a trip to St. Petersburg in Russia at your expense?"

"She did. She was in charge of my two older children."

"So that she became accustomed to luxury, and when you planned sending your two older children to boarding schools she became worried that she might lose her position?"

"That is true."

"And the anxiety preyed on her mind sufficiently to create a nervous disorder?"

Oh no, oh no, that's Boy you're talking about. I remained calm always. Except in my most private thoughts . . .

"That is quite likely."

"Consequently, the accused felt revengeful because of her possible dismissal, and when a crisis occurred on the marsh she could not control her temper."

"You are indulging in supposition again, Mr Thompson. What is your question?"

"Sorry, my lord. My question is, do you consider it to be likely that the accused lost her temper so completely as to cause the death of this unfortunate young lad?"

Mr Storrington took his time in replying, as if deeply reflecting the question. Then he said in a measured voice, "I think it would be likely."

"Thank you. That is all, my lord."

"Call the next witness."

But there were no real witnesses, Hannah thought in desperation. All these questions and answers were hypothetical and had nothing to do with the true facts. Although indirectly they had, for they sought to uncover her bitterness and her vindictiveness, knowing that everything would stem from those destructive emotions. They were too clever. She was no match for them.

In the witness box she could not raise her voice above a whisper, a fact that irritated the Judge beyond measure. He kept telling her to speak up, but some paralysis had affected her throat muscles. They thought she was pretending her nervousness just as she had pretended the reason for her desperate struggle on the marsh.

"You say Mr Storrington told you the guns were loaded?"

"Yes, sir."

"And, assuming he did so, you believed him?"

"He is a gun maker sir. He could make them fire. Why should he tell me they were loaded if they were not?"

"You are here to answer questions, not to ask them. Even if Mr Storrington made this assertion, which he denies, did he never indulge in, let us call it a little playfulness, which he would expect you to recognise and understand?"

Playfulness? Was that the word to describe those

passionate loving nights? No, she didn't recognise or understand the description. Something deeply coldly angry and unforgiving stirred in her. She lost her fear, she was no longer overwhelmed by the solemnity of the court, or shattered by her unbelievable catastrophe. Playfulness, indeed. Such as a cat exhibited to a mouse before the kill? She raised her head high and looked across the room to where Mr Storrington sat, well-groomed, composed, apparently untouched by any emotion except the obligatory regret for the death of a son. But now she, an inconsequential, almost accidental, woman in his life, had dared to be a nuisance, and refused to go away.

Let them decide whether or not she had hypnotic eyes. She deliberately fixed their full passionate accusing gaze on Mr Storrington, making their meaning so clear, that he began to frown, and make an uneasy movement. The powerful emotion sweeping through her brought her brilliantly to life. Her voice returned and she was able to say in clear ringing tones, "If he called it playfulness, I called it something else. It was downright wicked deception. Whatever the court thinks, or tries to prove, that is the real truth, and it will never be altered. Let him have it on his conscience. Where it belongs."

The Judge rapped, "Silence! Silence in court."

The stir, and the rustling, died away, and she knew that they all thought she was still talking about the gun, loaded or unloaded.

But Mr Storrington knew differently. She had penetrated his composure, she had seen the telltale flicker of anger, and knew now he would never forgive her, that indeed he would be relieved if she were hanged.

In indulging in her small revenge, she had convicted herself. She had illustrated what the prosecution had sought to prove, that she was a highly emotional person, with an uncontrollable temper, and that more than likely she was living in a fantasy world. As governesses were inclined to do.

What do women like this do, Charlie? I mean, dried up forever.

Nevertheless, her outburst had released her pent-up

bitterness. She felt fiercely glad and triumphant. Charlie Storrington had had a few highly uncomfortable moments. She would have been convicted, anyway. From the beginning she had been cast in the role of the victim.

The sentence of imprisonment, when it came the next day, was almost a relief. Easier, indeed, to endure than the image imprinted on her mind of Boy's white drowned face. That would be with her until the day she died . . .

19

Sarah

SARAH WOKE AT dawn the following morning. She put on her dressing gown and went out into the garden, walking on the dewy grass with bare feet. She knew that there was a trug in the shed where croquet mallets and garden chairs and old tennis racquets were kept.

The roses, gleaming with dewdrops, were ineffably beautiful in the first slanted rays of sunlight. She intended to cut every bloom and pile them all into the trug in a radiant mass, and take them to the hospital.

Charles had been half-conscious last evening. "Coming round well," the nurse had said. He would be completely conscious today and she intended to sit at his bedside or, if that were not allowed, at least in the corridor outside his door.

Jeremy came up silently behind her.

"What are you doing there? Stealing my roses?"

"Yes. All of them."

"You'll need a bucket to take that lot."

"That's right. We'll take the coal scuttle out of the dining room. But I'll need your help."

"After pinching all my roses you ask for help." But Jeremy was smiling and really looking quite human. "When are you planning to go to the hospital?"

"Straight after breakfast. And with no by your leaves from strict nurses. We'll just arrive."

"Mrs Storrington?" Jeremy asked tentatively.

"Oh, we'll be gone before she comes down. Explanations later. I'll take the blame."

Jeremy looked at the garnered harvest of roses. "If these aren't to die on the way we'd better start soon."

Sarah met a nurse in the corridor.

"I'm just taking these to Major Storrington," she said glibly.

"He's not allowed visitors." The nurse's eyes went to the overflowing brass coal scuttle of roses. "Oh my, have you robbed a florist's shop?"

"No, only Major Storrington's own garden. I'll just put these in his room. I promise not to disturb him."

"Well – don't let sister see you."

He lay flat on the bed, a sculptured white face, open intelligent dark eyes.

"Sarah?"

The voice was weak, its pleasure evident.

"Jeremy and I have stripped your garden."

"You're a pair of delinquents."

Sarah stood by his bed. "You're better?"

The faintest grin. "I can wiggle my toes – would you believe it?"

"Oh, God, how absolutely marvellous!"

"So – they say."

Sarah brushed his forehead with her lips. She didn't mind that he saw her tears.

"I'm off now. Before sister murders me."

"Sarah!" She turned at the door. "When – will you be back?"

"Tomorrow."

"Good."

She was gone just as a rustling uniform came down the corridor. Mission accomplished.

"Jeremy!" She was crying in the car. "It's bloody marvellous."

"Hope he notices Madame Louise," Jeremy said. "It's her first flowering.

"Then he would, I'm sure. I have a feeling he won't be missing much from now on."

The telephone in the evening, and the far-away voice.

"Sarah?"

"Yes, Charles."

"How's Dolly?"

215

"Fine."

"Good. Sarah?"

"Yes?"

"Were you planning to bury me with roses?"

"Jeremy wants to know whether you noticed Madame Louise."

"No, I didn't. I'll look."

Cressida, just back from London, looking unusually dishevelled, said, "Who's that?"

"Charles."

"But he's not supposed to speak on the telephone yet. He can't even have visitors."

"He wanted to know how Dolly was."

"Oh. He must be feeling better."

"Yes. He must be."

"Then why wouldn't they let me see him?"

"I shouldn't think he's up to visitors, Cressida."

"Are wives listed as visitors? More likely he told them he didn't want to see me."

"I wouldn't think –"

"Stop the humbug, Sarah. Don't you think I have eyes? A rosebed full of roses yesterday hasn't a single bloom left."

"Jeremy and I did cut them."

"There's no need to be furtive about it. It was a nice idea. I only wish it had been mine." She wasn't angry. She was only weary and unaccustomedly self-critical. "If you made Charles happy, Sarah, I suppose we owe you some gratitude. Dolly does, anyway. He apparently still has a father."

But not a mother? Sarah looked at Cressida's pale fatigued face and saw guilt and shame and a kind of dogged honesty.

"I can see Charles tomorrow," she said. "They've promised me that. I believe he can move his toes, which seems to be proof of success. But as soon as he's absolutely out of danger I'm off to Paris."

"For long?" Sarah kept her voice impartial. She hoped the sudden heavy thudding of her heart was not apparent.

"Maybe. I think you have a fair idea of the picture, Sarah. You're a very sharp girl. I can't go back to Charles's bed after all this. He doesn't want me anyway. We've both been – I suppose you could say tested too severely." She paused, pushing her damp hair up off her neck. "I thought I'd love a grand house like this. But I loathe it. I loathe it."

Later that evening Sarah rang Jane at her school. She pretended it was simply an ordinary call, not allowing Jane to sense her confused emotions.

"Hi, there. Dolly's been asking about you."

"Oh," said Jane flatly. "He's a bit daft, Mummy. Really."

"He'd like you to come again, though."

"I don't want to if he's always talking to someone you can't see. The girls here simply won't believe it. They say it's incredible."

"Oh, Jane, you're growing up. Yes, it's incredible, and yet not, when you know the story. His father's in hospital and we've had to keep it from him."

"Is Major Storrington getting better?"

"Yes, he's getting better."

"Will he still be in a wheelchair?"

"No. I don't believe he will be."

Jane's voice was young and warm. "Mummy, that will be nice, won't it?"

"I'll tell him what you said. And we expect you on your next long weekend. Remind me when it is."

"In two weeks. Mummy, is that old Nanny still wandering about?"

"I'm afraid so. But she won't be for much longer."

"Is she going to die?"

"Perhaps. More likely we'll have to send her to a hospital."

"I don't think she's good for Dolly," Jane said in her elderly way.

"Why not?"

"She's a witch. Really, Mummy. It's true."

Witch or not, old Nanny was still a human being and subject to human illnesses.

Agnes, the next morning, was worried.

"I didn't lock her in. Couldn't bring myself to. But she

hasn't come down to breakfast. I'd better go up and see what's wrong."

Sarah remembered hearing a thud in the night. But only a mild thud. A dropped book, or something knocked over. Not a body.

Nevertheless Agnes came hurrying downstairs to say the old lady was still in bed, but looking queer.

"She didn't seem to know me. She called me Barker."

"Who's Barker?"

"Search me. I think you should call the doctor."

"I will. I'd better go up myself."

"What's wrong with Nanny?" demanded Dolly.

"She's a bit tired. She's very old, you know. You'd better get into the library, my boy. I can see Mr Crankshaw's bicycle approaching."

Dolly scowled. "I'd rather go and look at Nanny dying."

"Dolly! What a thing to say."

"I meant it kindly, Sarah," he said earnestly.

Nanny wasn't in the throes of death, but she looked fairly close to that state. Her hands were scrabbling over the bed-clothes, searching for something.

"What is it, Nanny?"

"I can't find my pen."

"What do you want a pen for?"

"I want to sign my will. I'm dying, can't you see?"

There was a flash of brilliance in the deep-set eyes, a flash of impatience, and a ghost of long-past dominance. She must have had remarkable eyes, Sarah thought, and something shadowy stirred in her memory. What was she reminded of?

Anyway, the simple fact was that the old woman was in no state, either mental or physical, to make a will. She seemed so distressed, however, that Sarah decided to humour her, going to get paper and ball-point pen. The last item she was sure Nanny would scorn, but there was no point in getting ink on the sheets for the sake of an imaginary will.

When she went back the anxious fingers were still searching, and it wasn't until Sarah closed them round the pen that the old lady leaned back, relaxing.

"Point to where I sign, dear. I can't see." She breathed in frail uneven gasps. "I want to leave my sovereigns to Adolphus. They're his – by right. And the mouse – to Cissie – For Boy – no, nothing for Boy. Where do I sign?"

Sarah's breath was coming almost as unevenly as the dying old woman's.

"Here, Nanny. I'll help you."

She held the unimaginably fragile fingers round the pen, steadied them, brought them to the paper. Then, slowly and shakily, the signature appeared.

Hannah Knox.

"Is that name right, Nanny? Are you sure?"

There was a last luminous flash in the dark eyes. A flash of perfect intelligence. "That's quite right." The colourless lips quirked. "I fooled them, didn't I? Except Boy."

"His name was Joseph, Nanny. Didn't you know?"

"Not until the trial. They always called him Boy. And I was bad. I was wicked. But I didn't drown him. Although he never let me alone all these years."

The bright sunlight somehow made the neat attic room more creepy, more macabre. This old woman doing such long penance for her mild acts of revenge against a ruthless employer. Who had never escaped from her youth as the young impressionable governess, Hannah Knox, so bowled over by love and then so bitterly hurt and wronged . . . Who had become doomed to trail a ghost boy, like a shadow, behind her.

"I'm going down to make you a cup of tea, Nanny."

A deep sigh escaped the old lady. The thistledown head settled into the pillow. The paper with the scrawled signature fluttered to the floor.

Sarah saw that it was too late for the tea. Or for anything else at all.

Dolly was mooching about in the hall, looking bored.

"Haven't you time to play with me, Sarah?"

"I'm sorry, not this morning. Where's Joseph, anyway?"

"He's gone."

"Gone! Where?"

"I don't know. Where he lives, I suppose."

The startling knowledge was forming in Sarah's mind. "You mean he won't be back?"

Dolly shook his head. "Nope," he said laconically. "When's Jane coming again?"

"Oh – soon."

"Dolly swung an imaginary croquet mallet.

"I'm going to beat her at croquet this time. I'll hit her into the river."

He looked so carefree, so completely normal, so little affected by the departure of his invisible friend Joseph, that Sarah decided to tell him what had happened.

"Dolly – Nanny's dead."

"I know."

"Who told you?"

"Joseph, of course. That's why he had to go. To be with her in heaven, I suppose. I say, Sarah, couldn't we have a game now? I've got no one to play with. Oh, I know, Jeremy will."

He was out of the front door, whooping and shouting for Jeremy, a suddenly completely normal noisy small boy.

It was a kind of miracle. Sarah didn't know how to explain it to Charles the next day when at last she was allowed to have a conversation at his bedside.

"I can only think that old Nanny – I mean Hannah Knox – was consumed with guilt about Boy's death, and other things, and somehow brought Boy back and foisted him on Dolly. Who was young and susceptible."

Charles was as intrigued as Sarah.

"Hannah Knox! It's fantastic. When she came out of prison she must have changed her name to Henrietta Galloway. And then she cautiously only put in an appearance at Maidenshall after my father and grandfather had died, when no one would recognise her. She must have kept in touch with what was happening in my family."

"Returning to the scene of the crime?" said Sarah. "A kind of atonement? All the same, it must be blamed a great deal on Grandfather Charlie, Charles. He should have realised what a gullible victim Hannah was."

"Old devil," said Charles. "I'm glad Hannah struck back.

She must have given him an uncomfortable time, even if it was brief."

"Women had a raw deal in those days," Sarah said. "Or some of them did. Not your grandmother. She seemed to have it both ways, a husband and a lover. Well, Hannah's at rest now. I think we ought to have 'Depart in peace' put on her tombstone. Because she seems to have persuaded Joseph to depart, too."

"Thank God!" said Charles.

"You'd hardly believe the change in Dolly already. He had been such an oppressed little boy, but now he's noisy and extrovert. When he and Jane get together . . ."

"You make me afraid to come home. Where's our peace and quiet to be?"

Sarah took the long thin hand, holding it between her palms. Charles was still lying flat, but in a few days he would be allowed to stand. He looked worn and ravaged but serene. Serenity, Sarah guessed, was something he had learned over the past two years. There was no danger of him ever becoming a rampaging Grandfather Charlie.

"Cressida's gone to Paris, Charles. She did tell you, didn't she?"

"She did. In the kindest possible way. This has been happening for some time, Sarah. Long before you and me. But we'll manage, won't we?" He looked at her with anxiety. "Won't we?"

"No question," said Sarah, and repeated emphatically, "No question."

DOROTHY EDEN

AFTERNOON WALK

A woman has been kidnapped and is believed to have been driven through the streets of their tidy little town. This and police questioning sets the neighbourhood by the ears during these hot, brooding days of early summer. But it was the atmosphere in her own home that most upset Ella; threats from an unknown telephone caller, the feeling of being under surveillance and, above all, her distant husband's contention that she was becoming increasingly fanciful, forgetful and not careful enough of Kitty, their little daughter.

Rising doubts and fears force her into the confidence of her neighbour, Booth Bramwell. Maybe the heat was affecting her, but surely she hadn't imagined the dust-cloud up at the deserted house on the day of the kidnapping? It seemed that a little more than Ella's memory was failing her.

DOROTHY EDEN

THE MILLIONAIRE'S DAUGHTER

The unforgettable nineteenth century love story of a beautiful American heiress.

Christabel Spencer's life had been carefully planned before she was even born. For her father had decided his daughter should have everything. And as New York's newest millionaire, Harry Spencer believed that money could buy it for her.

And Chrissie was as beautiful as she was rich. Surely this combination would be irresistible to an eligible English aristocrat. But Chrissie knew she could not live without love – and she would find it at any cost . . .

DOROTHY EDEN IN CORONET

All these books are available at your local bookshop or newsagent, or can be ordered direct from the publisher. Just tick the titles you want and fill in the form below.

Prices and availability subject to change without notice.

CORONET BOOKS, P.O. Box 11, Falmouth, Cornwall.

Please send cheque or postal order, and allow the following for postage and packing:

U.K. – One book 22p plus 10p per copy for each additional book ordered, up to a maximum of 82p.

B.F.P.O. and EIRE – 22p for the first book plus 10p per copy for the next 6 books, thereafter 4p per book.

OTHER OVERSEAS CUSTOMERS – 30p for the first book and 10p per copy for each additional book.

Name ....

Address..

....